HIDING AMONG THE DEAD

CHRIS BAUER

SEVERN RIVER
PUBLISHING

Severn River Publishing
severnriverbooks.com

This is a work of fiction. Names, characters, businesses, places, events and incidents are either the products of the author's imagination or used in a fictitious manner. Any resemblance to actual persons, living or dead, or actual events is purely coincidental.

ISBN: 978-1-64875-497-5 (Paperback)

ALSO BY CHRIS BAUER

To grandson Evan and granddaughter Teddy. Dream big then go bigger. So proud of you already.

1

The stink from the river was badass intense, dizzying, even in the cold air, like rotting meat from a dead animal, odor as oppressive as wind resistance. It clung to them while their step van drove south on the Schuylkill Expressway. Why Grace felt she needed to comment on it considering their line of work, Philo didn't know. While he drove, she replaced the dead air with small talk.

"From skunk cabbage. They planted it up and down the Schuylkill River maybe fifteen years ago. It reduces sewer system overflow into the river during rainstorms. The smell sometimes finds its way here."

Maybe, just maybe, she'd stop there. Grace was never more than a thought away from going drunken-sailor nuclear. An overnight phone message put them on the road today. That and the slur recorded with it, from an Amtrak cop barking at a subordinate to better the din of an arriving ambulance on his end: *"I don't give a shit who else is coming. I want the Gore Whore here too...Oh, hello, Grace. Amtrak Police. Multiple fatalities near Zoo Junction. Call me ASAP at two-six-seven..."*

Every law enforcement agency in Philly knew Grace Blessid as the Gore Whore. The slur got them jobs, so the tough white Germantown woman didn't discourage it. It made sense: she had a nasty mouth, she toiled in a gory environment, and she'd acquired law enforcement contacts from a rumored prior career on the streets—and it rhymed. Philo had heard things far worse about female peers while in the navy, but rarely had these things come out of their own mouths.

Philo learned all this soon after he bought Blessid Trauma Services, the crime scene cleaning business Grace and her husband, Hank, had built from scratch. Grace Blessid was sick; she needed new lungs, like, now. After thirty-four years in operation the business traded hands, with Tristan Trout, "Philo" for reasons he hadn't shared, now the new owner.

"Smells bad as an unwashed cunt, doesn't it?" Grace said.

And she was Catholic.

"Really, Grace?" Philo said. "That's the image you're going for?"

"Tell me you weren't thinking it."

"You're killing me, Grace."

Grace, late fifties, kept her auburn hair under a large, tied-off silk scarf, today's colors Philadelphia Flyers orange and black, one end pulled forward to lay flat like a koi fishtail across cream-white cleavage her blue uniform didn't hide. At one time she'd been smokin' hot, her words. Now she was a little bit less so, with clear cannula tubing leading from her nostrils to the portable oxygen concentrator stuffed into the backpack at her feet. For the next four months, per the agreement of sale, she was Philo's on-the-job trainer, one of two. The other was Hank, her husband, his bulk currently planted in one of the two jump seats behind them, his earbuds plugged into Zeppelin.

They neared their destination, the expressway's Philadelphia Zoo exit. A second biohazard cleaning service had been at the site all night.

Philo was fifteen years absent his northeast Philly roots, and at thirty-nine was bruised from his military deployments but still looked cowboy lean and mean. He'd decided to return home, to blend in as a citizen. When he found a business suited to his proclivities and his disposition, he assembled the financing for it.

"Let there be no illusions, Mr. Trout," Grace said when they first met over drinks, leaning into her rheumy-eyed stare. "These chemicals will severely limit your life expectancy if you don't pay attention. Sad thing is, I can't sue myself. 'Course, I also liked my unfiltered Camels, so that didn't help." Grace couldn't still be a smoker and stay on a transplant list, which meant she fought her craving every day. "I'm cooperating, maintaining this charade, for my husband. He's not taking this terminal illness shit very well."

The business ran fine with three employees—Grace, Hank, and their protégé, Patrick—and would do so with the same number after the transition, meaning Hank, Patrick, and Philo. That is if Patrick, damaged goods in his own right, stayed stimulated and entertained, and if Hank wanted to stay on board. Grace's medical condition had turned Hank into a weepy sieve.

Belted in stiff as a storm trooper, young Patrick sat across from Hank in the step van, plugged into 50 Cent, his blue Tyvek biohazard suit the heaviest of heavy-duty over his uniform, his mask in place, too. Grace spoke over her shoulder, raised her voice.

"Warm in that suit, Patrick?" she asked, winking at Philo. They knew it was, even though the cold outside was brutal.

Patrick removed an earbud. "Only a little, ma'am." Standard answer, winter, summer, ice age, heat wave. He was a traumatic brain injury victim from an event that took his real identity and left behind the adult equivalent of a five-ten mound of Silly Putty. The hospital's neurological assessment: dissociative amnesia. Per the caseworker's notes: *"Found with no vitals a block from Pat's King of Steaks restaurant on Passyunk Avenue by Pat's employees, February 15, 2014. In a coma for four days. He doesn't know his name or age. Could barely speak when he returned to consciousness."*

Best guess was he was now midtwenties. Survived a bludgeoning, was left naked inside an open dumpster a few days after a blizzard dropped ten inches of snow. The trauma preceded his life with the Blessids, which meant it was more than three years ago. Patrick came with the business; no Patrick, no sale. What the trauma hadn't stolen from him, and what its aftermath couldn't hide, was his ethnicity. He was an Eskimo, or at least everyone thought he was. Philo had traveled the world during his military deployments, but Patrick was the first Eskimo he'd ever met.

"Aleut or Inuit," Grace said, correcting Philo back then. "Or so thought Catholic Charities. They said *Eskimo* as a word is pejorative, so we don't use it. No idea how he ended up in Philly. A tourist visit gone wrong, teleportation, who the fuck knows. 'Patrick,' from Pat's Steaks, near where he was found, was as good a name as any."

The end of Patrick's fifth day after his discovery, he disappeared from his bed at Pennsylvania Hospital. No one came looking for him, before or after.

A cold snap today, twenty-eight degrees would be the high, and this kept Patrick from oozing sauna-grade sweat inside his suit during their ride; Tyvek biohazard suits didn't breathe. At attention in his seat, he was the epitome of preparedness and concentration, ready for the job every time he left his apartment above the Blessids' detached garage. He removed his mask, sipped water from a bottle.

Grace's husband Hank removed his earbuds. "Today's job is hunt and gather, son," he said to Patrick. The Blessids had no children. They saw this man-child as son and grandson wrapped into one.

"Hunt and gather," Patrick repeated. "Then clean."

"Yes, son, there's always cleaning."

"Here's our exit, Philo," Grace said.

Their black 1998 Freightliner step van, boxy with a head-turning custom paint job, left the expressway and entered street traffic. On the truck's side panels and rear door were waist-up photorealistic images of the three Catholic popes who'd held the title since the Blessids opened their business in 1983. John Paul II and Benedict XVI were in their papal whites, as was Francis, a 2013 addition, each with their right hands raised chest high and poised to deliver sign-of-the-cross blessings to motorists as they sped by. The step van stopped at a red traffic light. A Ford SUV pulled alongside in the left lane.

The SUV's passenger window powered down while the vehicles waited for the light to change, releasing a most righteous ganja haze. A giddy teenager smiled up at Philo through it, struggling with loosening the belt holding up his pants. The stoner shimmied his pants down to his knees and presented two ass cheeks for close papal inspection through the open window—"Bio-clean this hazard, Pope-dudes!"—then dropped back into his seat in hysterics.

It wasn't like Philo was still a practicing Catholic, but no one got away with mooning the Pope.

Philo slid aside his window and summoned a serious scowl beneath his unruly brown hair, a rooster comb separating a dually receding hairline. He grabbed a stray rubber glove from the dashboard ledge and tossed it into the kid's open window, the glove landing in his exposed lap. "Enjoy the rash, kid."

It wasn't contaminated, but hell, the kid didn't know that. The traffic light changed, Philo turned right, then found off-street parking near the zoo.

A call to the Amtrak police got them onto the tracks. Their contract with Amtrak was a two-year deal carved up among multiple biohazard vendors along the railroad's Northeast Corridor, the route that ran from Boston to DC. Still cold, still cloudy, an icy breeze buffeted their faces as they walked, the four of them in blue Tyvek with goggles and headlamps at the ready above their foreheads, and filtered respirator masks hanging loose around their necks.

The train's eight cars—two power cars, six passenger—sat large and ominous ahead of them on the track, just past the curve and near the zoo entrance. Philo's eyes gravitated to the lower third of the silver-and-blue power car. Below the engine's red line, the wheels and undercarriage were caked black and gray with dirt, grease, and track grime —plus, hopefully, a certain something that a certain grieving family prayed they could recover.

This was yesterday's five p.m. 2167 Acela Express out of New York's Penn Station, which had motored through the slight curve around the zoo at eighty miles per hour until just before impact. Per the engineer's statement he saw three people on the tracks, a woman and two young children holding balloons, all holding hands. He sounded the horn and applied the brakes, which had no chance of stopping the train until well beyond the collision point. Closer in, the engineer saw the woman better—young, brown-skinned— and also saw a baby sling snugged up against her chest. She dropped down and lay across the tracks with the small children, their three helium balloons hovering. The victims disappeared in the undercarriage; the train did not derail.

Moving at the speed of Grace, her portable oxygen in her backpack, she and Hank trailed Philo along a paved walkway, and Patrick trailed them all, pulling a stubby all-terrain cart with pneumatic tires. Patrick eased the cart off the paved walk onto the tracks' stone ballast. The cart was stuffed with cleaning equipment, red hazmat bags, a short stack of empty twenty-gallon biohazard containment drums, solvents, gloves, soft brushes, wire brushes, tape, and tools. Tucked into a plastic bag somewhere was a large jar of Tiger Balm, which Grace swore by for smell management. An Amtrak maintenance supervisor trotted up to them.

"Who's in charge here?"

Philo gave Grace a questioning look; she nodded him an okay. "That would be me," Philo said, and introduced himself.

"Okay then. So Mr. Trout, let's go over a few things. You'll need to be thorough but quick. Service has been moved to another track, but the muckety-mucks want service restored to this one ASAP. Another biohazard company will work from the other end of the train as soon as they finish policing the tracks. I understand a spokesman from the woman's family called you guys. If you can do what they asked, we'll cooperate. Any questions?"

* * *

The local detectives cleared the scene as non-investigative. Showtime for Blessid Trauma.

"Patrick, you and I are going underneath. We'll shimmy from the power car back. Hank, lay the tarps over there for our biohazard control area. You and Grace can follow alongside us with the cart. Patrick, switch on your headlamp and get your phone camera ready."

Patrick fished his mobile phone out of a pocket, held it up, took a selfie, and showed it to Philo.

"You are one ugly dude, Patrick. Lock and load, buddy." Philo patted Patrick on the shoulder. "Cleansing breath, game face on. Let's go get dirty. And remember—no one better than you, Patrick."

"Sir! No one better than Patrick, *sir*! No one better than Patrick, *SIR*!"

For Patrick, the switch had been thrown. For Philo the chant was a mixed bag, recalling long, maddening daily marches from a once very serious, very disciplined, and very dangerous past.

They lay down on the stone ballast, Patrick softly repeating the mantra, keeping himself fired up, about to crawl into the belly of the beast. He lifted his breather mask in place over his nose and mouth, relegating his chant to humming and grunting. They shimmied underneath, dragging their bag of tools with them, he and Philo shoulder to shoulder.

Clearance under the nose of the train was minimal, the edge of the power car's front baffle scraping their chests as they wiggled past it, their headlamps on. They inched forward, their shoulders pushing against the rough-cut ballast under them. Polyethylene-coated coveralls and their uniform pants and shirts were heavy enough to protect them from puncture, but not heavy enough to soften the prickling discomfort.

The way Philo saw it there were three good things about this removal. One, it was outside, not in a confined, under-ventilated area like most of their jobs. Two, the weather was cooperating, with the frigid air limiting the immediate area to the more palatable smells of creosoted rail ties, grease and oil, and hints, mild only, of rat scat. Three, most of the heavy lifting from the four fatalities had been handled already. Forensics personnel, firemen, and the other crime scene cleaners had policed a stretch of track a full hundred yards beyond where the last few body parts were found. Whatever was left would be crammed into, hanging off, or maybe now frozen against the undercarriage of the eight-car train.

Which brought Philo to the one bad thing: the grieving Hispanic family, last name Marroquin. The info Amtrak had from a family relative was the young woman had recently lost her husband. The family's request was to locate a body part still missing, and to retrieve it as reverently and as carefully as possible; either that or confirm it wasn't there. In preparation, Philo supplemented his tool bag of normally less discriminating putty knives, tongs, chisels, and scrapers with two new instruments: a surgical scalpel and a bone saw.

Their order of work: take "before" photos; inspect each linear foot, wipe away blood and other body effluence, and carefully scrape off anything resembling a human body part and place it in a hazmat bag; clean with crud-removing, disinfecting solvent; take "after" photos; then shimmy forward another foot and repeat the process.

The undercarriage of the first power car contained, in no particular order, metal baffling, axles, steel wheels with wheel grease, traction motors, springs, tubing, large nuts and bolts, steel plating, and a myriad of other filthy surfaces. Their first discovery, inside a coiled spring, was a section of intestine glistening from crystallized internal moisture. Philo removed it with needle-nose pliers and tweezers and placed the pieces inside a red hazmat bag. After that, the hits kept coming. Lodged under an interior baffle was a severed child's foot in a no-name athletic shoe, and the back of a child's hand including knuckles and one hanging finger, the nail painted fluorescent lime. A popped Mylar balloon hung flaccid from an axle, the words on the balloon in Spanish and the string still attached. Tangled in the string, a baby's pacifier. And a ragged chunk of adult ass in jeans twisted around a steel tie rod, the butt crack the giveaway, already frozen in place by the extreme overnight temperatures. Philo used a pry bar to free the frozen ass-flesh from the frigid metal, needing to put his weight into it and ripping off a pocket on the jeans in the process, which liberated a piece of folded paper. He dropped his gloved hand on it before the icy wind could whip it away.

Gloves off, he unfolded the paper. In bold letters at the top, flush left: *US Department of Homeland Security*; flush right: *Notice to Appear*.

Ms. Therese Marroquin was being deported. Clipped to the notice was a small photo, larger than wallet-sized: a selfie of a smiling dark-skinned man in a white-sheeted metal-frame bed with an IV leading to his arm. Beyond him in the photo, the rest of the room was dark and stark and third world–ish, no furniture, with a slightly ajar steel door that was scraped and dented, cinnamon in color.

Muscle tendons and bone had jammed into the underpinnings of the next two cars. Philo tossed a second red biohazard bag out from under the passenger car so Hank could retrieve it. Hank used a Sharpie to label it with the location, date, time, "Blessid Trauma," and the specifics of their finds, in this case "misc. human parts." Hank passed the Homeland Security deportation notice and the photo of the Hispanic man along to the Amtrak cops.

They toiled quickly, efficiently, the second bio-clean company now working from the train's other end, professionals like Blessid Trauma, which meant there'd be little drama between the two contractors. Crime scene cleanup business in and around Philadelphia was plentiful.

Partway along the third passenger car, the last one they would clean today, Patrick saw it first.

"There," he said to Philo, steadying his headlamp. "Right there, sir."

A bald hand puppet was pressed face-out against the inside of the housing of a wheel bogie, frozen there like a sports pennant push-pinned into drywall, its tiny arms spread wide. One of the sleeves was flat, empty. Protruding from the other was a chubby, porcelain-like hand, same color as the puppet head. Both sleeves, like the rest of the outfit, were crinkly-stiff from the cold. Philo trained his lamp where Patrick pointed, then located a putty knife. On closer inspection he noticed a string hanging from its wrist. The puppet's blouse came into focus, a *Dora the Explorer* imprint. And on yet a closer look, it wasn't a blouse, it was pajamas, their bottom half missing, ripped away at the waist. And it wasn't a hand puppet.

From the neck up, here was a sleeping cherub, the baby's eyes shut, her skin still supple, her cheeks smudged with dirt and only a few scratches. From the neck down, save for an arm and a fisted, chubby little hand, the pajama fabric was empty. A balloon string was tied to her wrist.

Philo's deeper, filtered breath became a resigned sigh. He'd seen carnage as horrific as this before, during his prior career overseas, some of it just as graphic and unforgiving. Images with staying power. He eyed his partner to gauge its impact on him.

"You good, Patrick?"

"I'm good, sir," he said, no emotion.

Philo returned the scraper to a tool belt, unzipped a pocket, and produced the surgeon's scalpel.

"All right then, no one better than you, big guy. Just point and shoot. Get the 'before' shots, then we'll take care of this, okay?"

Patrick steeled himself, swiped his tongue across his top lip, and gulped in some filtered air. "No one better than Patrick, sir." He raised his camera phone. "No one better than Patrick..."

Click, click, click.

Philo poked at the shredded bottom edge of the pajamas with his scraper, separating the front material from the back, peeking inside. Room there for a puppeteer's hand had it actually been a puppet. The inside was instead filled by a tiny, gooey rib cage that dropped out and past Philo's shoulder onto the ballast, inclusive of stringy internal organs. The infant's bottom half had been found earlier that morning at the accident scene via a canine search, in weeds a short distance from the tracks, dashing the family's hope that the baby might have somehow survived. Which was what had prompted the request to the Blessids to please-please-*please* find the other half of their beloved newborn niece so they could attend to her arrangements properly.

"Patrick"—Philo pointed at the tiny rib cage on the ballast between them—"would you please, ah—"

"I'm on it, sir." Patrick turned onto his stomach and surrounded the baby's organs and ribcage with his gloved hands, scooping them up between them like a child collecting a wounded bird, and depositing them in a small hazmat bag destined for special handling.

Philo tugged gently at the infant's head, but it didn't budge, then he tugged more forcefully; still didn't loosen. He produced the scalpel, inserted it between the skull and the black metal plate it was stuck on to see if a cut of some kind could free it. No luck.

"Hank," he called. "Get me the hair dryer."

A long extension cord led back to their step van for juice. After a few minutes on high heat, the frozen blood turned gooey enough for Philo to wiggle the head. That's when he saw the curved metal hook behind it, embedded sideways just above the base of the child's skull.

He reached into the tool bag and retrieved the bone saw. He started at the top.

2

The medical examiner pronounced all parts of the infant dead.

Two ambulances that had parked just short of the rear of the train bookended multiple pieces of fire equipment. The firemen switched out some of their tools, took gulps of coffee, then steeled themselves before wandering back up the tracks toward the point of impact. Philo, their work completed, removed everything attached to his person in a particular order, Grace's safety-first-always voice in his head. He stepped out of his biohazard suit, stuffed his disposables into a hazmat bag, then climbed into a fleece-lined coat guaranteed to warm him better than the Tyvek suit. He found a Blessid Trauma baseball cap, snugged it up, then blew out as best he could, the soul-crushing, nightmarish, deathly air his lungs had sucked in from under the train, easing himself away from a meltdown. A canvas duffel laundry bag, tall and stuffed full of dirty Blessid Trauma uniforms, leaned against the back of the driver's seat. He blinked hard at the bag; acid rose in his throat. He turned his ball cap backward, and with lips pressed into a grim line he unloaded on it, throwing heavy-handed fist-bombs against the thick canvas, crushing it, grunting with each blow.

These...were KIDS, damn it. Innocent little ANGELS...

...What—a fucking—WASTE...

He exhaled, sucked in air to calm himself, good, crisp, head-clearing oxygen. He resettled his ball cap bill-forward, found Patrick at the rear of the step van. "You okay, bud?"

Patrick sat oblivious on the bumper, still in his hazmat onesie, the back doors open. His hands were in his lap. "I'm okay, sir, but..." He pushed the hood off his head and pointed. "Over there, sir. That guy. I saw him before."

"Okay. Is that a problem?"

"*Before,* sir. While I was in the coma, before I woke up."

Philo watched as an EMT a few tracks away manhandled his gear, tossing it with bad intentions into his rescue vehicle. Tall, wide, and looking disappointed, the guy dropped his butt down hard on the emergency vehicle's rear bumper, lit a cigarette, and sat staring at his feet like a benched ballplayer, the cigarette hanging off his lower lip. His eyes narrowed, focusing in the direction of the Blessid van; he exhaled the smoke. He straightened up, suddenly interested in them, or at least maybe in Patrick.

Patrick's personal history was scant. Given the attention, this was worth a short walk by Philo across the tracks for a chat.

"Hey. Philo Trout. Look, my buddy over there—"

"I know who you are," the EMT said, taking a drag. "Heard you bought out the Blessids. And I think I know *him,*" he said, pointing with his chin, "but my guess is he probably doesn't remember me." He raised his hand to greet Philo. "Lamar Cribbs."

A quick handshake. "So tell me then, Lamar, you say you know my buddy. Enlighten me. Who is he?"

"Oh. Right. No, sorry, I don't know his name. He was a Doe at the hospital. The emergency docs who first treated him, that's what they called him. Patrick Doe."

"Yeah, old news. No other insights?"

"Cracked skull, a subdural hematoma when they brought him in. I was an ER nurse back then. They drilled a hole and suctioned out the blood. He bolted the hospital after coming out of his coma, from what I remember. Had to be like, what, three, four years ago?"

"Three."

"He looks good. He ever learn his name?"

"No. Goes by Patrick Stakes."

"Too bad—young kid like that. Awful. But it looks like he filled out pretty good. Give my regards to him. I gotta get packed up. Today's been shitty. All our prospective business went into the red bags. How'd he end up with the Blessids?"

"A walk-on," Philo said. "They took him in, taught him the business, got close to him. The kid's a natural." He glanced across the tracks at Patrick, a protective reflex that accompanied the concern he felt. "But he's still not right. Struggles a lot because of the trauma. Other than that, he's a workhorse."

"Huh," Lamar Cribbs said. "So the Gore Whore has a heart after all. How's business? You keeping her clients happy?"

A shout pierced their quiet conversation, from a contentious Grace inside the Blessid van. "Philo! How about hurrying it up?"

"Heh," the EMT said, "that's the bitch I remember. Still wears the pants. Suppose I'll see you 'round, Trout."

"Philo!" Grace called, doubling down on the bitter. "Goddamn it, *now!"*

Philo arrived at the Blessid van, stepped inside and slid the door shut. "You need to cut that shit out, Grace. Last I checked, you work for me now."

Grace's scowl didn't let up after his ass hit the tufted seat. She took a hit of oxygen then cursed right through his verbal stop sign. "Why the fuck you talking to that guy?"

"Calm down, Grace, you'll hurt yourself." He would not out Patrick as a reason. Worker bros stuck together. "Look, he just wanted to wish me luck with your company."

"Fat fucking chance, Philo. He's a wolf guarding the hen house. What did he want?"

A concerned Patrick unhooked his seat belt and squatted between Grace and Philo in the front seats. "M-my fault, ma'am. I, um, told Mr. Trout I thought I knew him. Not sure from where, though."

"He knew you from the hospital," Philo said. "He was a nurse in the ER when they brought you in."

Patrick got animated. "He was? What's he know? What's his name? I wanna—"

"Sorry, bud, nothing more than you already know. Just that the ER docs did a good job patching you up. His last name is Cribbs. Knew nothing else about you, before or after you left the hospital."

Grace was done holding her tongue. "Fucking blood-sucking ghouls. He works for an ambulance outfit tied to that goddamn body parts surgeon Dr. Andelmo."

Philo recognized the name. The successful doctor fronted a consortium of partners sponsoring a new urgent care services company local to Philadelphia and its environs. Their TV advertising presence was significant, like the law firms and big-money pharmaceuticals.

Grace continued, unadulterated: "That zombie prick Andelmo's facilities are popping up everywhere. Someone needs to fry that man's unethical ass. Working with him in the ER got Cribbs and all the people around him fired."

"For what?" Philo asked.

"Some patient at Andelmo's hospital, a Philly house painter, died due to complications from a lung condition. When the family claimed his body, some of his organs were missing. Heart, lungs, pancreas. The explanation was the organs were 'donated for education.' No family consent. The cavities were stuffed with newspaper. Andelmo dodged the allegations, but the rest of his staff was nailed. That Cribbs guy was one of them. I'm shit-sure he's trying to work his way back into prime-time hospital nursing. I don't trust any of them, Philo. This business is crazy enough already."

Her cough kicked in, a smoker's hack but worse, her face reddening, clearly painful. "Word gets around (ackkk) you're associating with them, people get the (cough) wrong idea."

"Okay, Grace, I got it. Jeez, just relax, you'll cough up a lung." Soon as he said it, he wanted to take it back. "Sorry, Grace, not trying to be a wiseass."

"No worries. But listen to me. Those guys, and some of the other rescue outfits, there've been rumors of complicity. Bounties on patients, alive or dead, based on leads."

"Patrick—" Husband Hank interrupted Grace's diatribe, grabbing and pointing the melancholy kid toward the empty jump seat. "Have a seat so we can get going, son. Philo, maybe we could break for lunch now?" Hank winked at Patrick, a conspiratorial thing. Today was a big day for Patrick.

"Sure, why not," Philo said. "Let's go get this guy his birthday lunch."

* * *

Philo, Grace, and Hank each had a cheesesteak, the sandwiches in their wrappers in their laps, the three of them staying warm inside the truck while it idled curbside next to Pat's King of Steaks. Traffic cones guaranteed them rock-star parking; the Pat's Steaks guys had been expecting them. A special bond here, with Patrick enjoying the hell out of his "cheesesteak wit" as in "with onions" at a picnic table under the overhang, two Pat's sandwich guys keeping him company on their breaks.

Philo ate, his head still locked onto speeding trains versus flesh and blood people. A glance at Patrick, then a glance up the street while horrific thoughts gathered and took aim at his heart, piercing it, letting the horror ooze out.

...Cold outside, but the zoo was open. Their desperate mother took them to see the animals, some special last thing she wanted them to enjoy. Then, in an instant, gone, all of them, balloons tied to their wrists, obliterated by an eighty-mph train, their severed body parts crammed into the wheel housings, spinning inside until ground into little pieces, or jettisoned onto the ballast, or into the weeds. Skin, bones, organs, heads...

...violent, gruesome, nightmarish—

...hacked bodies—

...sorties in Afghanistan—Libya—

...a raid in Abbottabad, Pakistan—

"Philo. You okay, Philo?" Grace asked.

"Some really nasty shit back there on the tracks," Philo said, not skipping a beat. "No worries."

Grace breathed through her hacking while she rewrapped what was left of her sandwich and dropped it into the same greasy brown bag it had arrived in. She reached for more oxygen. After three or four deep breaths she retrieved an unfiltered cigarette from her pocket, stuck it between her lips and sucked on it, unlit.

Today was February fifteenth, a date that served for Patrick's birthday, the day he'd been found in the dumpster. Grace smiled absently in Patrick's direction from inside her closed window, engrossed like a concerned mother watching her son. Outside, Patrick shared grins with his benefactors, chuckling with his mouth full, gesturing with a French fry, and sitting there in the cold, carefree as a young person should be in his early years, like he was at a hot dog stand at the beach with his buddies in midsummer.

"He's stuffing his face," Grace said, "and he'll do it again tonight when we take him to a nice restaurant for a sit-down meal and a birthday cake. Steak sandwich now, steak tartare later. The kid's an animal when it comes to eating. Likes steak as bloody as they can make it, and sushi."

Raw meat and fish, she said, a freak for both. Patrick was a living public service commercial for Alaska.

"You going to try again?" Philo asked her, changing topics.

"Meaning?"

"Help him find his true identity?"

"Why? He's seems content, doesn't he?" she said, a sideways comment meant to ease her conscience, her emotions still mixed; she'd told Philo as much before. "Hank and I are done with it. We did what we could. Three years of newspaper ads, a local TV profile, postings with missing persons networks, facial recognition, fingerprinting, cold-calling police departments in Alaska, all over Canada. All dead ends. No missing persons reports found on him anywhere. It's like the kid dropped out of the heavens into that fucking dumpster. Patrick still pursues it, is still hopeful. His call to stay with it I suppose, but I hope he stops. 'Course, I admit I'm a little biased."

Grace was tough on the outside, but on this topic, she wore her heart for all to see. She was afraid that if Patrick found his identity, he'd leave.

"You ought to do the DNA thing," Philo said.

"Fuck DNA testing. The cheap tests only give ethnicity. Too much on our plates at the moment, Philo. We'll be out of the business soon," she said, sniffling and coughing. She hacked hard into a tissue, which camouflaged her tears. After her tumult subsided: "And my, um, my wait on the list—it's just not working out."

The lung transplant list. For her, thirty-seven months and counting.

A furtive glance over her shoulder. Behind them Hank sat with his head back and a small pillow behind it, resting, his phone earbuds on. She straightened up and thrust out her chin, regaining control.

"Yeah, fine, I'll think about the DNA. Maybe we can pay for more extensive testing, but…"

The "but." Philo completed her thought, didn't share it: *But if I do, I might lose him.*

"What the hell, Philo. Yeah, okay, we'll think about it," she repeated, trying to convince herself. Then, with her bitch back on: "That EMT you were talking to, he's one of them." She sucked on her unlit Camel, expelled nonexistent smoke and flicked invisible ashes.

"Grace, please," Philo said, "a little less chatter on conspiracies today."

"Ambulance companies chasing people who aren't quite dead yet, Philo. That's who he works for."

"Isn't that the whole ambulance idea?"

She ignored the comment. "Some of their patients make it, some don't. Some of the EMTs contact that Frankenstein prick Andelmo to let him know what's coming in, then maybe even dial down their service a little to hasten the inevitable. A for-profit transplant specialist. Andelmo's the ringleader."

One thing that was true about this surgeon, who was affiliated with a few Philadelphia hospitals, was he was in a ton of trouble, with the press already convicting him in the court of public opinion. Made public were a number of malpractice lawsuits; patients getting routine procedures who had died on his table. For one, an appendectomy, for another, a gallbladder —both patients, coincidentally, organ and tissue donors. Andelmo had questionable associations with influential people in need of all sorts of transplants—wealthy people and celebrities—who suddenly got them. All of it remained innuendo until a criminal case could be made. Something the Philadelphia DA was apparently pursuing.

"Lose the 'Frankenstein' BS, Grace," Philo said. "It stopped being funny after the first ten times I heard it."

Hank, from the back seat: "What Philo said, honey. Give it a rest, please."

Grace narrowed her eyes at her husband, then she caved. "Only because you said please, doll."

Dr. Francisco X. Andelmo, Grace's "zombie" doc, was a neurological surgeon in his early fifties, with positions in two Philadelphia hospitals plus other hospital relationships south of the border. That was the extent of what Philo knew about him. Good guy, bad guy, Philo didn't know, didn't care, and had no reason to think he ever would. But to Grace he was the antichrist.

Philo put up with Grace's conservative rants from the beginning, and he wouldn't stop now. She'd been a good sport about playing through her disease, a hardship factor that upped her standing in his eyes a thousand-fold. Plus, she, too, was on one of those transplant lists the celebrities and wealthy people seemed to bypass, so it wasn't like she didn't know what she was talking about. But her "in general, if it walks like a duck rants" and her in-particular attitude toward government overreach, had begun to grate on him.

Philo balled up his sloppy sandwich wrapper and found an empty paper bag for it. "You check the messaging service to see what else we've got for today, Grace?"

"A Philly cop car. It's in this neighborhood, three blocks up. A perp accident, in the perp seat." She tucked her Camel away into a blouse pocket, watched outside as Patrick took his Pat's Steaks buddies through some well-executed, straight-outta-Compton special goodbye handshakes.

Red flag language for Philo: perp mess in a cop car. Police lawsuits had surfaced around the country, cops suing their cities for having contracted hepatitis and HIV from contaminated crime scenes. One outcome of the legal actions was increased work for the crime-scene cleaning industry, cops not wanting to contract diseases, cities not wanting to settle lawsuits if they did.

"Grace, if this is a few cops tuning up a perp, call them the hell back and tell them to clean up their own mess."

"Relax. The guy threw a tantrum in the back seat, took a dump, horked up his lunch, then pounded his head against the glass. PCP, maybe meth, bath salts, maybe all of it, the cops weren't sure."

Her fingers returned to her blouse pocket, retrieved the Camel she'd given up a minute earlier. She reinserted it into her mouth and went through the motions again. "You need to cut the cops some slack, Philo, the crap they put up with. Hank, honey"—she reached back, tapped her husband on his knee—"this squad-car thing, you and I are up. Would you mind handling it for me, doll? I'm just not in the mood."

Hank leaned in next to her in her seat, concerned. "Grace, honey, you think maybe you should—"

"I need to just not do this next job is all I need to do, sweetie, so relax." She cupped his cheek. His eyes welled; she swiped at a tear with her thumb. "Just not feeling it now. I'll be fine, love, just...It'll all be fine."

Two minutes down Passyunk, then a left onto Washington. Philo parked in front of the cop car, an unmarked Chevy Impala, a detective's car, so he felt better about it. Less chance there'd been any funny business in the back seat. The rear doors were ajar, and they could see some of the perp's brown and pinkish redecoration efforts caked onto an inside door panel.

Philo and Grace answered texts, and Patrick stayed connected to an online game app. Hank worked the job, the blood, the feces, and the puke all as promised, and no doubt sweat and tears also, but it was all apparently perp-initiated. Except for the tears part, where a depressed Hank, working alone, was also a contributor.

3

Kaipo Mawpaw lifted the cha siu bao with her chopsticks, admiring its dense texture. Stuffed inside the soft bread-bun was diced barbecued pork tenderloin mixed with Cantonese sauces, the last dim sum of her five-course meal. On Oahu this dish was called manapua, which meant "delicious pork thing." Kaipo took a tentative, inquisitive bite, then she took a less dainty bite to finish it. She devoured the second bun with gusto. She placed her chopsticks on the table, poured herself more tea.

The Happy Empress Cantonese Restaurant dining room was tiny, only seven café tables, each decorated with a wine-red tablecloth, a burning yellow candle, and two white cloth napkins, but its take-out business was robust. The stream of customers was constant, passing behind the drapes that hid the glassed-in hallway.

Tonight she was one of only two dining room patrons. At a second table an elderly Asian man tossed toothless smiles and furtive glances her way between slurps of soup and hearty bites into large, meat-filled dumplings, the food no match for his hardened gums. The smile was respectful, not leering—she knew the difference—and wasn't meant to elicit conversation, was offered instead only in reverence to her wholesome, natural Polynesian beauty. For Kaipo this was refreshing, and so dissimilar to the usual reception she got whenever she met friends for drinks, from trolling men or curious women, all looking for a change in their partners short-term, to someone a bit more...formidable. Kaipo oozed femininity yet was not a shrinking violet. At five ten, her well-proportioned femininity was far from a shrinking anything.

The male waiter delivered the check then bowed once before retreating to the kitchen. *No charge, with our compliments,* it read at bottom, which was how all her checks read at this restaurant for the few years she'd frequented it, coincident with the same number of years she'd spent on the mainland. The free meals were not a privilege she abused. She ate here only once a week, on Thursdays, the day her clandestine employer had requested. It was a visit that meant, on occasion, a few subsequent days and nights would be busy, with her doing what they wanted her to do and getting paid handsomely to do it. With her dinner check came a handful of after-dinner peppermints and one very special fortune cookie. Dipped in chocolate and absent any cellophane, she would enjoy the fortune cookie dessert first.

She pushed her hair back over her shoulder, cracked the cookie open with a fork, the milk-chocolate encasing it not fully hardened. When she pulled it apart, the soft chocolate made the pieces stringy, like chocolate saltwater taffy; the dessert couldn't be any fresher than this. Inside, the tan strip of paper bore her fortune. She lifted it to her nose to savor its fragrance, strawberry, its lettering red and glistening, further enhancing the aroma. She flattened it against the tablecloth to view the message.

The words on the small strip were in cursive, handwritten with decent penmanship. She read the instructions, then she fed the paper into her mouth and ate it, too. Its wafered texture was sweet and fruity and as edible as the scent suggested.

She raised her attention from the dessert plate. The old Asian man had put aside the ripped cellophane from a standard pre-packaged fortune cookie that accompanied his dinner, his gaze now moving from her empty plate to her hands to her face, his gumming of his cookie slow, ponderous. To her, his apprehension looked like fear, and this fear might mean he knew something about her, her connections, maybe her avocation. Or somehow maybe he knew the instructions that were in her fortune cookie. To her, he was suddenly now, sadly, a danger.

She told herself he was old and his life was behind him, to ease her conscience about what she would now need to do to him.

4

Philo hung up after listening to the overnight messages in the Blessid Trauma office. He patted himself down, made sure he had everything, his phone, his keys, his wallet, and the Sig Sauer 9mm handgun tucked into the crook of his back, inside the waist of his uniform pants.

"I don't get it," Grace said.

The fabric recliner inside the paneled office at the back of the garage had cigarette burns visible from across the room. Grace leaned back in it, her feet up, resting, adjusting her red-white-and-blue Philadelphia 76ers headscarf. For her, today would be a down day that she hadn't put up a fight about with her doting husband Hank, something she needed after yesterday's Amtrak suicide adventure. Hank would stay in the shop to babysit her. It was help he needed to give, Philo knew, as much as help she needed to receive.

Blessid Trauma Services occupied a two-story, four-storefront building in Philadelphia's Germantown section, was originally home to a bar stool manufacturer. Lockers, shelving, storage tanks, chemicals, and biohazard equipment occupied the wall space surrounding the vehicles parked inside. The step van sat beside a Ford Econoline van, the Econoline black but unmarked for more discreet jobs. The third vehicle was Philo's Jeep Wrangler. The business entrance was a glass door that opened onto busy Germantown Avenue.

"And what is it you don't get, Grace?" Philo said, frustrated they were having this conversation again. He expected to be on the road with Patrick by 7:15 a.m. today, headed for a job in Port Richmond.

"One," she said, "the fact you actually have a concealed carry permit, and two, that you're packing today. And three, why the hell you won't talk to me about it."

She hadn't noticed, but he was packing every day. "Fifteen years in the military, Grace. Stop looking for other reasons."

"Yeah, Philo, but that was then, this is now."

She watched the news, right? Radical Islamists, the Taliban, Daesh. Terrorism knew no space or time boundaries. For Philo, what was then, and half a world away, could easily be now, and right here. "Grace, please, not today."

"Fine. Maybe I don't even give a fuck. Maybe I'm even glad to see it, considering who you're seeing today."

On the message service last night had been a call from a Dr. Andelmo, deemed by Grace to be *the* Dr. Andelmo of recent organ trafficking infamy, alleged. The doctor's call was pleasant, like follow-up calls people typically received from hospitals following their procedures, checking on a patient's condition.

"Look, Grace, the EMT saw Patrick, remembered him from the ER, and this doctor heard about it. These people saved Patrick's life. When he bolted he dropped off their radar. They're curious about him, or maybe have some info on his identity."

"That news got to the doctor awfully fast, Philo."

"Traveled at what, the speed of the wireless airwaves, like every fucking phone call out there? Someone alerted the doctor and he called to check up on Patrick, that's all it is. It's what doctors and hospitals do."

"Ulterior motives, if you ask me."

"Whatever. We're done here."

Patrick poked his head into the office, already hazmatted head to toe in luminescent blue, carrying yellow gloves. Philo rubbed his sleep-deprived eyes at the bright colors, being tired a common condition for him. "Patrick and I will start that project in Port Richmond, then we'll shoot down to see his doctor around noon. Let's go, Patrick."

Grace liberated the cigarette in her pocket, tucked it into a corner of her mouth, spoke out of the other corner. "He's not his doctor, Philo! After this visit, Patrick needs to have nothing to do with him..."

* * *

An elderly man named Norman had called the cops. He hadn't seen his friend, Phoenicia, at the Port Richmond senior center in weeks. The police had investigated, then called her niece in Detroit, the "person to call in case of emergency" from what they'd gleaned from Phoenicia's purse. They then notified her friend Norman with the bad news: Phoenicia had been found deceased in her second-floor bathroom. The niece's internet search subsequently directed her to Blessid Trauma Services; Philo provided a ballpark estimate over the phone. Blessid Trauma needed only a small deposit.

"You might consider using your home insurance to cover part of the remediation," Philo had advised her

"Why do you say that?" the niece had said.

"Just a hunch," he'd said, not volunteering what a body decomp could do to a room, floor, whole house.

They parked at the deceased woman's address, in front of a house nestled deep on a lot with silver chain link fencing boxing in its weedy property and a garage in back. The fence was utilitarian, the kind often used to contain a dog.

"Yes, my aunt has a dog," the niece said when Philo called to say they'd arrived. "The police didn't find him."

The small, detached Arts and Crafts two-story might have at one time been considered charming. Its shingled exterior was now a washed-out gray, with chipped masonry steps that led to a red-brick front porch and outdated silver aluminum storm windows and doors. The front gutter had detached from the roofline and hung low, emptying into another crooked gutter hanging lower than the first, slanting farther down into a claw-footed porcelain bathtub in the side yard. Here was a life-size version of *Mouse Trap*, the 3-D board game.

The driveway led to the single-car garage at the rear of the property. Philo stopped the step van alongside the front porch. The smell, the one a person never forgot, entered the van's interior through the vents. Patrick found the Tiger Balm and applied a liberal glob under his nose. He retrieved a portable caddy full of cleaning supplies from behind their seats and sat it on his lap, ready to receive his one-sentence pep talk.

Philo slathered his upper lip with the balm then bro-slapped his partner's chest twice.

"No one better than you, big guy."

"No one better than Patrick," Patrick repeated.

They entered the yard through the gate near the bathtub. Icy brown water topped off the tub with a thick, glassy, dead-leaf crust. It was the third day that temperatures had dipped into the twenties. Liquids left outside in any receptacles, if not frozen solid already, would be soon. A north-south crack in the tub's white porcelain hinted at its near-frozen contents, with dirty water drip-drip-dripping through the crevice and making a run for it along the thick, dark brown icicle that had already formed, connecting the tub to the ground. They stepped onto the porch, the floor's wooden slats creaky, the path to the front door scuffed through the wood stain, exposing bare planks underneath. The house key left under a flowerpot let them inside.

Hot, stifling heat greeted them, the radiator pinging from somewhere under stacked cardboard boxes of Christmas tinsel near the front picture window. First order of business was to find the thermostat.

Phoenicia was apparently a hoarder. A surprise of sorts, only because the Detroit niece hadn't mentioned it, but not uncommon with the elderly; maybe the niece didn't know. Readying the entire place for re-habitation could take days, to clean out and neutralize whatever was growing in here. A few more steps inside the door, a careless Philo elbowed a picture frame to the floor, the glass shattering. He shook away the shards and picked up the frame.

"Sorry, ma'am."

A photo of Phoenicia, Philo reckoned. Heavyset black woman dressed for church, fancy hat, bulky suit jacket over a pink blouse, dark skirt, a Bible in her hand, and a smile good enough for an *AARP* magazine cover.

The worst thing for a crime scene cleaner was to see a photo of the deceased. It personalized the project.

Patrick found the thermostat in a hallway. "Turn the heat down, sir?"

"Turn it off for the time being."

"Okeydokey, sir."

What was of interest, and the reason for them being there, was the house's lone bathroom, upstairs. But surrounding them on the first floor was the homeowner's detritus, evident throughout the living and dining rooms. Pigs and angels. Everything pig, everything angel. Pig salt and pepper shakers, pig and angel ceramics, pink piggy paperweights, bookends, statues, books about pigs, books about angels, angel costumes, angel wings, empty and full angel-hair pasta boxes, baseball cards for players named Angel, vinyl records and CDs by artists named Angel. And on two legs, a fiberglass pig-snouted butler, adult-size, in a tuxedo and holding a tray, ready for guests to rest their drinks. Sitting unrefrigerated on the kitchen counter were packages of—surprise—bacon, with squirming maggots. The porcine and angel memorabilia adorned the walls, floors, ledges, and furniture, and was also stuck to the ceiling by way of plastic characters tinted glow-in-the-dark green. Assaulting Philo and Patrick's Tiger Balm noses was the mother of all odors, strongest near the stairs, coming from the second floor.

"I'm going up," Philo said, adjusting his mask. "Join me when you're ready."

In bedrooms one, two, and three: if-pigs-could-fly wallpaper, pink stuffed pigs, collectible dolls in angel costumes, and on one unmade bed, pink piggy-themed sheets with food crumbs that supported a small ant colony. At the end of the hall was the bathroom, its eye-watering bouquet beckoning. He opened the bathroom door.

Whoa. Death and gravity in cahoots.

"Gravity, Tristan," Philo's elderly grandmother had once told him, gumming her way through the syllables, *"is no longer my friend."*

True that, especially when seated on a toilet.

The cops had found Phoenicia, the forensics notes said, her bulk seated there, her top half wedged between the toilet tank and the wall, her body propped up until it began melting from decomposition. Her last known sighting had been two weeks and two days earlier, at the senior center. The coroner decided the date of her last visit to the center worked fine as the date of her death, and that she'd died from a coronary. In over two weeks of decomposition, gravity had done its thing.

From what Philo could tell, the coroner's office had taken enough of her body to legitimately say it was Phoenicia in her closed casket. Left behind was a toilet full of soupy internal organs and waste, and on the tile floor around it, gooey black blood mixed with what was probably more liquefied human being.

"Seen it before, sir," Patrick said, now behind Philo in the bathroom. "And I seen bodies before they took 'em, too."

That's all Philo needed to hear. "Really? Good. So Patrick, how about you—"

"Good training for you, sir," Patrick said, not letting him finish. "That's what Grace told me my first time. 'Good training, Patrick. You can handle it.' That's what she said. And I took care of it, sir. You can do it. Good training for you too, sir."

"Um—"

"No one better than you, Mr. Trout, sir," Patrick added. Philo was pretty sure his about-face and retreat hid a smirk.

"Wise guy," Philo said under his breath.

Philo produced a bottle of disinfectant. He sprayed the mound inside the toilet. Its surface rippled like a wind gust across a lake. Maggots.

Easy fix, he thought: flush the toilet. He twisted the handle, realized his mistake immediately. The commode started overflowing.

"Aww, FUCK!" Philo reached for the shut off valve under the tank, steadying himself with a hand on the plastic toilet seat. Another mistake. The seat snapped, and Philo slipped shoulder deep into the maggoty innards inside the toilet bowl. His scream was prehistoric, lengthening into uncontrollable gagging, and culminating in the elimination of his stomach contents in the bathroom sink.

* * *

Philo changed his Tyvek suit. After Patrick fixed the clog with a plumbing snake, the toilet flushed, and the remainder of the body sludge that the coroner hadn't wanted disappeared into the sewers. The bathroom generated one hazmat bag, two thirty-gallon biohazard containment drums, and two layers of flooring with the third, glued linoleum, also contaminated. They boiled water and used a shovel to pry the flooring up for removal. Four hours later the bathroom was spotless, top to bottom, from scrubbing with antiseptic and enzyme cleaners.

Philo called his customer, the woman's niece, from the front porch.

"We're finished, ma'am. I'll work up a quote for taking care of the rest of the house. You'll need to let me know if you'd like to be here when we do it."

"Fine," the niece said. "Did you find Marco?"

"Who?"

"My aunt's dog, Marco. He's an older dog, a midsize spaniel mix. Any sign of him?"

In the kitchen they'd disposed of two dog bowls, one containing canned dog food and live maggots, the other an empty water bowl with caked, dead maggots, but, "No. No dog. But I can't guarantee he isn't inside the house mixed in somewhere with your aunt's things."

Patrick humped the last waste drum out the front door, dropped it onto the porch floorboards, and rolled it on its edge over to the steps. Philo ended the call with the niece and reset the heat thermostat to fifty degrees to keep the pipes from freezing. He helped Patrick guide the drum to the van, where they hoisted it inside.

"We're going to bid on cleaning the whole property," he told Patrick. "Gimme a few minutes while I walk the perimeter." It was also to make sure that, as he'd already reported to the niece, there was no dog.

Philo entered the unlocked garage—no car and not in need of a biohazard clean—then he completed his circumnavigation of the house. No need for their services outside, and still no Marco. Back to the step van.

The engine running and the heat up, Patrick waited inside, his head down and earbuds on, mesmerized by an online video game. Philo climbed in, slid the door shut.

"No issues in or around the garage. We'll quote on cleaning the inside only. Yard's beat up, like the dog spent a lot of time out here, but no sign of him."

Patrick stared past Philo's shoulder. His eyes widened. "Uh-oh."

"Uh-oh what?"

"There, sir. *There.*" Patrick pointed.

Philo turned, focused, noticed only the crimped rain gutter. Still hanging low, still terminating in the cracked bathtub. "Where? What?"

"That brown icicle, sir, coming from the bottom of the tub, it's, it's—"

Not an icicle, now that Philo looked at it. Looked more like frozen leg of dog.

* * *

One swing from the sledgehammer and the porcelain tub split in two. Beneath the crunchy leaf topping, Marco the Dog's body was encased at the bottom of a bathtub-shaped block of dirty brown ice. Poor Marco, who no doubt had been thirsty rather than looking for an ice bath. Philo lightly rapped the ice block on its side a few times with the sledge, not knowing why he was being so tentative, the ice chipping but otherwise not cooperating. He put his back into an overhead swing. The block separated, giving up the dog's stiff body like a gooey chocolate Easter egg.

"Patrick, get me a fifty-gallon. We'll put him in with some of the ice. He'll keep that way until we can get him to the bio waste drop-off. Patrick? Yo, Patrick?"

Patrick was nearly catatonic, staring at the dog's body amid the chunks of split ice on the grass. After a moment, he broke the trance.

"I think I had a dog when I was a kid, sir."

5

One scheduled stop became two. Patrick needed it to be this way, and Philo complied. The planned stop was at a hazardous waste facility in the Kensington section of Philly, open to anyone with a biohazard dumping permit. Everything from today's job should have exited their truck in Kensington, but it hadn't, not after Patrick's pleading. Their second stop was the neighborhood animal shelter.

"I'll pay for it, sir," Patrick said. He rolled the biohazard container with the dog's remains out of the truck. A shelter employee directed them to the rear entrance.

"Relax, Patrick, the company will pick up the tab."

"No. I'm taking the ashes. They're for me, so I wanna pay for it, sir."

"Patrick—"

"No one better than Patrick, sir. I'm paying for it. Done deal, sir."

They were ushered inside the rear door, where an attendant talked money. Three hundred bucks for cremation, a stained walnut urn, and an engraved plaque. Without a plaque, two forty-five. Turnaround time for the ashes, a week to ten days.

"No need for a plaque, right, Patrick?" Philo said.

Patrick agreed, but wasn't fully convinced. "Maybe later, sir. When I think of something to put on it."

Philo watched him retrieve the cash, twenties, tens, fives, then ones—each denomination from a different hazmat suit pocket—watched him peel the bills off. More uniform pockets probably meant more cash, maybe in higher denominations. "You carry a lot of cash, Patrick?"

"Yeah. It's so I don't get beat into another coma."

Back in the van, Patrick put his earbuds back in. They entered traffic, headed south to meet with the ER doctor at Pennsylvania Hospital. Four miles from their visit with Dr. Andelmo, it would be long enough—fifteen minutes in traffic—for Philo to do some gentle probing.

"Remember anything else about your dog?"

Patrick hummed along to the noise in his ears, a rhythmic rap track. He lifted his head, stared unfocused out the front window and removed an earbud, his look distant. "His name was maybe Poy, sir. He looked like Marco. Brown and white. Poy sounds right. Yeah. Maybe. I'm not sure, sir, but Poy sounds good."

"Where was this?"

"Um..." He raised his head again, was now in full ponder mode, his face contorting. In front of them the dense noon traffic on Columbus Boulevard was at least moving, their original ETA to the doctor still looking good. "Umm..."

Philo held his breath, wanting him to go deep, to dig inside that dented melon of his, to find the name of a town, or a street, something.

Patrick's head drooped. He returned his interest to the phone in his lap, his enthusiasm gone. "We became a state in 1959."

Alaska. Somewhere in the Aleutian Islands. A canned response. The reflex equivalent of *I don't have a fucking clue*. Hundreds of thousands of godforsaken square miles. No record of him there, alive, dead, sick, or missing.

"Okay, sport, we're close to the hospital. Ready to say hi to Dr. Andelmo?" Philo resisted saying "again," as Patrick had no recollection of being in the ER with this man the first time.

"Ready, sir. No one better than Patrick, sir."

Inside the parking garage, Philo ran his hand through his hair, tamping down his rooster comb top and the side tufts that belonged behind his ears. He checked himself in the rearview, then assessed Patrick. Not bad, the two of them tradesmen-chic in their luminescent blue uniforms. Patrick's light brown face had skin as thick and shock-absorbing as whale blubber; something pro boxers would kill for. Still, an off-center dip the size of a revolver's gunstock menaced his head just above his hairline, a distance above his left eye.

Philo expected this meeting to be about Patrick's progress, the doc no doubt wanting to hear someone tell him he'd done good by bringing Patrick out of the coma, considering all the bad press Andelmo had received recently. If one could ignore the allegations and instead key on what Grace had shared about Patrick's treatment, the doc came off sounding like a hero.

A beaming Dr. Francisco X. Andelmo waited for them inside an office near the ER, his smock personalized in a red longhand script above a breast pocket. His eyes were friendly but dark, their corners crinkled by deep crow's feet. His nose was wide above a capped, glistening smile, and below that, his upper torso looked buff under his tailored doctor whites. Remove the smock and replace it with gold bling and a wolf-toothed necklace on a bare chest, he could have passed for an aging Mayan high priest who colored his hair. Patrick and Philo sat across from him and one other doctor, a Dr. Barry Heineken or something, someone Philo now didn't give a damn about, because Dr. Barry wanted Philo to leave the room.

"You're not a family member, Mr. Trout," Dr. Barry said. "You're his employer. You shouldn't be here. You don't have a horse in this race."

The comment hung out there, its pointless stupidity making Philo squint. He waited for Dr. Andelmo to straighten his associate out. When that didn't happen, Philo's mood spiraled, escalating from puzzled to incredulous to barely being able to contain his temper.

"Where the hell are you and *your* horse from, Barry, Mars?" His stare drilled a hole into the bridge of the balding little fuck's nose. "Patrick's here because I drove him here, because he doesn't drive, because he can't drive, because no one will give him a license *to* drive. Because he doesn't know his name. No family members are here because he doesn't know if he has any, and if he does, he doesn't know who or where they are. Isn't that the whole damn point of this visit? To see how he's doing while he tries to get his life back on track?"

"Dr. Heinzman to you, Mr. Trout," the doctor said, stiffening his jaw. "Head of transplant medicine here, and the hospital's chief administrator. And I don't care for your tone. If you don't leave this office, I'll call Security—"

"Listen, *Barry*, you pompous fuck, if you think I'm leaving Patrick alone with you, you're more confused than Patrick."

Patrick remained calm, a stoic presence belying his intellectual shortcomings. Dr. Andelmo keenly observed the exchange, and Patrick's demeanor during it, which seemed unaffected by the heat coming from Philo. The Latino doctor stayed out of the disagreement until finally addressing his colleague. "Barry—calm down, Barry."

Philo smiled. Not Dr. Heinzman—*Barry*.

A little dressing down from your associate, Barry-boy, you giant sack.

"Your point is well taken, Mr. Trout," Dr. Andelmo continued. His diction was formal, precise, his accent confirming him as Central or South American. "No one is here to discuss any malfeasance, or anything detrimental to your employee-employer relationship. Barry, Mr. Trout is clearly here as a friend of, and representative for, Mr. Stakes, not as his employer."

"But Dr. Andelmo—"

Dr. Andelmo waved his hand at his protesting colleague and addressed Patrick directly. "Mr. Stakes. Can Mr. Trout be here while we speak with you?"

"Er, yeah, sure."

"That handles the HIPAA requirement, Barry. Perhaps it would be best if you leave me your notes while you get back to the business of running your hospital. All I want to do as his former physician is to check on his condition. Just leave him to me please."

With Dr. Heinzman gone, the desk in front of this neurosurgeon and alleged organ trafficker—Philo had googled him after Grace's tirade—now held folders with pages and pages of hospital forms, notes, and charts. Posted outside the office door were two security guards who arrived soon after Dr. Heinzman's exit; they stood peering through the glass at them. Dr. Andelmo left his seat and closed the blinds.

"There. A little more privacy for us. My deepest apologies for my associate's behavior, gentlemen. HIPAA requirements dictate that administrators err on the side of caution. So. Patrick." He refolded his hands on the desk. "It has been a while. Three years, I see. May I call you Patrick?"

An attempt by the doctor to bond. Patrick responded. "Yes, sir. You can call me Patrick, sir, because that's what people call me. Patrick Stakes."

"Wonderful. First, I appreciate if you'd leave your phone number with us for any follow-ups, Patrick. So. I am sure you are wondering why I asked you here."

The doc emerged from behind his desk, raised his stethoscope to his ears, and listened to Patrick's heart and lungs. "It is to see your progress for myself, considering you left my care in such a hurry the last time. To see how you are assimilating despite your challenges. A colleague of mine called yesterday, and he said he saw you at that tragic Amtrak train suicide near the Philadelphia Zoo. That must have been horrible."

"Yes, sir, horrible. Messy. Sad. Sir, what does 'assimilating' mean?"

The doc took Patrick's vitals while hitting all the right marks conversationally, explaining himself to his former patient. He then shared his satisfaction at how Patrick was managing to fit in, leading a productive life despite the brain damage and the loss of practically all his memory.

"Patrick, I am curious. How did you end up working for Mr. Trout?"

"'Cause of Mr. and Missus Blessid. They were at this place in, ah, South Philly, near, um, um..."

Philo offered him a prompt. "The Italian Market, on Ninth Street. Not far from Pat's Steaks, right, Patrick?" Affirmative, Patrick's beaming face told them.

Philadelphia's Italian Market was block after block of open-air stalls filled with fresh fruits, vegetables, meats, fish, spices, and some restaurants smart enough to be located nearby, plus, it was the origin of the iconic footage of a jogging Rocky Balboa forever emblazoned into everyone's memory. For Philo, Stallone's *Rocky* bordered on a religious experience.

"The Blessids were cleaning up after a crime scene," Philo said, continuing when Patrick didn't. "There was a violent murder in a second-story apartment overlooking the street vendors. The forensics people—cops, detectives, a coroner, even CSI sometimes—they do the investigating, but secondary responders, biohazard people like us, we do the cleanup."

"Yeah, a crime scene," Patrick parroted. "I was outside, sir, looking for something to eat." He scrunched up his face, the memory not a good one. "The kidney was mixed in with Joey the Butcher's meats."

A puzzled Dr. Andelmo looked to Philo.

Philo explained. "Patrick was living on the street, homeless, a hungry kid who the Blessids later learned had been hanging around the Italian Market for weeks, around the open stalls, because that's where the food was. He'd picked a human kidney out of the meats and seafood displayed there on shaved ice; maybe it looked like a bloated rib eye. There'd been a messy execution upstairs. A shotgun blew someone out the second-story picture window, onto a cloth awning that split under the weight. Some of the victim landed on the street. The coroner collected the body, just didn't get all of it. On one of the Blessids' trips outside, Patrick handed the kidney —er, I should say, what was left of the kidney—to Grace Blessid."

"Joey said I should give it to Grace, sir. It tasted different than the other meats," Patrick said.

Philo patted him on the shoulder. "I understand, Patrick."

"Joey threw up 'cause he saw me take a bite out of it."

"Okay, we got it, Patrick, thanks."

They waited for the doctor's reaction; this couldn't have been something he heard every day. The dead air finally got the best of Philo. "So, Doctor, he's looking great, isn't he? You need anything else from him? You have any new info on him?"

The doctor finally spoke. "Your mistake about the kidney, Patrick," he asked, "it was fortuitous, yes?"

"He means lucky," Philo said to Patrick.

"Yeah, lucky. Grace took the rest of the kidney and asked me if I needed a job. She said if I had a job, I'd be able to buy my own food instead of stealing it, maybe even cook it if I wanted. I said yeah, gimme a job, please."

"I see." The doctor clicked his ballpoint multiple times, his smile gone. "Patrick, in the ER you were frostbitten, bloody, and unconscious, and whatever signals your brain was giving you"—he checked his notes—"what came out of your mouth was gibberish. Nonsensical things, or so we thought." He turned to Philo. "The delirium—it was expected, considering his bloodied skull. But his mouth was bloody too, his lips caked with it. That blood, Mr. Trout, was not his."

Philo shrugged. "Sorry, Doctor, but that's old news. The cops investigated, went searching for the bastard whose blood he was wearing but never found anyone. None of that helped him get ID'd."

"Inside his mouth, Mr. Trout. The blood was on his teeth and tongue."

Philo's head tilted. His confused facial expression preceded his question. "What's your point, Doc?"

"Hearing about this kidney," Dr. Andelmo said, "that concerns me. One of the nonsensical things he said during his delirium was, and I quote from the transcribed notes, he said, 'I ate a pinky.'" He turned toward Patrick. "Have you ever heard of kreatophagia, Patrick?"

"Um—"

"Of course you haven't. It means having a raw meat obsession. And eating raw meat can make a person very sick. Some foolish people think a raw meat diet is a good diet for them, but it isn't. Tell me something else, Patrick."

Patrick turned his attention from the doctor, his look to Philo pleading and confused. Philo patted Patrick's forearm, gave him a "don't worry, it's all good" nod.

The doctor continued. "Have you experienced any nocturnal wanderings?"

"Huh?"

"People with traumatic brain injuries—bad knocks to the head, like you had—occasionally sleepwalk after the trauma, even become violent during these episodes. Have you awakened in places where you didn't know how you got there?"

He squirmed in his seat, rubbed his head, glanced at Philo. "No," he said, sounding unconvincing.

"There's no wrong answer here, Patrick. I'm only looking to assess your condition, son. Do you sleepwalk?"

"No," he said, more forcefully this time. "No, sir. Nope."

"Fine. Do you know what cannibalism is?"

"Wait, what?" Philo sat up straighter, his fuse lit. "What the fuck, Doctor? Where'd that come from? He made a mistake with the kidney, okay? It's not like the kid's got everything sorted out. Christ. Sometimes the simplest shit gives him trouble, and now you're filling his impressionistic head with this crap?"

"Please, Mr. Trout—"

"Fuck you, Doc. C'mon, Patrick, we're leaving."

Good doc and bad doc, just like with cop interrogations. Philo was pissed he hadn't seen it queuing up that way with these two pompous pricks. Hearing about the kidney, it was like a light went on for Dr. Andelmo, a direct salvo at Patrick. Philo started the truck, let it idle.

Cannibalism, though. Really? Cannibalism?

The truck left the parking lot, easing into traffic. "Patrick, I need to know. You eat raw meat?"

"No. Maybe. Not much. Sometimes."

"Which is it? You eat raw meat or not?"

"Yes."

"Well, stop doing it. It'll make you sick."

6

Kaipo packed up after finishing with her last client, a male TV news anchor living in an art deco high-rise condo in Center City Philadelphia. Bundled for the cold in a warm coat and crocheted dangle hat, she left via the news anchor's private elevator, pulling her folding table in its cart. At street level she entered the park at Washington Square, on to her next appointment in the same neighborhood.

Factoid: Hawaii as a state boasted the second lowest percentage of obese adults in the US behind Colorado. Every personal trainer on the Hawaiian Islands hyped this stat, using it to attract transplanted mainlanders to their practices, their clients desperate for transformation from obese ogres to gladiator ninjas ready to flaunt their new bodies in their island paradise. When Kaipo was younger she'd been no different as a trainer, selling her services to much the same population, until she decided to swim upstream to the source, the mainland itself. She had parlayed her Hawaiian brand of training and massage therapy into a small business employing four Hawaiian trainers in addition to herself, and she had set about attracting well-heeled customers to her growing stable of clients.

"But why Philadelphia?" the philly.com health editor interviewing her had asked. "Why not the glitz and glamor of the West Coast? Why not New York?"

Kaipo had taken the interview soon after she'd hung out her shingle, conducting it from her apartment home office via Skype. Her long, straight black hair was clipped atop her head, an easy early morning rise-and-shine solution; no one would notice her bedhead. Her pouty features were captivating, with full cheeks and lips and bright, confident eyes. "High demand here," she'd answered. "Apparently no one else from the Islands wants to set up shop in Philadelphia."

A lie. A big, deadly lie. True, there were no other freelance Native Hawaiian personal trainers in Philly—her business employed the only other four—but this was because an influential group of Hawaiian businesspeople had arrived in the city years back, preceding Kaipo, and had set up their own establishments: restaurants, coin-operated laundries, dry cleaners, corner groceries, and car washes, plus illegal gaming and high-end escort services. This influential group was the transplanted Hawaiian mob. Nicknamed the Enterprise, or Ka Hui, they had been eradicated, reportedly, from their native island soil in the late 1990s. But reports of Ka Hui's death had been greatly exaggerated. Italian wiseguys, the Russian and Chinese mobs, Mexican cartels, each had storied presences in all the urban environments on the US mainland. Ka Hui instead took advantage of its obscurity, its rumored demise, and the unlikelihood of such an obscure pairing, a Philadelphia–Hawaii connection, to make quiet inroads into the city's neighborhoods. There was now a network. It had income, it had soldiers, and it had a support staff.

Which included Kaipo Mawpaw, a striking personal trainer and massage therapist. She'd been recruited while still in the Islands, also while she still had a cocaine and pill problem, something her clandestine employer leveraged to secure her interest. The leverage: We'll help you kill the addiction monkey. Let us do that for you—or else. Simple intimidation, but a business deal as well. So what was in it for them?

They liked her extracurricular work, a certain expertise, and she couldn't perform it when she wasn't sober. So their help became intensive psychoanalytic therapy with a twist: a therapist on their payroll worked on her head to subdue her cravings while her employers worked on the heads of her drug suppliers, as in—the twist—if you gave Ms. Mawpaw any drugs, you'd be beheaded. She'd relapsed four times, involving four different dealers. After three dealer heads surfaced around the city, the street began going out of its way to not sell to her. The fourth dealer was still at large. Kaipo had at last, after one year, ten months, and twenty-two days—693 days clean in total—fully embraced her new sobriety.

Ka Hui, "The Enterprise," flourished. So did Kaipo's personal trainer business. When other entrepreneurial Hawaiian trainer types relocated here they were soon persuaded to un-relocate. After seeing the gory outcome of these persuadings, plus her personal involvement in a number of other unrelated jobs, Kaipo's avocation as Ka Hui's mob cleaner-slash-fixer had been solidified.

She was not an assassin. As a benevolent businesswoman with scruples, or so she fashioned herself, she'd kill only for self-preservation. Much like last night's dilemma: the old man at the Chinese restaurant. She'd caught up to him on the street, his gait slow, deliberate, a shuffler. She pulled him into an alley and put a gun under his chin. He didn't scream.

"My money is in my jacket pocket. I don't have much," he'd said in broken English. His eyes were cloudy, full of cataracts. *"I smell your dinner, your perfume, and your rotting tooth, but I will never know your face. Take my money, but please show me mercy."*

She'd made a mistake, she'd told him, and she let him live.

Kaipo now retrieved a phone from her right coat pocket, called ahead to make sure her appointment was ready for her. In her left pocket a second phone buzzed, a TracFone disposable.

She answered it. "Yes?"

A male voice. "Did you find last week's fortune cookie satisfactory?"

"It was delicious. Thank you."

"Good," came out elongated, the caller giving in to a scratchy hack and sniffle, adding, "your meeting has been moved up." In the background on the caller's end, a bone-chilling scream reverberated in their ears. "We'll be ready for you in two hours."

The caller's hack-sniffle, Kaipo knew, was nasal cancer. For starters, an unusual diagnosis. Even more unusual, it was stage 4. Lymph nodes and elsewhere. Terminal. Dry snuff tobacco wasn't normally a killer. Which meant that Olivier 'Ōpūnui, the caller, fit into an extremely small percentage of users. His habit had him sniffling into the phone after their call ended, a muffled hot-mike moment suffixed by a spoken "oh, good-ness," that, Kaipo surmised, came after he looked at whatever his nose had expelled into his tissues. Then came the lengthy, familiar *sniff-f-f* she'd heard and seen him execute a hundred times before. Out with the diseased and bloodied snot, in with the finely ground snuff tobacco, until his nostrils consumed the pinch he'd taken between his thumb and forefinger. A filthy habit, and a chic affectation in the circles Olivier traveled, but Kaipo hadn't made the mistake of thinking the affliction diminished his allegiances, instincts, or physical capacity for violence. Her handler was a mobster. Healthy or not, he followed orders, or he would die in the attempt.

She retrieved her right-pocket phone and rescheduled her next appointment.

* * *

Kaipo pulled her Chevy van under the *Grand Opening Feb. 29* banner hung across the side of the building. Remnants of figure eights from muddy tires had christened the newly tarred parking lot of the car wash. Out of her vehicle, she pushed through a whitewashed door made of thick opaque plastic cut into a two-story garage door of the same composition. She pulled her small cleaning cart through the portal, into the interior.

This abandoned car wash in Olney had been reclaimed and retrofitted to perform as a six-dollar express wash with free vacuums. Its Quonset hut footprint was ideal, and the new car wash was less than two weeks away from opening for business. Glistening, standing water on an interior floor indicated it had been used already, no doubt today.

First in line inside the building were heavy fabric rag-strips in faded green, hanging as tightly together as matches in a matchbook, a thousand-legged Cthulhu monster look-alike for swooshing and scrubbing vehicles passing underneath. Behind the rag-strips were side and overhead brushes in Cookie Monster blue and Elmo red. Large painted bands of red, white, and blue barber-poled the aluminum pillars and the overhead scaffolding that housed the hot wax sprayers. Beyond that, industrial strength wide-angle air blowers. Front to back it was a carnival of car love that tunneled through the dinge of the old Quonset hut's interior, soon to get a steady diet of road dust and dirt and late winter salt.

Kaipo removed her wool gloves and dangle hat and tucked them all into a pocket. She blew into her fingers; it was chilly in here, could see her breath. And lately, as the old Chinese man had noticed, her breath had a distinctly unclean dragon-mouth edge to it, from a decaying tooth needing a crown. She popped a Tic Tac and continued absorbing the surroundings.

Twenty yards into the tunnel was her reason for being here. A figure sat slumped in a chair under high-ceilinged spotlighting, unmoving, near the car wash exit. Add this to her toothache, and her contact's handle, Olivier, and the images echoed Laurence Olivier's movie-dentist's venue, plus his question to Dustin Hoffman's tortured Marathon Man: "Is it safe?" From an intimidation, torture, and murder perspective, the people who paid her and Olivier were in a similar business. She was here to remove the evidence, and the aftermath, of their obscene use of this place.

Her first time here, she could see the attraction, knew they'd use this location again, and maybe other car washes, for this kind of work. High-pressure hoses and sprayers, scalding water, a covered drain trench, and a waterproofed, stain-resistant cement floor. Kaipo wheeled her chemistry cart along the tire guide rails that ran the length of the building, stooped to move past the Elmo brushes overhead. On the other side of the brushes, her eyes concentrated on her object of interest, seated under the liquid hot wax sprayer. The chair with the slumped body was adjacent to the drain. She stepped closer, her cart behind her.

Some of his sepia-brown skin was gone, boiled off to expose his musculature in spots, his skeleton in others. There could be little question about the efficacy of the car wash's hot wax nozzles; a blend of wax and skin formed a mound on the floor that reached above the man's ankles. Alongside him now, she still couldn't smell the body, the stink masked by the thick, sweet odor of the wax. She dipped her finger in it; still hot. She eyed the drain trench, which cut a wide channel inside the tire guiderails, its silver-black grating flush with the floor. Straining, she gripped and tilted a section of the metal grate covering the trench to gauge its weight, then she lifted a four-foot piece of it off the channel and set it aside.

The trench was a foot deep. In it, preserved in wax below her, was more melted human being. She tucked her hair inside her stretchy biohazard cap, spread some Tiger Balm on her upper lip, put on a mask, and stuck her head and a flashlight inside the trench to see down its length. The channel ran forward, toward the car wash exit, and was mostly clear except for what looked like wax and body effluence that had gathered near its end. Farther down, she removed the grate to see where the channel connected with piping destined for the public sewers. A high-pressure hot water rinse from a maintenance hose would clean up the trench and the drain nicely, and push along whatever mess that had already accumulated, plus the additional mess she was about to create.

Kaipo returned to the front of the car wash track and poked her head out the door to confirm there was no audience. Back inside, with the press of a button, the car wash garage door lifted. She backed her van up to it, opened its rear doors. Inside, on casters, was her pressure cooker. She slid a short ramp from the van's undercarriage and unloaded the cooker from the van bed, onto the car wash floor.

Commercial quality, with a stainless-steel tub and a 150-quart capacity, size-wise the cooker's exterior mimicked a car wash industrial vacuum on steroids, and was a hand-me-down from her employers by way of one of their restaurants. A small metal plate stamped onto its curved exterior wall listed its specs in both Chinese and English. She hit the garage door button again. The door slid back down to the floor, Kaipo and the pressure cooker inside.

In her biohazard suit now, she squeezed on medical-grade nitrile gloves. Kaipo rolled the cooker the length of the car wash and set it up over the drain, next to the body.

Sodium hydroxide, or lye, heated to 300 degrees with sixty pounds of pressure per square inch, would liquefy a body in a few hours and leave behind a flushable residue the consistency of maple syrup. Her head covering in place à la a 1950s spaceman, she peered down her nose at the victim. He was wrapped tightly in the chair by multiple bungee cords. When she unwrapped the cords, the unsupported body leaned forward then toppled to the floor.

There were cavities where organs should have been. No heart, no lungs.

She poked at the body with a broom handle, separating the husk from other internal organs. No kidneys or liver either. No eyes.

An execution with feeling. A torture in retribution for some heinous act, but the organ harvesting was new territory for her employers. They were recycling the trash for money, every reusable organ exploited.

They paid her to dispose partial bodies the same as for disposing the whole ones, but the organ-harvesting thing was over the top. A new, obscene direction for Ka Hui.

No time to process this now. She needed to get to work.

Kaipo unrolled a plastic tarp, gripped the severed upper torso under the shoulders and dragged it on top. Something pink on the side of the black man's skull got her attention: a Post-it note attached—stapled—to an earlobe. She jerked it off with one quick rip, the way she'd remove a Band-Aid.

Handwritten on the note in 'Ōlelo Hawai'i: *E waiho ke po'o ma ke pākeke polū.* The translation, *Leave the head in the blue bucket.* Below that, also in Hawaiian, *You're welcome.*

The *You're welcome* presupposed her thank-you, but for what, she didn't know. Kaipo looked more closely at the skinned heap that was the upper body of the victim.

God no.

She pushed the broom handle through what was left of his wax-covered lips, levering jaw muscles hardening from rigor mortis; his mouth opened. There she found what she hadn't wanted to: two silver front teeth.

Monte, the last of her drug dealers.

Threats by Ka Hui had long lives. This one had lasted one year, ten months, and twenty-two days—693 days in total—coincident with her sobriety date. This was dealer number four, the one attached to her last relapse.

"So sorry, Monte. You didn't deserve this."

Resigned, she found her machete in the van, returned to the body "Or this, either." *Whap.* His head separated from his torso with one coconut-splitting swing.

The pressure cooker powered up. She strained while she hefted Monte, minus his head, into the cooker, then seasoned the stew with the lye. The head she deposited into a biohazard bag, would leave it as directed in the blue bucket next to the office. Ka Hui's machismo bullshit, with its messages for the street, had always been so overly dramatic.

While the pressure cooker hummed and popped and gurgled, it was time for a little break. Kaipo patted down her sweaty face and retouched her makeup, then settled in with some reading on her e-reader in her van for the next few hours while the lye did its work. After, she would wash out the cooker and use a hose to rinse all the sludge the length of the trench to the drain, turning what little was left of the victim into sewer meat. By then it would be dinnertime. She'd grab some local Mexican takeout and eat in her van.

* * *

After dinner she keyed a text into her left-pocket phone, to Olivier, staying cryptic: *It's safe. It's very safe.*

But the cleanup had been unnerving. At a younger age, Kaipo had lost two important people in her life, each from a different side of the organ-transplant equation. Her mother, when Kaipo was a teen, needed a heart transplant that never came. And Kaipo's drug-addicted lover sold his own body parts to stay high, then committed suicide when he ran out of parts to sell. Ka Hui's new black-market endeavor was a problem for her.

7

Philo parallel-parked his Jeep on the street in the Mayfair section of Philadelphia. Diffused, yellow-hued lighting from two spotlights on motion sensors bathed the front steps leading to his row house plus the house's microscopic front lawn. He humped his plastic bag of groceries up the gray steps to his front door.

He'd gotten lucky. When he'd moved back to Philly, the two-story row home where he'd spent the first eighteen years of his life was for sale. He closed on the house, moved in, then emptied out his long-term storage unit and hauled its contents over to the house: family items, pictures of his deceased mother when she was healthy, other keepsakes, specifically his father's massive WWII leather-bound steamer trunk with its wood struts and brass appointments, covered with decals and stencils from the USN's Pacific war theater. Guadalcanal, Okinawa, Hawaii, the Philippines. He made the mistake of telling his VA shrink how fortunate he thought all this was, being able to live in his boyhood home, surrounding himself with family memorabilia. His shrink pronounced these feelings abnormal, citing textbook "needing to return to the womb" bullshit. Philo fired his shrink.

He'd had little idea what was in his dad's trunk beyond a US flag and the old man's naval officer's uniform, but he was correcting this oversight in small doses. Absorbing it all at once, that his father's honorable military life could be stuffed into the drawers of a four-by-two-by-two-foot box, would have been too painful otherwise.

The house was three resales removed from his time there as a kid, in a section of the city that was "changing," which was white-people speak for turning nonwhite. Hearing neighbors whisper this pissed him off. Not willing to embrace diversity? Then move the fuck out. Many had done just that, in mass quantities, and the ongoing exodus had made the house a steal.

He pulled open the tan aluminum storm door. Loose mail sitting short of the brass mail slot at the door's base slid out underfoot, onto his welcome mat. He gathered it up. Soon as he inserted his key, the mail slot cover popped up to bang his ankle, shielding a cat paw strike not visible to the naked eye. Lucky for him the strike contained no exposed claws, this because he wasn't the mailman. He jammed his shoe against the brass cover to keep it from flipping up a second time, felt additional strikes against it from one pissed-off cat.

"Step away from the door, Six."

Meow.

"Cut the shit, sweetie. Do it. Now."

Meow.

Philo pushed through, letting the storm door snap shut behind him. Six the Cat clawed her way into his bag-filled arms, cuddled his neck, then purred in Calico ecstasy. She moved onto his shoulder while Philo punched in a few numbers on a security system keypad. "Good to see you too, sweetie," he said. "Let's eat."

It would be dinner in the living room in front of the flat screen. For Philo, a pint of freshly cooked spicy corn chowder and a takeout Caesar salad with grilled chicken. For Six, canned tuna and all the salad croutons she could guilt Philo into giving her.

He sipped a scotch for dessert, found and neutralized his snail mail, then policed the litter box in the basement. Cat shit in the trash, it was time to hit the equipment. In gym trunks and a light T-shirt, he fired up the space heater, else his middle-aged bones would catch a chill. Six skittered down the steps to join him, got in some reps at her cat scratching post, then sat back in awe and purred in time to Philo's grunts as he attacked the heavy bag with fists and feet.

He toweled himself off. Tonight was laundry night, or so he'd told his attorney girlfriend, Lola, which was the reason she wasn't here. Doing laundry tired him, and she was okay with this as an excuse; she wanted him at peak performance when they slept together.

LAUNDRY was stenciled in small black letters on the tiny door to a squat locker-styled cabinet, a piece of white basement furniture that sat between the washer and the dryer. He snapped the door open and lifted a pimpled plastic container the size of a toolbox from the middle shelf, bypassing the liquid Tide and Downy. He humped the kit to a workbench, flipped open the lid, turned on a TV for company. Inside the kit, carbon cleaner, bore polish, solvent degreaser, brushes, gun oil.

"Doing laundry" would take him three hours, all of which would be spent watching cable news while he worked. His row house had six rooms plus a bath and a half, a finished basement, and a garage. Ten places where he could park his ass at different times during the day or night. Ten places that each needed a gun. The handgun he carried and his sometimes ankle-holstered derringer brought his total pieces owned to twelve firearms. He'd start with cleaning the shotgun he kept in the basement.

Another unsettling news story on the TV screen: discovery of a home-land terrorist plot, this one in Michigan, its tentacles reaching north into Canada, east into Pennsylvania and New England. All bad actors, part of a radical Islamist group, including some who were homegrown. Vengeful fucks just like Al Qaeda overseas, terrorizing the infidels. Common, maybe even ignorable, abstractions nowadays. Except for the ones that weren't. The ones out there with long memories who maybe disliked him and his military brethren personally. The ones with grudges that had merit, fueled by his past deeds and one very visible, successful mission.

Twelve guns. Not too many. Maybe not enough.

* * *

Lights out, bedtime. Philo louvered the slats to the living room window shutters open enough to watch the night, empty and cold, outside his front window. Snowflakes swirled around the tops of streetlights, blowing haphazardly as they feathered Unruh Avenue ahead of a light snowstorm moving in. A few sober souls bundled against the brutally frigid night braved the weather on foot and pushed up the sidewalk from the bus stop. A few others with only a vague notion of where they were going did likewise, fortified for their trip home by last call at a pub around the corner.

Aside from the windows, there were three ways into his house: the first-floor front door, an aluminum jalousie door off the basement that opened to a short alley, and the door from the garage, his driveway and backyard the size of a storage pod. While in the house, he kept the security system off. He was a light sleeper. He'd know sooner than any security company if there were a breach, and an alarm scaring off someone wanting to make a name for himself was not the preferred option; the asshole would only come back. If Philo weren't quick enough to stay ahead of a law enforcement response, the response wouldn't matter; he'd be dead by the time they arrived.

He removed his finger from between the window shutter slats. The love seat reclined, and he settled in so he could give his eyes and head a rest. The La-Z-Boy faced the picture window, front row seating situated for exterior viewing, not for living room conversation. He unfolded his long body, spread himself out across the open recliner, and pulled the wool blanket up to his waist. A loaded Sig Sauer went to his lap.

This double recliner was more comfortable than the one in the basement facing the back door, so tonight's four-plus-or-minus hours of sleep might be sounder. Six hopped onto his chest and balanced herself on her way down his reclining body until she reached his feet, then she dropped back onto the floor. She'd go through this routine in reverse in the morning, parking on his face until he woke up. When he slept in the living room, she occupied the cat bed next to the mail slot, unless she whined to go out.

Meow. MEOW...

Philo let her out the front door. An outdoor cat was an independent cat. Better she learned now, just in case.

8

The Blessid Trauma truck hit a highway pothole that made the four of them bounce in their seats. I 95 in Philadelphia was perpetually under construction, with uneven pavements, zigzagging tight lanes, and stretches without shoulders, terrorizing its everyday travelers with white-knuckle moments and frayed nerves.

Once inside Northeast Philadelphia they abandoned the interstate in favor of Route 13, Frankford Avenue, two lanes of worn blacktop made claustrophobic by narrow sidewalks and storefronts close to the street on both sides; their destination would keep them just inside the city limits. Philo shared a breakfast story about today's bowl of Frosted Flakes and the hairball garnish his cat had added to it, soon realizing that, shit-God-almighty, he'd fucked up by mentioning that he had a cat.

"Cats," Grace said, then mimicked a gag. "For people who like open boxes of shit in their kitchen."

"Basement."

"Whatever. You stay in this business long enough, you'll smell enough cat lady homes that you'll lose the cat."

"Copy that, Grace."

Cats topic dead. Good.

Patrick murmured something from the jump seat, into his filtered mask.

Philo checked him in the rearview, didn't pursue it, but Hank did, speaking loud enough to better the road whine. "You say something, Patrick?"

Patrick stopped tapping at the games on his phone to lower his mask. "Yup. What's the cat's name, Philo sir?"

Philo pretended he hadn't heard him.

"Philo," Hank said, louder than Patrick, "your cat. What's his name?"

"It's a she. She's a Calico. Six. Six the Cat."

"Odd name for a cat," Hank said.

"Guess I'm just not a Tigger or a Garfield kind of guy."

A quarter-mile farther along the blacktop, an excited Patrick pointed at a tandem bus approaching a bus stop. He pulled off his mask as they drove past. "That's the Sixty-six. A SEPTA trackless trolley. *Double* sixes, Philo, sir. Ha!"

Patrick had a keen interest in Philadelphia's public transit system, the cheapest way he had to get around the city by himself. He'd memorized all the routes, and on their trips to jobs they would often hear in detail how public transport could do just as good a job getting him there as their van.

Patrick spoke louder, this time more insistent. "I think it means something else, sir."

Philo didn't follow. "What means something else, Patrick?"

"Your cat's name. It means something else."

"Yeah, well, the names people give their cats don't much matter, bud. It's not like they answer to them."

"They mean something to their owners, sir."

Too close for Philo's comfort; he needed to end this conversation. He flipped on the radio, hummed along to some Neil Young, and paid special attention to the traffic. Patrick lifted his mask back onto his nose and mouth and found his earbuds, shutting himself down. He connected one earbud, raised the other, was snugging it into place until—

Mask off again. "I know what the name means, sir," Patrick said.

A millimeter from a clean getaway. "You do, do you?" Philo nonchalanted a wink at Grace, dismissing the question.

"Yeah. It's to make people think there's a one through five."

Philo forced a patronizing nod and a chuckle, like this was a cute comment. Problem was, in one regard it was true; a regard he didn't want to have to explain. Time to shut the topic down tight.

"That's, ah, pretty good, Patrick. But the reason for the name is top secret. If I told you"—he smiled back at him in the mirror—"I'd have to kill you, bud."

"Then don't tell me, sir."

Another day, another biohazard job, with Blessid Trauma on their way to an abandoned car dealership dormant for decades until it was resurrected in the nineties as a chop shop, where stolen cars went to become black market car parts. Philadelphia's Northeast Detectives unit had put the chop shop out of business almost as soon as it opened. The dealership's three-acre parking lot, a dismal piece of real estate, its blacktop buckled, the lot's cracks and craters claimed by ambitious winter-hearty weeds, was empty behind an ancient *For Sale or Lease* sign. They drifted past the dealership's former showroom, worn, gray plywood covering its tall windows. Philo guided the van around back of the building and shut the engine down next to a metal door with the word *PARTS* stenciled above it. Inside, Philo knew from the call, promised to give new meaning to *chop shop* and *PARTS* as identifiers. "How appropriate," he said. "We enter here."

Grace eased herself out of the step van, a bit shakier today, Hank by her side. Philo exited and stretched, his eyes taking in the exterior of the building. Its painted white cinder block construction stopped above the second story just short of the roof, where corrugated metal began and continued north to the roof's overhang, rusted over and stuffed with leaves and twigs in nooks that would become bird nests in the spring. Behind the short strip of parking spaces facing the overhead doors was farmland that extended multiple acres, the churned earth frozen, fettered with the remains of threshed cornstalks. Farther yet in the distance, at least two football fields away, was a housing subdivision.

It was private back here. A good place for people to enter and leave a building to do things they didn't want other people to see behind a number of closed garage doors, their plastic window construction painted black from the inside.

Bio-suited up, Philo and Patrick led the way. They shouldered the stodgy *PARTS* door open. A bright shaft of natural sunlight blinded them once inside, angled from a skylight two stories above the empty auto parts counter. They shaded their eyes, kept them lowered while they traversed a dusty floor toward a metal interior door painted in caution-tape yellow. Above the door, a rectangular plate in the same yellow carried the black-lettered message that belonged with the cautionary color: *Service area – No customers allowed.*

Philo grabbed the door handle, needing two hands to get it to budge. Once inside, another blinding skylight. Their hands shielded their eyes. A few steps past the intense shaft of sunlight, they lowered their arms.

Ten service bays in total, the first eight empty of anything they'd need to remedy, the space tidier than the area fronting the *PARTS* counter. The service area's walls, a dingy paper-bag brown, did not impress. The hydraulic car lifts had all been engaged, all raised by their single silvery pistons a foot or so off the floor. Other ceiling skylights lit the long room, dusty specks swirling in their shafts, the morning sun casting everything outside them in featureless shadows, their footsteps echoing. They approached the ninth and tenth car bays because this was where the action was.

Two metal single-bed frames with chipped white paint were centered on the last two car lifts and raised off the floor the same height as the other lifts, their mattresses waist-high. Blood-spattered sheets, latex gloves, bloodied gauze and gauze sponges lay on the first mattress. On the second, a dark-skinned body lay splayed under similar blood-soaked debris. The body had gaping holes, the head no eyes. Disgusting to see, it was worse to smell. Patrick checked his pockets for his Tiger Balm, started working it under his nose before handing the jar to Philo. Philo applied a generous dip above his lip until—

A hand, attached to a large man, dropped onto Patrick's shoulder from behind.

Philo wheeled, his greasy fingers ripping the offending arm away from Patrick and twisting it, a chicken-wing, bent-thumb combination that forced its owner to take one knee then two when Philo applied more lever-age. The man's head was now inches from the floor. Philo reached under the man's dangling suit jacket, removed a gun from a shoulder holster and pointed it at the back of his head. "Don't even breathe."

The former owner of the gun groaned. "Badge, wallet, coat pocket. Cop. Live crime scene. You can't—be in here…"

Dark suit, white shirt, red tie, heavyset, and from as unflattering a position as this, his upside-down jowls looked flabby enough to choke off his air if Philo were to lower him any farther. Philo drew the gun back, slid it out of reach. He found the guy's wallet and flipped it open. Inside, a detective's badge; the shield appeared legit. A friendly, with accessories and a coat sleeve now smudged with Tiger Balm.

"Sorry, Detective. Philo Trout, Blessid Trauma Services." He wiped his greasy fingers on his uniform pants, offered his hand. The detective begrudgingly used it to help himself up. Philo returned the badge and let the detective retrieve his gun.

Patrick was beside himself, his mask off, his face lit up bright as a kid at a magic show.

"That was some move, Philo sir!"

Philo's victim caught his breath, coughing until his throat cleared. "I thought…you two heard me behind you. Lorne Montgomery, Northeast Detectives, Philly police. It was a slick move, cowboy, I'll give you that. No accounting for"—his head swiveled, checking the rear of the shop, his voice rising—"my missing goddamn partner, goddamn it."

The shop area was empty of cop partners, goddamned or otherwise. The detective narrowed his eyes, sizing Philo up. "Where the hell did you *(cough)* learn that?"

Patrick answered before Philo could, grinning. "If he told you, sir, he'd have to kill you."

"Patrick"—Philo gave him a look—"you need to relax, buddy. Don't pay any attention to my friend here, Detective. You rattled him."

Less wary now, Detective Montgomery turned sheepish, using a hanky to rid his person of Philo's greasy grip. "Look, my partner doesn't need to know what just happened, okay, Trout?"

"Fine with me."

The detective gestured. "What about Happy the Clown?" He eyed Patrick's blubbery, giddy face. "Doesn't look like he's from around here."

"From Alaska; a long story. His name is Patrick," Philo said. "He sees you're a cop. He'll behave."

"Fine. My friggin' partner is, is...Hell, I still don't have a clue where the hell she is, damn it."

A door slammed, followed by a raised, condescending female voice. "Use your words, Lorne," echoed across the shop area. A woman in a smart skirt suit and pumps approached them, Grace and Hank trailing her, Grace panting while she walked.

"Glad you could break away from your gabfest, Ibáñez," Detective Montgomery said. "I was about to remind Mr. Trout here that the dead body in here means this crime scene hasn't been released yet."

She ignored the comment, made direct eye contact with Philo on her approach. "Detective Rhea Ibáñez. I had someone call you about this job."

"Yes, you did, Detective, and we're glad to be here. Blessid Trauma is ready to go, which means we're on the clock. If you want us to sit until you complete additional forensics, sure, we'll sit, but like I said, we're on the clock."

Striking ebony eyes and glossy black hair in a bun—both were impossible to miss because she'd gotten right into his face, at least as best as her diminutive stature would allow. A close talker, with butterscotch on her breath.

"Great, another smartass," she said, staring Philo down as best she could from her disadvantaged position. "What should have happened here was one coroner should have been able to process both bodies, but there was a complication. Sorry, we were too aggressive in guesstimating the time we needed you here. You say you're on the clock so have at it. Two homicides. You can take care of the first bed; that crime scene is released. Just make the space presentable; the city owns the property. But stay away from the last bay. Another medical examiner is due here any minute."

"Will any of these garage doors open?" Philo asked. "I want to back our truck inside."

"Probably haven't been opened in twenty years."

Philo scanned the garage door nearest them, the framing cracked, screws and metal plates holding the door's panels together. The black paint on its plastic windows, thick with multiple coats, was chipped in spots, tiny rays of sunlight slanting through them.

A noisy *snap-clack* pierced the service area. They turned, watched

Patrick engage an upturned latch, and listened as horizontal levers disengaged from one garage door's side rails like swords releasing from their sheaths. Patrick then worked a crowbar between the door and the smooth floor. The framing creaked as the door's steel rollers moved, raising it off the floor by six inches. He dropped the crowbar, grabbed a door handle and lifted.

Philo joined him. Flecks of cracking black paint rained on their heads and arms while they shouldered the door up until it would budge no more. Philo sized up the opening, decided there was room enough for the step van to fit underneath. Patrick grunted his approval, his adrenaline still coursing—"WOOOT!"—and followed it up with a primordial yell that dropped a few octaves—"WOOOOT! *Woooot!*" The celebratory display turned physical, foot stomps and bent knees moving him outside the garage, one heavy stomp at a time, his hands slapping his chest, his crows misting into cold-air breaths like a chugging steam train. It ended with him in a crouch and his hands on his knees, another caveman grunt piercing the quiet behind the dealership.

"*WOOOOT!*"

"What the hell was *that?*" Detective Montgomery said.

"My guess is it's a ram-it-up-your-ass war chant from a twenty-plus-year-old Alaskan," Philo said, not fully convinced.

* * *

The abandoned dealership's water wasn't turned off, and according to the detectives the Philadelphia Water Department was stymied as to why. A gift horse, as far as Blessid Trauma was concerned. Functioning spigots and drains, a serviceable sink and a toilet would make treating the space a hundred times easier.

Detective Ibáñez chatted Philo up. "We got lucky on this case, Trout. Teen goths looking for somewhere to do their goth stuff discovered the crime scene."

"*Light slivers*" was how one of the goth girls explained their discovery, the detective said, checking her notes. "They investigated lights in the building around midnight, wanting to 'understand their origin,'" Ibáñez air-quoted. "Slivers of light that, and I quote, 'punctured the dark nightscape, interrupting our midnight campfire time. We crossed the frozen tundra because we had to know what was in there, creating all that negative energy,' end quote."

The detective pointed to the horizon a few hundred yards away. "They live there," she said, "in that neighborhood, were hanging outside on one of the cul-de-sacs when they decided to investigate."

Philo saw sunlight glinting off roof flashing in the distance, could picture what she described, considering the spot the detective had directed his attention to even now had someone silhouetted near it, a lone figure facing their way. But the teens could see this far only if they...

"...used binoculars," the detective offered. "Without them, they wouldn't have noticed the light from inside the building 'puncturing' anything."

"But then again, what about—"

"I know, electricity. There's water here, but no electric service. Whoever was in here had their own power source. A car battery would handle it."

"Not your problem, Philo," Grace said, entering the conversation. "Let's stay on topic, shall we, Detective? We'll clean up that bed, and then we'll wait for the other M-E to do his thing so we can clean up the second one. Thanks for the input. Let us get to it."

Grace had more feedback for Philo and delivered it privately. "Here's my take. Whoever was here last night was doing what we're doing now, cleaning up after a bloodbath, but was doing it for a different customer. The mob, a gang, or whatever they want to label them—some kind of criminal element. The teens surprised him."

"How you figure that?" Philo asked.

"Follow me."

Grace retraced her steps, reached an iron grate embedded in the floor between the seventh and eighth car bays. Hank was there, crouching next to it, said to them, "Check this out."

He'd removed the grate with a socket wrench, exposing the mouth of an embedded drainpipe eight inches or so across. Philo squatted and looked in, grimaced, and quickly snapped his head back. "Grace, you got any more—"

"Yes. Here." She handed him a jar and Philo two-fingered more of the balm onto his upper lip. He leaned back in, saw a stubby log of brown human flesh wedged inside.

"That's not a hot dog wearing a helmet in there, is it?"

"Nope," Hank said.

Hank raised his head, gazed the length of the service area; Philo did the same. The grates between the bays were all off and to the side; Hank's doing. "No more human remains, no nothing in the rest of them. Clean as a whistle. "

"So the other four drains are—"

"Spotless." Hank said. "Only one is clogged. What are the chances any of the drains in a building this old would be squeaky clean without someone's intervention?"

Zero, Philo thought.

The areas around them, the floor, the hydraulic lifts in all eight of the other bays, looked clean also. Too clean.

"Christ. Whoever spooked the guy here last night," Grace said, "caught him in the act. Otherwise all ten bays would have been cleaned and there'd be no crime scene."

Five large drainpipes serviced the ten bays. Two were clogged with human remains, the other three with no obstructions other than some interior rust, like they'd been bleached, maybe even snaked as well.

"My money says those other car bays had activity," Grace said, "just like these last two. Someone cleaned 'em up."

The two detectives were across the room, huddled by the bed with the body left behind. Philo called to them. "Hey. You guys need to see this."

* * *

Detective Montgomery escorted the second medical examiner to the remaining body. Detective Ibáñez responded to Grace's summary about the drains. "Appreciate the insight, ma'am, but we already luminoled the other lifts and the rest of the garage."

"And it showed nothing, right?" Grace said. "All he had to do was use oxygenated bleach as the cleaning fluid. It screws up the hemoglobin so luminol won't pick it up. But my guess is you already knew that."

"Thank you, Ms. Blessid. We'll take it from here. And keep your thoughts about special bleaches and penises in drainpipes to yourselves, please. If anyone on your team chirps to the media about this, you'll never get another gig with the city. Do I make myself clear?"

"Sure, Detective, no worries. But if the luminol didn't show any blood, that's telling me something else."

"And that would be?"

"That you're dealing with a professional. A fixer. A Victor the Cleaner type."

"Yes, same as it told us."

Patrick popped his head out the back door of the step van, the truck's rear now inside the garage opening. "Victor the Cleaner! Harvey Keitel! I saw the movie!"

"Yes, Patrick sweetie, Harvey Keitel," Grace said. She shrugged an apology at the detective. "He's kind of a patron saint for this business. We like him even though Victor was one of the bad guys."

"And we detectives don't," Detective Ibáñez said. "Don't forget, Ms. Blessid. Privileged info. No leaks."

Behind them in bay number ten, the coroner did his work, his phone to his mouth recording his observations. "Deceased is a dark-skinned male, possibly Latino, appears to be late twenties to early thirties, found reclining in a bed. Fresh stitches along one side, climbing to the middle of his back. Gaping chest cavity." The doctor touched the stitch marks. "Probable organ donor, not a recipient, similar to deceased Doe Number One."

This, Philo understood now, was the complication Detective Ibáñez had mentioned. Organ donors here, as in plural. An illegal organ trafficking operation, where two people died. The deaths appeared unintended judging from the deceased's fresh stitches on one part of his body prior to someone cracking open his chest cavity and leaving it that way. But how many other surgeries had there been? Chances were, judging from the attempt to sanitize the other car bay areas and drains, as many as eight. If the cops hadn't already suspected how busy this place had been, they did now.

Patrick hauled the last few red hazmat bags of gore-soaked rags into the back of the van, the Blessid team finishing up the first bay. He, Philo, and

Hank sat on the truck's bumper on a break, munching snacks. After the body was removed, they'd get back to it. Grace took a catnap in the truck.

Espresso-coffee-bean-energy power bars: a caffeine fix for Philo, considering there were no Dunkin' Donutses close enough for a visit. "Not bad, Patrick," he said, eyeing his half-eaten snack. "Good choice."

Philo ran his gaze around the interior of the repair area. Battered wooden workbenches with vises lined the service area perimeter. A gray-brown pegboard clung to the wall, with one fan belt, a tin funnel, and a sixties Chevrolet calendar affixed to it with the *See the USA in Your Chevrolet* tagline at bottom, a Norman Rockwell reprint.

"I like the cinnamon," Patrick said, chewing the snack bar.

"Me too, bro."

And facing them across the service bay, Philo now noticed a cinnamon-colored door, the one that brought them into the service area. On the *PARTS* counter side, the door was yellow and free of significant blemishes, but on this side the paint was cinnamon-y, a chipped and pounded reddish-brown coat nicked enough to expose its gray primer underneath in spots. He hopped off the truck bumper and crossed the bay to get a closer look.

Philo ran his hand over the door's battered metal plating. Long scrapes and scratches and dents, some of the dents deep enough to expose the bare metal beneath. Wear and tear marks common for a service garage, decades' worth of them, some of the battering probably dating from as far back as the fifties. Except—

He pulled back to study it from a few paces away. He knew this door.

"Detective Ibáñez," he called. "Over here."

The detective left her partner's side, self-conscious, Philo thought, of Philo's interest in her approach. He hadn't meant to stare, but she was a small woman who really filled out her blouse.

She arrived, got into his face again. "What is it?"

Her close talking—it made sense. At this close a distance, a person could only appreciate her face.

"This door here," Philo ran his hand over a few of the dents. "You guys know about the Amtrak train deaths from the other day? The female suicide had a photo in her pocket. This door was in it."

9

Kaipo raised her binoculars. Her toothache was gone because her problem molar had been neutralized: an emergency root canal this morning. The fallout, aside from the anesthetic wearing off, was that it made her late to this surveillance. She stepped up from the blacktop onto the curb, then onto a lush, residential grass lawn.

The curb connected two sprawling split-level homes on a cul-de-sac, part of a large Bucks County housing development at least a few decades old. She adjusted the glasses, using them to peer between two homes on large lots with mature plantings and meticulous landscaping. The view was unobstructed across an empty cornfield that ran behind the houses. This side of the field was lower Bucks County, the other side Philadelphia, where she and her toothache had been last night, cleaning the service bays of an abandoned auto dealership. With this sightline she understood, could now fully see, how a distant light source against a black backdrop might prove too enticing for bored suburban teenagers to ignore.

Her exit from the last night's scene had been premature, precipitating this cop-sponsored biohazard response. The new cleaners were still there, had arrived before she'd found this distant vantage point from which to observe them. She had no idea how long their truck had been in place behind the dealership, backed up to one of the garage doors; doors she knew from the inside only. She made another binoculars adjustment.

Movement, but not what she expected: a garage door lifted. The doors to the bays were painted shut, and so old she thought opening them would be impossible without the wood frames crumbling. One person in a biohazard suit drifted outside, next to the truck. She traded her binoculars for her phone, zoomed in, pressed *Record*. Here was an excited cleaning tech whose job seemed to really do it for him, overly demonstrative, *dancing* —as the cliché suggested—like nobody was watching. She waited, soon recorded more video that included three more cleaning techs, two men, and a woman.

Last night, while inside the building, muffled voices, young, serious, had surprised her only a few feet away, on the other side of a garage door. She and her monster toothache were not in the mood. She had handguns powerful enough to obliterate whoever was out there, plus the door in between, but those guns were in her van. The handgun she carried might or might not have done the job. Either way it would have been sloppy, creating more work. Plus, there was this other thing: she wasn't a cold-blooded murderer. So she'd taken a simpler approach, had banged against the doors like a disgruntled elderly neighbor, which scared them off. Then she picked up after herself in a rush, the job not done. The two bodies she'd been cooking left with her, crammed into the cooker; the other two she'd had to abandon. After she had driven off the property, she stuck around to watch from across the street, to see if anyone had called in the building trespass, and they had, because it generated a police response.

Her phone away now, she swung the binoculars right then left along the rear of the building. More activity: two people carried a body bag out an exterior steel door, over to the coroner's vehicle. A knot twisted in her stomach thinking about that corpse. Latino male. Someone who'd decided on a risky, drastic way to make a pile of cash by selling a part of his body.

Unfortunately for him, the surgery went south, the host on his way to becoming a corpse. The mob surgeon had quickly harvested more of his organs, guaranteeing that outcome. There'd been four dead she'd needed to address—out of how many total donors, she didn't know—left by the surgeons or butchers or whatever the hell these people were. It had prompted her to text her mob contact Olivier about it overnight. His response had been quick:

Disposables. Plenty more where they came from.

Her next text fessed up about the dead donor she'd been unable to remove from the scene. Olivier made her wait twelve minutes for his answer.

Incompetence. It does not become you. Pono 'oe ke hana maika'i.

The translation was, "You must do better."

What was this? Absolution? Would there even be a next time? Or would she not see any more new business, which could then only be interpreted one way: she was a dead person walking. Until she received a new assignment, she'd sleep with one eye open.

She stayed another five minutes with her binoculars raised. Her new focus was the police van arriving, parking next to the biohazard truck. What she had hoped to avoid, she hadn't: the cops were doing another sweep of the bays. They'd soon learn the operating theater had been crammed with considerably more organ donors than three.

There was also the matter of the two decomposing bodies she'd been forced to take with her. They were still in her van, only partly cooked.

10

Philo dozed in and out of sleep on the loveseat recliner in his living room, a few feet from the front picture window. His Sig Sauer lay across his lap.

CRASH.

Upstairs. The house shook, the second floor jolted by a thunderous thud. Shattered glass ricocheted off hard surfaces in a confined space; had to be the bathroom.

He launched himself from the recliner, groggy as fuck, bounced off a tall lamp, then a bookcase, stumbled his way toward the stairs in his swim shoes, a sleeveless tee and camo pj bottoms.

At the foot of the steps he still processed the noise, his head clearing enough to feel the steel of the Sig in his hand. He leaned a shoulder against the wall, the handgun arms-length and chest high, with him listening, concentrating, willing away the remaining cobwebs.

"Lola, that you? Lola, honey? You okay?"

No, no, it wasn't Lola, his girlfriend was gone, had left earlier, pissed off when Philo just wasn't feeling it. He checked his watch. One forty-seven. He needed to focus.

The skylight, in the upstairs bathroom—that was the breach; the entrance to the house he rarely thought about. Fucking thing never opened, not during the eighteen years he lived here as a kid or the six years after, when he still used to visit, and also not since he'd moved back in, the cranking mechanism gummed up from inactivity. But it was another way to get into the house, because all that separated the bathroom from the elements at roof level was glass. Seventy-year-old glass, not tempered to resist shattering. Glass that was no doubt now all over his tiled bathroom floor. Someone would soon step on it, something he'd hear if he listened hard enough.

No crinkling-tinkling footsteps, no other noises.

He eased one foot onto a carpeted step, pulled himself gently up, went for a second step, then a third, his raised gun leading him, its safety off, its trigger with so light a touch that worn fingerprints could fire it, just the way he liked it. The bathroom's closed panel door appeared in his sights, each step exposing more of it, eggshell white, many paint layers applied by his dad, then subsequent homeowners, the glossy paint reflecting the glow from his Sock Monkey nightlight in the hall. The nightlight lit the door as far north as the handle.

Top of the steps now. He swiveled to see bedroom two, swiveled again to see bedroom three, both doors open, then another body-swivel to bedroom number one in the front of the house, lit poorly by another nightlight. No visible threats, and still no noises from anywhere upstairs.

The closed bathroom door, had he left it that way...?

He reached for the doorknob.

Hard push, or soft and slow?

He shoved the door back and stiff-armed his raised-gun entrance, assumed a military stance. Glass shards were everywhere, sink, tile floor, bathtub. The cold, starry night was evident through the broken skylight, the air inside already frosty, his breath visible. On the floor was a cinder block and spider-webbed breaks in the floor tiles under it. He took a step forward, his swim shoes doing their job on the sharp glass, their molded rubber soles flexible, thick, paying dividends for him yet again—

The opaque shower door was ajar—room inside for one person comfortably, two intimately, where he and Lola had been earlier in the evening. He stepped closer to it, snapped the shower door open toward him. Empty.

Behind him he heard it, turning too late, guns sliding out of their leather holsters, two thugs with one each, their arms stiff as they reached them into the doorway, their firepower red-dotting his body. Fuck. The skylight breach had been a diversion.

"Drop your weapon," one thug said, the man brawny under black thermal outerwear, with black slacks and black shoes, his white face the only part exposed. "Do it. If we were here to take you out, you'd be dead already."

Philo felt his Sig's trigger, its magnetism, its yearning, its wanting his finger to show it the faintest twitch, but he breathed down his adrenaline and did as asked, turning the gun around and setting it on the sink. There was always the handgun under the fake tissue box on the toilet tank.

The dark-costumed toady retrieved the forfeited gun. He motioned at the toilet. "Have a seat."

Seat down, Philo sat. Behind him on the tank, the tissue box beckoned.

"Thank you, Mr. Trout. Someone would like a word with you." The thugs parted to let a third man enter. Business-suited and bulky, he smelled of alcohol. No gun visible, but something might be under the jacket. It was now a bit crowded in here.

"Hello, Philo," Mr. Business Suit said. "To help in securing your trust, and to prove my sincerity, I'll tell you my real name. You might remember it. Wally Lanakai."

"Sorry, chief," Philo said, "but that's not doing it for me."

"Think LA, August 2001, the Barrio. Your last fight."

Philo narrowed his eyes in concentration. That night had been a fucking cataclysm. He was lucky he'd gotten out alive.

Yes, Wally Lanakai. Banker, fight promoter, and manager. Hawaiian money guy. Philo never met him, but the name was synonymous with promoting the best illegal bare-knuckle boxing matchups of the day.

Shit. He suddenly knew what this was about.

"I didn't take the purse," Philo said.

Forty-three thousand bucks. Largest purse ever, winner-take-all, for young Tristan Trout, age twenty-three at the time. Undefeated in sixty-four fights, all won by KO. He was a bare-knuckle street-fighting prodigy from Philly, none of his contests lasting more than five minutes. He lost the pretty-boy name Tristan around fight number twenty, the new nickname not of his own doing, became "Philo," after Clint Eastwood's late seventies movie namesake and bare-knuckle brawler Philo Beddoe. His undefeated record had evoked the comparison. That, plus a lean physique and an Eastwood-inspired rooster-comb hairline.

Philo's bare-knuckles talent: it was all in the leverage and the pop, Chuckie Fargas had told him. Chuckie was his best friend from childhood, and his fight manager. *"You've got both, Philo baby. Long-arm leverage, big wrists, and fists that explode on impact, plus a Marciano chin. You're gonna make us a ton of money."*

That night, in the empty Barrio tire warehouse, Philo had figured, yes, he would do that, he would make them more money than they'd ever seen before, by notching win number sixty-five against Wally Lanakai's sumo-size bull of a fighter from Hawaii. It was all good, *"...all in the leverage, Philo baby, all in the leverage."*

And Chuckie had, indeed, leveraged all of it. He stole the money. Wally's and the money gathered from the crowd of bloodthirsty drunks who had shown up. Chuckie was gone before the first punch was thrown. The fight never happened.

"Chuckie boosted the purse," Philo said to his unwanted houseguest. "Not me."

"Yes, we know. Took us a while but we found him. You might have heard, maybe?" Wally let his smile and the insinuation sink in for Philo.

Philo had heard. RIP Chuckie Fargas, 2002 or thereabouts.

"We retrieved what was left of the money and went looking for you. We did find you, but we backed off."

9-11 had hit. The World Trade Center. Philo quit the fight game, quit civilian life, quit fucking civilization, period, and enlisted in the navy, in honor of his late father, a retired USN pilot who'd turned full pacifist in his later years, but still retained his hatred for "those sneaky bastard Japs and their goddamn Datsuns." His father was a passenger on American Airlines hijacked Flight 77, the one that hit the Pentagon.

"Yeah, well, I was busy back then."

"I know. Accept my sincere thanks, Philo, for your military service. But now you're out. You're what, thirty-nine? You still look good. Real good. Bigger than you were back then."

Yes, he was a full twenty pounds bigger, in all the right places, a solid two ten and in kickass shape. "What's this about?"

"You owe me a fight, Philo."

Philo smiled. "You're funny, Wally. You break into my house, and you go through all this hotshot mobster bullshit with your pussy posse here, just to get me to fight again? You wasted your time. Find someone else. I'm a businessman now."

Glass crunched underfoot as Wally's two offended toadies leaned forward into the doorway again, posing. Philo didn't flinch. Wally spread his arms to stop them; they stood down.

"Like it or not, Philo, you're the gold standard in the sport. A legend. People still talk about you. Fifty-seven and oh, all knockouts, all under six minutes—"

"Sixty-four KOs, five minutes or less."

"Forgive me, champ," Wally said, "for not giving you your props. It's not like they keep these records on ESPN."

Champ. A title reserved for the professional boxing elite. One lament Philo always had was he'd never turned pro. His pacifist father would have disowned him if he had.

"I'll get the record right when I talk the fight up, Philo. I have a fighter—"

"I don't give a shit who you have, I'm not interested. How'd you find me? And why not just ring the doorbell?"

Wally's jowly chin tightened. "You're making it easy for me to dislike you, Philo. Almost as easy as it was to find you. You're living in your parents' house, genius. And I don't ring doorbells."

So Philo was. Living here was for sure a subconscious death wish. Fuck the psychology of it. Wally Lanakai was the least of his worries, hadn't even been on Philo's radar; other more worrisome enemies were, but only to a point. You had to die sometime.

"As I was saying, the guy I'm promoting—he's destroyed everyone out there, and has no one left to fight. As much as I've talked you up, he'd like to meet you, champ. Meet you," Wally's sly smile was also a taunt, "so he can knock you out."

Same bullshit boxing promoter Don King pulled with boxers past their prime. Tell them how good they were, then tell them how someone had dissed them to get them all fired up, and stoke them into fighting again. Self-serving, money-grubbing asshole.

But Philo wasn't past his prime. Philo was more dangerous now than he was in his midtwenties. No matter. "Get out of my house, Wally."

"I understand your reluctance, Philo, really, you being rusty and all—"

Philo's tissue box gun was calling him. Hands at his sides, he rose from the toilet. "Get—the fuck—out. Now."

Two raised guns again.

"You are being stubborn, Philo, so let's say we do this. First, here's two thousand bucks, a thousand for the bathroom, a thousand for your front door." Wally dropped the cash into the sink, on top of broken glass. "Now let's talk about that biohazard business of yours. You bought it from the Gore Whore, right?"

Grace's nickname. It apparently had legs on the other side of law enforcement, too. This got Philo's attention. "What's your point, Wally?"

"She sold it because she's sick, right?"

Philo didn't respond.

"Needs new lungs, right? On the transplant list for what, more than three years?"

The man had done his homework. "Again, Wally, make your point."

"I can help with that."

11

The Hawaiian thugs were gone, had left the way they entered, through the front door. No real mystery how they managed the rooftop breach: an extension ladder, a cinder block, and a glass skylight. A ladder raised anywhere along the city block would allow someone to walk across the tarred flat roofs of twenty homes to any skylight in seconds.

But the front door locks needed investigating. The mechanisms were blown out, sitting in pieces on the floor, and Philo hadn't heard any such noise while he was upstairs. He examined one of the locks, then realized why.

"Captive bolt pistol," he murmured.

Also called a stunbolt gun, cattle gun, bolt gun. Pneumatic. It rendered cattle unconscious by using compressed air to shoot a stainless-steel bolt into their brains. The bolt could also penetrate door locks. Quiet, effective, and trendy, a new unregulated weapon of choice. He'd used one himself, more than once. He shouldered his front door closed, now slightly off plumb, would need to rely on the tiny push-button lock for the rest of the night. He stuffed dishrags into the two holes where the lock used to be, to keep out the cold.

The damage to his house was to the front door and bathroom only. Except where the hell was Six?

"Six? Six, sweetie?"

Upstairs, downstairs, the basement—no sign of her. If she'd gotten out, he'd find her purring at the front door at some point, cold and hungry.

By three thirty a.m. the tile floor in the bathroom and the hardwood floor just inside the front door were shop-vac clean. He settled into the living room recliner again with his Sig Sauer back in his lap, then texted Grace to let her know he'd be sleeping in today. They had no jobs until the afternoon.

Wally Lanakai: a mob fight promoter from Philo's crazy past. People like Wally were out there, many not liking that they'd lost money each time Philo knocked their guy out, some wanting another shot if they could find him. Still, worrying about people from that part of his past wasn't what warranted his sleepless nights. Potential blowback that had queued up from fifteen years of clandestine military missions, however, did.

Wally would make the arrangements, would accommodate Philo's schedule, and he promised a fifty-thousand-dollar winner-take-all purse, all details that were of consequence but still only the barest of interest to Philo, even the money. What did it for him was what it meant for Grace and her condition.

Philo had watched his mother die; him fifteen, her forty-eight. Cigarettes. Lung cancer. Chemo, radiation, remission, then it traveled. Brain cancer, hospice, and a return home when there was nothing more they, or his father, or he, could do. The emptiness he felt—the helplessness...

But with Grace—Grace was dying, and he could do something about it.

Wally's promise was there'd be two new lungs awaiting her, regardless of the outcome of the bout. Philo would talk with her and propose a what-if, but he'd leave out the sensitive parts, like anything to do with the fight, or a Hawaiian wiseguy claiming to also be an organ broker. Her need to know would pertain to the availability of the organs only, and how a transplant might happen. The less she knew, the better.

Across the street from his house the aura from a lamppost bathed the sidewalk and the parked cars paralleling the curb in amber. The row homes behind it, identical to Philo's, stood tall in a wall of shadows. Outside, it was quiet and cold, with a trickling of car traffic, and foot traffic that was nonexistent, until—

A pedestrian entered the lamppost's amber cone, his hands in his coat pockets and his hooded head down, puffing frosty air onto his chest as he pushed against the cold. No sway, looked sober; not a stray from one of the bars. He stopped under the lamp, turned to face the center of the street, shifted from foot to foot on the sidewalk, shaking off the chill. Philo sat up and opened the shutter slats another millimeter to watch. The pedestrian inched himself closer to the curb, still hopping from foot to foot. He left the curb and crossed the street, toward Philo's house. Philo was now on high alert.

A cat strutted inside the perimeter of the amber lamplight.

Six.

She slipped between the stranger's legs, hitched up her back, clawed at his shoes and rubbed herself against pants that were, what, gray? Blue? Part of a uniform?

Six leaped into the man's arms, stopping him in the middle of the street. She nuzzled his shoulder, then his exposed chin until he couldn't help himself and started petting her behind her ears. His head back, a grin emerged from inside the hoodie shadow, slight, goofy, young...

For fuck's sake.

Patrick?

Philo yanked at his front door with both hands, unsticking it from the doorframe with a *pop!* It spooked Patrick, who dropped Six and took a hard right, heading back the way he'd come. The cat sprinted toward Philo's steps.

Philo cleared his gun, tucked it into his waistband, and stepped around Six onto the front steps. "Hey, no, wait—"

Patrick made a run for it.

"Patrick, stop! HEY! C'mon, Patrick, no one better than you, bud..."

Patrick halted. He turned to face Philo, appeared lost, frightened. Philo met him in the street and guided him up his steps, his arm around him.

"Dude. Let's get inside."

* * *

Philo's guest picked the raisins and walnuts from the top of the sticky bun, put them aside, broke off a small piece and took a bite. Under-cabinet lighting dusted the granite countertop and rimmed half the perimeter of Philo's kitchen, the other half lit by a hanging ceiling lamp that cast a soft, diffused light onto a round acrylic table. Sunrise was still a few hours away. The two men were seated next to each other, Philo with a mug of coffee, Patrick nursing a glass of milk to go with the day-old bun. He was delivering disturbing news about Grace. She'd been taken away in an ambulance overnight.

"When?"

"Don't know, sir. Midnight maybe. Hank called nine-one-one. He went with her."

"You didn't?"

"I was on a trolley when Hank called me, sir. My phone woke me up. Hank was crying."

A few things were buried inside those comments that would require more prodding. Philo started with asking why he hadn't gone home or to the hospital.

"I was out, riding the bus."

"I got that. Why not—"

"I came here instead, sir."

"Where is Grace now? What hospital?"

"Eisenstein."

"*Einstein?* In Olney?"

"Yeah. I can't eat any more of this, sir."

"Then don't. How come you came here?"

"At the car dealership today, there was, um, it was...and Grace, she's really sick, sir. Hank said she was coughing up blood. And stuff's messed up, sir, and, and..."

Patrick gritted his teeth. Philo watched the anger rise, saw his chest inflate, deflate—inhale, exhale—saw his breathing shorten, the rage building. Patrick's eyes blasted open, looking larger than their sockets. "...and, *and...*"

He pounded the table with his fist, his eyes like a madman's, lost, pleading while he spit his words, "...and I don't—know who—I am, sir!"

"Okay, Patrick, okay. Easy, bud, easy. Try to calm yourself."

Patrick's breathing slowed, his man-boy eyes now spilling over, his heartache pouring out through them. "I need to figure stuff out, sir. I just need help figuring all this stuff out..."

"I know you do. Relax. Finish your milk. Then we'll take a ride."

"Where?"

"To see Grace."

* * *

They were in Philo's Jeep at four thirty in the morning heading across town, traffic nearly nonexistent. Philo nudged Patrick gently with a few softball questions to get him to open up.

"Grace and Hank. They've been really good to you, haven't they?"

"The best. Grace worries about me, sir. I tell her not to, but she does. I want her to get better."

"I second that, Patrick, and she wants that too. She's strong, and she's fighting hard to keep it together, for Hank and for you, but she's almost sixty years old, and for a person her age with her physical problems, sometimes attitude alone just isn't enough."

He'd researched lung transplants. What Philo found was, she would never fully recover. The prognosis for lung recipients was good for the first year, a four-in-five chance of surviving, but after three years it got considerably poorer, survival only a little better than one in two. Organ rejection could be slowed but never stopped, plus the side effects from the drug therapy often caused kidney damage and diabetes.

"Why are you out so late at night riding SEPTA?"

"I look for things when I'm not asleep."

"What kinds of things?"

"Things and places that might make me remember, sir."

SEPTA's bus, train, and trolley system covered much of the city and had a reach into other nearby counties as well, even across state lines into New Jersey and Delaware. Like Grace had said, Patrick was on a relentless mission to rediscover his past, assuming his past, longer term, had something to do with Philadelphia or its surrounding environs.

"Any memories of things in my neighborhood?"

"No. Yeah. Maybe. I check out all the neighborhoods, sir. Today at our cleanup job near the Sixty-six bus route, something was...Something there made me feel good."

"Something at the car dealership."

"Uh-huh. So I went back."

"At two in the morning?"

"Yeah. And sometimes when I'm on the bus I fall asleep then wake up in my seat. Other times when I wake up, I'm not on the bus."

"What, like in a dream?"

"Not a dream, sir. For real."

"So you *are* a sleepwalker. Why didn't you tell the doctor this when he asked?"

"His questions made my head hurt, sir."

"Yeah, mine too. Interesting."

"Yeah. And confusing, sir."

Philo never believed in that sleepwalking shit, unless it was carryover from taking a sleep aid or was drug influenced, yet he was fairly sure Patrick wasn't capable of lying about it. "You take sleeping pills?"

"No drugs. I smoked one of Grace's cigarettes once, sir." He made a face. "Made me throw up."

"Fine then, you walk in your sleep. Where are you when you wake up? Outside? Inside? At home?"

"Sometimes at tourist spots. Other times at places like tonight, at the car dealership."

"Hold that thought." Philo steered the Jeep into the hospital parking lot, found a space a distance from the main hospital entrance. They exited his Jeep. As they walked, Philo returned his full attention to him.

"So what I'm hearing is you wake up at jobsites and other places not knowing how you got there."

"Um, no. Yes. Sometimes."

This was a yes, Philo was learning. Here was an example of sleep-walking to the extreme. "You tell anyone else about this, Patrick?"

"Grace and Hank know about the SEPTA rides, not the sleepwalking, 'cause they'd worry about me. I don't have any other friends, except for maybe you and the guys at Pat's Steaks. Didn't tell them either."

Philo had to analyze this. He didn't want to keep info from the Blessids, as invested as they were in Patrick's wellbeing, but with Grace in the hospital this wouldn't be a good time for them to hear about it.

"I'm thinking you best not talk to anyone about your sleepwalking or your late-night SEPTA recon trips, okay, bud?"

"Why?"

"Just don't. Especially when we're on a job. People don't need any more reasons to think we crime scene cleaners are weirder than we are. Got that?"

"Okay. I need coffee, sir." Patrick lowered his hood, rubbed his eyes, then dipped his fingers into the dent in his head that had precipitated his confusing life as a brain-damaged amnesiac; he massaged it.

"We'll get some inside. Let's see what we can do about cheering up Grace and Hank."

"Sir?"

"Yes?"

"She needs more than cheering up, sir. She needs new lungs."

"Soon, Patrick. Hopefully, soon, she reaches the top of the list."

Which list, controlled by whom, manipulated by whom, from *the* list or from some other list, legal or not—at this point Philo didn't care.

He and Patrick added sugar and milk to their takeouts. Philo sipped, studying Patrick. Such an enigma. "Patrick?"

"Yeah?"

"What at the dealership made you happy today? The place grossed me out."

"I dunno. The smell, I guess."

That, to Philo, was almost always the most difficult part of the job. "Then why use the Tiger Balm?"

"The dead body smell makes me sick like it does everybody, sir. The other smell I like. The sweetness from inside a body when it's opened up. Animals have the smell inside their bodies, and people have it, too. From blood and the stuff inside. There was a lot of that smell around those car bays today, sir."

From internal organs. Multiple donors had been there, undergoing some kind of guerrilla surgery, getting sliced open to give up one organ or another, or in the cases of the bodies left behind, Philo surmised, any organ that could be worth something on the black market.

"Sir, can you hand me a few more packets of sugar for my coffee, please?"

Patrick and raw meat and internal organs. In Philo's head now was Dr. Andelmo, that judgmental, cannibal-conspiracy-loving fuck.

Philo tossed him the packets. "No talking to people about liking that smell either, okay, Patrick?"

"Okay."

12

Two partially cooked bodies were crammed into the pressure cooker that was in turn crammed into the cargo area behind Kaipo's seat in her van. She was now about to make a stop where she knew she wasn't welcome.

Hawai'i was an upscale steakhouse in Center City, Philadelphia, where customers enjoyed seventy-five-dollar custom-aged, hand-selected USDA steak straight from Hawaii's Parker Ranch, plus traditional island dishes like Kalua pig and poke, a Hawaiian version of sushi. Today's customers needed to remain clueless as to whatever else would be passing through the kitchen while they ate. The alley where she parked ran the length of the mid-rise city block. Kaipo ran an extension cord from her pressure cooker to an outside outlet. Her stew needed another half hour before she could dispose of whatever hadn't cooked, the plan being to feed it into the restaurant's Sledgehammer 5000 commercial garbage disposal.

She pounded her fist on the restaurant's back door. It opened, and the Italian sous chef's surprised look turned to alarm. He poked out his head, checked left and right down the alley, leaned back in, then blocked her entry.

"No. Not today, Kaipo. No, no, no. If you want a meal, you must eat with the customers in the front. Get out."

Kaipo ignored the objection, was already re-familiarizing herself with the gleaming kitchen's capabilities over the chef's white-smocked shoulder. "Not here to eat, Plenio," she said with no eye contact and no love lost for this pissant second-in-command. "Where's Icky?" She strained to look deeper into the kitchen.

Plenio was shorter than her by a head, was a young and flimsy food nerd, and had no chance of physically stopping her from finding Icky herself, but the two large hair-netted men busy with food prep behind him could, plus the staring dishwasher, a new guy who stopped mid-scrub to check her out.

"Mr. Ikaika is out front," he said, "in the dining room with our guests. This is highly irregular and is the absolute poorest of timing. You must leave."

Her appearance there was always poor timing, considering her avocation, but what was it that made *this* visit the absolute poorest, she wondered?

Not for long. Two sedans carrying no identifying markings arrived, their tires stutter-stepping and stopping short, blocking her van's exit. She retreated from the door stoop onto the blacktop, where she watched one of the drivers march up and produce a badge for the sous chef lookout, Plenio.

"Department of Public Health," the badge's owner said, his team of three technicians crowding in behind him. "We're here to inspect the restaurant's premises."

The SWAT team approach was all show. The restaurant's Hawaiian owners boasted an enviable string of never having failed any of the health department's unannounced inspections, this because there was no such thing as an unannounced anything when it came to inspecting her mob employers' establishments, a call always preceding a visit. Still, she got a chuckle out of her timing. The cooker off, she discreetly unplugged it from the outlet.

"You seem to have your hands full," she said to Plenio, who was now barking orders to the staff. "I'll wait out here. Tell Icky as soon as he's done with these folks I need to talk with him."

"I'm busy right now, Kaipo, it will have to—"

"Do it, Plenio. You keep me waiting, Icky won't be happy. You're watching those health department guys hunt down mice and roaches you already know they won't find." She picked out a spot on the stoop and sat, would keep an eye on things while her e-reader kept her company.

A chunky, oval-faced Hawaiian man in a Hawaiian shirt, white shorts, and loafers without socks, exited the restaurant's back door, totally underdressed for the weather. The costume was the saddest of stereotypes, but it was good for business.

"'Sup, Kaipo?" Icky lit a cigarette, offered Kaipo one.

She declined. "Icky, I need a favor." She gestured with her head at the rear of her vehicle, the door slightly ajar. "See the pressure cooker in my van?"

"I'll see that cooker and raise you another cooker from my restaurant," Icky said, satisfied at how clever his bad self was. He sucked hard on his cigarette. "We get a new one at the end of the month. The way I hear it, you get the restaurant's old one as an upgrade. The one you're getting is a beaut, Kaipo. Higher tech, bigger capacity. A faster, more even cook." He glanced at her van again, something just now clicking for him. "Wait. Why the hell is it here?"

"The job I had the other night was too much for it. Took too long, and the stew didn't cook enough. I need access to your garbage disposal today."

"Are you shitting me? And with these Health Department people here?" He tossed his cigarette at the pavement. "This is a high-class establishment, Kaipo. I can't be having you cart any of your slop into the kitchen."

"Relax. You stuff the equivalent of full sides of bone-in beef down that thing every day. It's a disposal, not a broiler. It'll do fine. I just need some chopping power. We'll wait until they leave."

"Kaipo, damn it, no."

"Let me run a hose through the door and into the drain after the inspectors are gone. Ten minutes tops and I'll be outta there."

Icky lit another cigarette, sucked in the smoke through an if-looks-could-kill frown, still in assessment mode.

"Look, Icky, it'll be fine. You're the best, bud. Next time I speak with Olivier, I'll tell him that. And soon as my replacement cooker's available, let's get it done. This one needs to be retired."

They both knew the frustrated fat Hawaiian had no choice. He marched off, his cold breath and cigarette smoke trailing him into the back door of the restaurant, oblivious to the *This is a smoke-free establishment* sign posted overhead. The door opened again and he popped back out, his face grumpy, to flick his cigarette in the direction of her and her van, then he disappeared back inside.

She had more to mention to him, specifically about things she was seeing over the past few assignments. She'd hit him up about it after she was finished dealing with today's mess.

Her cleaning jobs had always dealt with recycling the trash. Cleaning up after bad actors who Ka Hui had removed from the environment. Always a fine line for her, what she did and how she felt about it, and how she compartmentalized the brutality, but these people knew the risks of being in the life. Except these new assignments involved remediating innocent, victimized people whose only significant crime was they were poor. The little guy. Yes, she had a *very* specific question for Icky after she was finished with the disposal.

* * *

The heavy-duty, Gilmour-28-series, three-quarter-inch-wide pro-golf-course hose had the girth for the job. After the Health Department left, Kaipo connected the hose to the bottom of the cooker and threaded it through an open window, across the kitchen floor, and into the wide expanse of the garbage disposal's mouth at the bottom of a massive sink. Icky had cleared that part of the kitchen of its staff. She signaled him to switch on the disposal, then she threw the pressure cooker's ignition on and hustled back inside the kitchen. It was all good, Kaipo mused, as the cooker and disposal hummed through their jobs. Icky stood beside her, motionless, sweat gathering on his forehead.

He patted his face with a hanky. "Don't you need to be outside so you can turn that thing off if anything goes wrong?"

"In a minute. Got a question for you. Your dishwasher—is he new?"

"What? I have no fucking idea, Kaipo. Maybe." Icky was considerably underinvested in the conversation. He leaned over the disposal and grimaced when it occasionally stopped its purring and coughed, needing to grind through some small chunk more formidable than the pablum that most of it had been, crunching through it in a ferocious manner. "Where's that stuff you put under your nose for the smell, Kaipo? I need it."

She handed him her balm. "What happened to your other dishwasher?"

Icky fingered a glob below his nose. "How the hell would I know? These guys come and go. Minimum-wage disposables."

Disposables. That word again. He was toeing Ka Hui's party line.

"Sure, Ick. Right. Minimum wage. That's funny. You probably pay them half that, under the table."

"Hey, I don't set the market. It's their choice to come here. They don't like it, they can get a second job, or they can go the fuck back to Mexico or Venezuela or wherever the hell they came from and starve."

Kaipo's major point, coming right up. "Or they can supplement their income by selling off parts of themselves, right? A kidney here, a cornea there? Except the surgery sometimes doesn't work out."

"What the fuck you talking about?"

"Your old dishwasher. I saw him yesterday."

"Pedro? How about that. How's he doing?"

At the car dealership Kaipo hadn't been sure, but she was plenty sure now. Seeing a new face here had confirmed it. "Not well," she said, pointing to the gurgling garbage disposal.

She left Icky hanging, headed quickly outside soon as the chug-a-lug noise started, to turn off the cooker's laboring motor, the cooker now empty of its contents. She propped the hose's disconnected open end upright, spilled bleach in and ran water from an alley garden hose through it, then she stuffed it with other bleach-soaked and biohazard enzyme-soaked rags. She reentered the kitchen to do the same with the hose's other end, to rinse it out with kitchen sink spigot water and bleach, then stuff it with more biohazard-killing rags.

"Turn your disposal off, Icky, we're done. Ick?"

Icky stood solemnly over the sink's drain, his hands folded, offering a prayer on Pedro's behalf. He blessed himself then flipped the disposal's switch off, the kitchen faucet still running.

* * *

The first thing Kaipo did at home after the car dealership fiasco was find the Blessid Trauma website. Something, a niggling intuition, or maybe a sixth sense drive-by, had suggested she search for it after she'd re-checked her phone photos. Specifically, the photos from the distant vantage point across the cornfield of the techs who cleaned up after her short-circuited attempt at purifying the dealership.

The small company had a basic website describing their services and the people who performed them, some testimonials and FAQs, and a "What Do Crime Scene Cleaners Do?" primer. Plus, something out of the ordinary: a page dedicated to one of their current employees, with a riveting story about him being a trauma-induced amnesiac with a brain injury, searching for his identity. For Kaipo, the sixth-sense niggle was strong here.

She'd retrieved her phone, thumbed her way to the footage she took of the cleaners and their dancing-like-nobody's-watching technician making a spectacle of himself.

"Mr. Patrick Stakes. Well, aloha."

The story was touching, but it wasn't quite correct. She decided she'd help them correct it with what little she was sure of. Starting with her next assignment, none of the commercial crime scene cleaners who were any good at what they did would miss her hidden message, yet it would mean something to only one of them.

13

Hospitals. Visiting them was not Philo's strong suit. He'd had to make too many visits in the past, in and out of the States. Makeshifts, M.A.S.H. units, even third-world facilities. Too, too many. Colleagues sick, colleagues missing limbs, colleagues dying. Colleagues dead and needing identification when their country disavowed knowledge of who they were, or where they'd served, or what had killed them.

"You okay, sir?" an observant Patrick asked, entering the hospital elevator first. Philo was lagging.

"I'm good. Thanks, bud."

They found Grace in a double room with no roommate, resting. Wires, tubes, beeping machines, low lighting. Everything Philo did not want to see, and yet he was glad to see it all turned on and working, doing its job. The alternative always sucked.

"Grace. It's Philo and Patrick." Philo moved in a little closer. "'Sup with this shit?"

"Patrick, honey," Grace said in a whisper, reaching, "come give me a smooch, please. Philo, you can fuck off," she said, winking at him.

A spontaneous lung collapse, an attending said. No trauma involved. Nothing any more specific than that, according to the docs, but after they took X-rays of both diseased lungs, they reinforced that she needed something to shake loose on the transplant horizon almost immediately. Hank sat forlorn in a side chair, unshaven, his hair a mess, his eyes unfocused, looking lost.

"Hank." Philo patted him on his shoulder, gently squeezed it. "I'll sit with Grace while you and Patrick get something to eat in the café." Philo handed Patrick a twenty. "Order some breakfast for yourselves, Patrick. Bring me back an orange juice, please. No hurry."

They left the room. Philo leaned in, made direct eye contact with Grace. "As far as fucking off goes, there'll be none of that, on my part or yours," he said. He gave Grace a peck on her cheek while he squeezed and held her hand. He still held it while he stood over her bed.

"Philo," she said, laboring, "my skin was blue before. Fucking. Blue. Color's coming back now, and my breathing's a little better, but for how long?" Her eyes welled. "Be good to my guys, Philo, please. They mean the world to me."

"Will do, Grace, but you're not going anywhere just yet. The prognosis is good for releasing you in a day or two."

"Releasing me to what?" she said, her voice weak. "Really, Philo, to what?" A tear rolled down her cheek, onto her pillow. She swallowed; her eyes were pleading. "You bring your gun with you today?"

He squeezed her hand hard. "What the fuck, Grace, you can cut that shit out right now. If I hear any more drama like that, I'm right the hell outta here. Besides, you still owe me some training, and I'm going to hold you to it."

He leaned in and gave her a caring hug. When he straightened up: "I've got some news. Just listen, no comments. Think you can do that?"

Grace nodded, gulped in some air, her breath still short.

"Good. I've been checking with some connections of mine. There's a strong possibility you'll get access to a pair of lungs shortly. No guarantees—"

"But—"

"Shut it, Grace, you're listening, remember? No guarantees, but the military's got some recourse in this area, even has its own lists. I'm waiting for a call back about arranging the location, as in what surgical facility we would take you to for the procedure. We won't know the date because, you know, that's a function of when the organs become available. But we'll get the location ironed out soon."

Her lips clamped into a straight line; her eyes narrowed. Her rebuttal was firm but soft, about all she could manage. "I will *not,*" Grace poked the back of his hand with her finger, "have *anyone* pull strings to make this happen, or take organs from someone else who's entitled to them. You hear me? *Will. Not.* No funny business, Philo. I won't agree to it."

Philo was ready for this as a response. "No pulled strings, Grace. Promise. I have people who owe me." He wrapped both his hands around her one, smothered it, and he focused on her tired eyes.

"And now, you'll be one of them. You'll pay me off by getting healthy enough to finish our transition contract. After that," he said, "you can chow down on all that self-righteous BS you feed yourself and check out if you want to. But I hope you don't. Your guys need you."

"Philo—"

"Look, I'm just being selfish, Grace. I still need your help with the business. *Your* business. The business you spent your life building with your husband. This guarantees—or is the closest I can get to a guarantee—that I get it."

She eyed him, analyzing his pitch. He knew, that *she* knew, there was more to his plea.

"I see," she said.

He didn't want her to make him say it, that this sexy old prickly bitch of a woman had somehow wormed her way into his hardened, ooh-rah heart. Didn't want her to make him say that, like Hank and Patrick, he needed her, too. There'd been little room most of his adult life for caring about people, for caring about parents. He'd screwed up too many times, had disappointed them ad nauseam. Maybe now, here, he could start making up for it.

Someone had to speak. "I won't tell Hank or Patrick about this," he said, "because you don't need anyone else pressuring you. I won't say anything until it's close to happening."

Not telling Hank or Patrick about prospective organ availability was a promise he could keep. Everything else was a fabrication. A separate military organ-donors-and-recipients list did exist, but he had no access to it other than if he himself needed a transplant. Him forcing her to earn out this "favor" by still training him, and him needing said training—all bullshit as well. Convincing her everything was on the up-and-up, including arranging an operating room theater and doctors she wouldn't question, that might prove difficult. But if she learned Philo had scammed her *after* she received the transplants, it wasn't like she could give them back.

He'd had her to himself long enough. A nurse popped in, confirmed he wasn't the husband, and waited for him to leave. He made his pitch again. "Say yes, Grace. Let's just do this. You've suffered enough. We can make this happen. How about it?"

Touched and teary-eyed, she disengaged their hands so she could recover his with hers.

"For the business then, and for my guys," she said. "Okay, yes, let's do this." And with her whisper of a smile, she let Philo's soft-heartedness off the hook.

Outside her room, Philo fished out a business card. He tapped Wally's number into his phone and keyed a text, was determined to play through his watering eyes.

Move the fight up. Tell me how the surgery will work.

14

TWO WEEKS LATER

Chinese food on a Thursday evening, the usual time and place for Kaipo. Her chocolate-covered fortune cookie was on a plate in front of her. Great presentation, on china, and warm, fresh, and so gooey it looked like it had been dipped in a fondue before it had been swirled with its sweet, decadent strawberry sauce. She'd meet this dessert artist someday, to personally commend him or her for creating these masterpieces with such five-star flair, inclusive of their private cryptic messages.

Why couldn't that day be today?

Kaipo did a quick about-face in her chair to see if she could get a glimpse.

Her Asian waiter disappeared through swinging, salmon-colored doors, the doors more pleasing in appearance than the set of doors beyond them, aluminum-clad and battered, leading to the kitchen. Another waiter entered. In his wake, the ambient lighting revealed a lone male standing in the shadowy no-man's-land between dining room and kitchen, observing her. Black hair slicked with mousse, white uniform jacket, black pants, and a long, thin, and tanned face. Also Asian, with a hooked nose and a mustache. Dressed here as a cook, he somehow didn't fit the profile, as interested in getting a glimpse of her as she was of him. The doors continued swinging, but after a few passes he was gone.

She cut open her chocolate-covered fortune cookie, using a fork to separate the pieces and eat them while reacquainting herself with her surroundings. Two couples at the front window, nearest the street, enjoyed each other's company, one couple holding hands beneath their table, the other sipping cocktails. Kaipo read her cookie's fortune. Finally she had a new assignment, a job for next week. She let out the relieved sigh she'd been holding in for days. Ka Hui had forgiven her perceived incompetence, the abandoned dealership job sloppy, unfinished, and necessitating that they relocate their operation.

She tucked the message into her mouth, and discreetly let its strawberry-flavored consistency charm her taste buds as it dissolved on her tongue. One thought came to mind: Did her dessert artist know the significance of these fortunes?

A new thought, a disturbing one, from an odd text she'd received this morning while at a client's home in another Philadelphia high-rise.

Businessman needs after-hours cleaning services. Name your price.

A huge red flag. No one outside Ka Hui knew she was a mob cleaner. Here was someone with the poorest of judgment who had to be on the inside of Ka Hui's supply chain, and who was now making an egregious mistake.

She'd held off responding until she saw she had a follow-up request from the same texter, suggesting they should meet this evening—

...for a drink. Non-alcoholic of course. Center City. Non-binding.

Casual tone, light, thoughtful, yet also professional. So natural for her to receive an inquiry, maybe even innocent, but any mention of services she might provide outside of personal training and massage was careless and dangerous, more so for the person who had contacted her than for Kaipo herself. She knew what she would do, *had* to do. And after she did it, she had no control over the outcome. This was someone who knew her background, also knew she was in recovery, which meant someone close to Ka Hui's management. She texted the only response she could, knowing this was what her current employers would want:

Where and when?

His return text:

Tonight at 9. The Franklin Bar.

A Rittenhouse Square subterranean speakeasy. She wasted no time in texting her handler, Olivier, to give him the heads-up about this breach. His response:

Enjoy your Thurs night dinner. Will get back to you.

And Olivier did get back to her with a text while she sipped her tea.

A proxy has been arranged for that meeting. You need not attend.

Standard protocol was that any further instructions from Olivier regarding her newest assignment were TBD, but after the Franklin Bar attempted-hookup time passed, the instructions she'd receive wouldn't be much more than time and location, and maybe quantity of victims.

She left her tip for the waiter, glanced again at the doors that shielded the dining area from the unpleasantness of the kitchen; no one had returned to the no-man's-land in between. Time to leave so she could go home and catch up on some rest, maybe do some reading while this breach was handled.

* * *

At nine thirty p.m. Kaipo's Franklin Bar suitor texted her because she was late for their appointment. Ninety minutes after that, she received another text from the same number. This one, she was sure, was not from her suitor.

It is safe.

She put the phone away. Her other phone buzzed with another text that included an address.

We're ready for you to make it safer.

* * *

Her destination was a residence on Elfreth's Alley, a tourist attraction in the Old City neighborhood of Philadelphia with significant sightseeing notoriety. She was on her way there in her van, a little after eleven thirty p.m.

As "the nation's oldest residential street" according to the National Register of Historic Places, Elfreth's Alley dated back to 1702, its present thirty-plus homes built in the mid-eighteenth and early-nineteenth centuries. She found parking a block away, on a different street.

Snow fell as she walked, a late-night dusting of the Philadelphia waterfront that was moving inland. Elfreth's Alley had room for foot and bicycle traffic only, no cars, but occasionally, young crotch-rocket motorcyclists dared the cops on the beat to catch them zooming along its short stretch. Red poles three feet high anchored the sidewalk in front of every house, emphasizing the no-motor-vehicle ordinance. Tonight there was no danger of that type of interference, the surfaces too slippery. Well-appointed brick fronts graced each of the two- and three-story early American homes, most with attic dormers. Kaipo guided two large pieces of wheeled luggage up the street on the slate that separated the brick sidewalk from a wide cobblestone stripe in the center. She wore a skirted business suit accessorized with a shoulder bag, her long black hair braided and away from her face. She caught snowflakes in her mouth, falling snow still a wonder to her even after three years on the mainland.

The home was a double, two row houses redone as one, and it was for sale. She checked the price online before she entered it, just for grins: reasonable at under $800K for 3,500 square feet in so hallowed a location. After tonight's activity and her visit, the price would drop.

"Safe" for this job meant "eliminate connections to us." She could make things safe from identifying the participants, but recently, in consideration of Ka Hui's newest venture—organ harvesting—eliminating all traces of these events had become a challenge.

Her low heels crunched the snow underfoot, squeezing out little white tufts, her rolling luggage leaving sloppy wet tracks behind. A lockbox hung from the doorknob. She punched in the code Olivier gave her and removed the key; she unlocked the door.

Inside, it was an open-floor plan, with living room, dining room, and kitchen connected by tongue-in-groove "rare red-heart pine flooring" per the real estate listing. The mess wasn't on the first floor, far as she could tell, was most likely on the floor below street level, accessed by a set of beautiful interior stone steps that wound their way downward.

Downstairs, the exposed stone foundation walls supported a curved, distressed red brick ceiling above three dramatic spaces: an unfurnished rec room appointed in brick top to bottom, an alcove with a hot tub, and next to it in a small room, a sauna. The lid to the circular hot tub was set aside, exposing gurgling water and something large in it. She peeked inside.

A floater.

She moved to the next room. From the doorway she switched on the light. Body number two. The multi-person sauna was a slaughterhouse, the gore overwhelming. She backed out and returned to the hot tub room.

Here too, the gruesome had ruined the room's ambience, with bubbling red water buffeting a naked body floating face down. She removed her gun and its holster from under her short sport coat, setting them aside within easy reach.

Kaipo pulled on a pair of nitrile gloves, reached in, and nudged the body's shoulder, slowly rotating the floater to expose an ear-to-ear throat cut, the blood still leaking from the slice and circling the body's upper torso in the water. The woman's face was distorted but her ethnicity was discernible: reddish-brown skin probably from south of the US border, anywhere from thirty to fifty years old. Kaipo rotated the body to get a better look at the damage. Holes throughout, many organs missing. Hopefully the throat cut ended the drama quickly for her, before the organ removal. An intended victim, or collateral damage? Kaipo guessed the latter. Someone unlucky enough to be on site as a potential witness when the chickens had come home to roost for the victim in the sauna; maybe a housekeeper. Regardless, after the maid's new Colombian necktie, the organ-harvesting vultures had swooped in.

Kaipo returned to the sauna, another striking room. A long cedar bench extended wall to wall. At the end of the bench was the sauna's heat source, stones that were still warm, in a box raised off the floor, the box level with the bench. Draped across the bench, with a face buried in the stones, the second body also had chunks missing, but the parts had been hacked out at haphazard angles, different than the maid's.

She assessed the sauna mess; this one would be less work for her. When she'd heard the address—Elfreth's Alley—she knew not to expect a simple lift and drop into the cooker. The narrow street and the home's internal configuration wouldn't permit it, the cooker not a consideration inside the house. No, these bodies would require transport, which meant dismemberment, and with this one, here in the sauna, the process had already been partially completed, evidenced by what was strewn around the cedar bench and floor: many of the body's internal organs, tenderized nicely in the sauna heat. They hadn't been surgically removed, were instead savagely torn from their cavities, or so it appeared. This was not an organ harvest; it was more like a wild animal feeding frenzy that had been interrupted.

Her phone vibrated.

Olivier.

"Yes?"

"Are you on site?" Olivier said. A gravelly hack, with no apology, then he blew his nose.

"Yes."

"You are wondering what happened."

"Yes."

"We needed pictures."

"For marketing?" she asked, a vague question, as in was this expected to deliver a message to a mob competitor?

"In part," Olivier said. "And partly because one of our contractors requested it. Your instruction is to remove the floater only. Everything in the sauna must stay as is, to be discovered by the *(cough)* authorities. Let me know when it is safe."

"Wait," she said. "I have a question."

She needed to choose her words carefully, to speak so only Olivier could understand her. Phone conversations traveled the airwaves; the airwaves attracted prying ears. Plus, she needed to be respectful. "This new program. Its donors sometimes experience unexpected outcomes. Are the company's other businesses not performing well enough? Why this new venture?"

The phone was silent for five, six, seven seconds, then a guttural snicker. The snicker turned giddy, almost feminine.

"Your question reminds me of Michael and Kay. You know, Pacino and Keaton? Like Michael Corleone said, 'Don't ask me about my business, Kay.' I can still see him slapping his hand on the desk in that scene, yelling at her, 'Enough!' Ha! *(cough)* You should assume that just happened on my end, but without the trite yell.

"This one time I'll answer your question about the business, then we close out this discussion. The other businesses are performing quite well. But cheap raw materials and leveraged outsourced support generate high margins, and high margins always interest us. That's all you need to know." The call ended.

A rebuke, somewhat lighthearted, but mostly not. Below the surface: *Don't screw with us, Kaipo. You know what we're capable of.*

Netting it out, and ignoring her discomfort, this would be a reprieve in her workload. The ghoulish male body parts mess in the sauna, per Olivier, needed to stay where it was. Only the female needed remediation. A throwaway domestic, probably an undocumented immigrant. A cheap raw material, per Olivier.

She opened one of her luggage pieces, removed her circular saw, a one-piece hooded Tyvek suit, footies and goggles, some chemicals and rags, and a roll of heavy plastic sheathing. She got to work, measuring each cut to maximize the space in the second suitcase, then adjusting the pieces with further cuts as needed to make them all fit.

Finished, she wiped off her mask with an enzyme-treated rag, lifted the mask above her head, and sat on a lounge chair she'd covered with heavy plastic. Her phone gave her the time: one twenty-two a.m. One more task, then she could pack up the rest of her things and leave. It was something she'd decided to do for herself at this and future jobs until further notice; an outcome of her ogling the Blessid Trauma website.

The sauna interior, top to bottom, was finished cedar—walls, ceiling, and raised floorboards resembling shipping pallets, cut to fit the space. Underneath the pallets were layers of flooring: vinyl, then hardwood, then brick, a drain passing through all of it. She knew the floor's constitution because she'd tugged a corner of it up, because this was where all liquids settled at a crime scene. Here one would find the human sweat, the blood, and the other body refuse, all of it going layers-deep if left to fend for itself, becoming a longer-term biohazardous nightmare. Cleaners who knew their stuff would clean the drain plus dig deep into the flooring to solution the biohazard, sometimes even carve out and remove the underlayment if necessary. Whatever service the cops or a homeowner would use to clean up this toxic space, to do it right, the cleaner would need to pull apart the floor and clean all layers containing seepage. This was where she left the message. She'd do it again at future sites—some crime scenes meant to be discovered, some not—expecting at some point that one cleaning service in particular would be assigned one of the jobs. The website info, about the personal trauma this Patrick-Stakes-from-Alaska young man had experienced, hadn't flipped the switch for her, but his warrior dance at the car dealership had.

She'd seen the celebration before, a haka at a graduation event for US military training, in Hawaii.

The kid was Hawaiian, also might be a soldier, and was apparently unaware of either of those facts.

The bag with the reconfigured maid stuffed inside was heavy. A muscle in Kaipo's back grabbed as she dragged the luggage piece step by step up to the first floor. She returned to the basement for the second bag and one last look inside the sauna, for a confirmation about the victim.

She lifted his head. Asian, with a hooked nose, tanned face, moussed hair and a mustache.

Oh my.

Here was her off-stage admirer from the Chinese restaurant tonight, the one who watched her eat her dessert. Another mob contractor who wanted her to do for him what she did exclusively for his and her mob bosses. She could have gone for a guy like this. Attractive, and for him to be such a great dessert artist, he was probably a good cook as well. A pity.

Out of her biohazard overalls, she now appeared as she'd originally entered the house, a professional woman in a skirted business suit. Kaipo slid the suitcases out the door, locked up, and returned the key to the lockbox.

A glance left then right, then she started her trek back up Elfreth's Alley. New snow had fallen. She retrieved her phone, stopping to key her parting cryptic "all-clear" message to Olivier. A hesitation before she sent it, discomfort, again, from a sixth sense.

She turned in time to catch someone standing under a streetlamp half a block away, where Elfreth's Alley ended at an intersection. He danced from foot to foot, tamping the snow while keeping warm, watching her, her studying him as intently as she would a painting. Behind him a SEPTA bus slowed while driving past. She heard the wheels squeal when its breaks engaged as it neared the corner. Her admirer hurried off, the bus doors wheezing open then snapping close.

She couldn't give chase on foot, her baggage the reason, but she might cruise the streets a bit in her van in search of that bus. She'd been seen leaving a job. This would need to be addressed.

15

Tonight at her condo apartment in Conshohocken, Lola had been crazy-nice to Philo sexually, even after he'd been preoccupied and again less than attentive to her during their lovemaking. Then he announced his news: he was making himself scarce for a bit; Blessid Trauma was about to get very busy.

She swung her legs over the side of the bed, slipped on some panties and a sleeveless white tee and left the bedroom, headed for her kitchen at the end of the hall. The kitchen light went on.

"It's temporary," he called after her. "I'll be off-grid a coupla weeks, three weeks tops. They released Grace Blessid from the hospital, but she's still out of commission."

Philo knew Lola couldn't care less how shorthanded Grace's illness made him. She'd heard too much about the Gore Whore's affliction already.

A kitchen cabinet closed, not softly. A ceramic mug kissed the granite countertop with equal gusto, then he heard dripping coffee, then nothing. She'd gone cold, had tuned him out and slipped into the now-quiet midnight recess of her kitchen. Her Zippo lighter snapped open, flicked once, and snapped shut. If she was smoking, she was thinking. About him and her. Her, with him. Them as a couple. Life, and love, and sharing, and other deep thoughts, which meant he was fucked.

It was the new project. His plea to her had been for understanding, that the project would demand all his attention. An old grain elevator on a pier near the Navy Yard in South Philadelphia was scheduled for demolition, but it needed biohazard curing beforehand. Blessid Trauma did deals like this before, was accredited to prepare smaller warehouses and corner stores for repurposing when property titles changed hands, but never a deal this large. Lola's rebuttal, a repeat of every past conversation they'd had about his busy schedule, was she was plenty busy too, with her high-profile legal career, and she was tired of being an afterthought.

Grain elevators at waterfront docks were a simple concept. Buckets scooped up large quantities of loose grain at pier level, ran the grain up a conveyor, and deposited it into silos multiple stories high, ready for redistribution inland. This one elevator was last operational in the midnineties: six above-ground levels, one below, over one hundred eighty feet tall and backing up to the Delaware River, the rubble surrounding it making the multi-acre property appear post-apocalyptic.

Implosion of the building was scheduled for late April. Biohazard remediation would prevent a repeat of the disastrous 1956 explosion and fire that destroyed another Tidewater Grain Company grain elevator, one that was next to the Schuylkill River. Philo researched it. The force of that blast was the equivalent of eleven hundred pounds of dynamite, and required six alarms plus fireboat support. Three dead, eighty-five injured. The blast and fire rocked block after block of downtown Philadelphia, and was felt miles away in the suburbs. The cause: grain dust, which was highly explosive. The summer after the blast and the fire, a small crop of corn grew out of the ashes, nature's response to the disaster, a bit like stuffing daisies into soldiers' rifles.

A casino consortium planned to develop the property on the waterfront. A demolition company had the contract to implode the building, and they in turn subcontracted to feeder outfits like rubble removers, metal and wood recyclers, and Philo's biohazard restitution company, Blessid Trauma.

He'd waited to fess up to the project until after their Friday-night lovemaking, his timing more from procrastination than self-interest. Regardless, she had to hear it tonight. He didn't tell her, couldn't tell her, the more significant reason for his limited availability: that he'd decided to fight bare-knuckles again, and he needed to train. She was an assistant district attorney in the Philadelphia DA's office; she couldn't be party to it, bare-knuckles boxing being illegal and all.

The grain elevator demolition was undeniably real, now part of the local news cycle. Needing help for the massive remediation job was also real. The part about needing to work twenty-four seven, with little time for recreation, that too was true, but it was also an excuse. After busting his ass all day on what he knew would be a monster of a project, Philo would need to go to a gym to reawaken his boxing appetite, to get his game face on; to resurrect and sharpen dormant skills, and focus on Wally Lanakai's fifty-thousand-dollar proposition.

The Hawaiian mobster put his underground promo machine in motion quickly, locally and internationally, and was honoring Philo's request that he make the fight sooner rather than later. It was set for a Saturday night in early April, three weeks from tomorrow. In pro boxing, this was almost too short a notice for getting into fighting shape. Not so for bare-knuckles matches, where training for your next fight was often the number of minutes your previous fight had lasted. Three weeks' notice was a palatable luxury—but only for someone who fought a lot more recently than fifteen years ago.

He'd already heard rumblings about the fight at a few watering holes in South Philly and the Mayfair section of Northeast Philly, and was proud of himself for keeping his identity and his ego out of the conversations. The bar chatter had been entertaining, warts and all:

"Undefeated Northeast bare-knuckle brawler. Fucker's coming out of retirement."

"The kid rose from the ashes of 9-11, been out there executing ragheads in the Middle East, now he's back."

"...doesn't stand a chance. Fifteen years since he was last in the game? No fucking chance."

There was a convenience to the excuse part. Philo wanted a break. From being a couple with Lola; from Lola and the phenom she herself was becoming.

Lola Pfizer. Probably the best thing that had ever happened to him, and he was blowing her off. An incredible mind with a hot-shit legal career. A stunning redhead, other physical gifts as well. A bundle of energy in bed, a dynamo on the local scene, and a woman who'd make a fine politician one day, her associates kept telling her, and that was the problem. She was listening to these people, and Philo had never met a politician he didn't want to punch in the throat.

She was wise beyond her years, too, and wise way beyond Philo's, even though he was older than her by almost a decade. She knew what this temporary absence thing meant for their relationship better than he did.

He pulled up his jeans, climbed into his sweater, and found her in the kitchen, still chilling. It was nearing one a.m. She lit another cigarette then sipped coffee at her center island, contemplating her mug, a spotlight illuminating her hands. The cigarette went to an ashtray, the smoke swirling before her faraway eyes. She ignored his entrance, played with her lighter, snapping it open and closed, open and closed, until he spoke.

"Lola, honey."

He told her more. How he would need to scramble, might even need to parcel out some of the work to other biohazard companies, or at least add some help. That the project was dangerous, and it was making him anxious, and people were counting on him, and he was feeling a lot of pressure, and yada yada yada. The more he added, the more he sounded uncomfortable as hell about...something. Lola knew it, and he knew she knew.

"Methinks," she said, "the weasel doth protest too much. I've had enough of this." She flicked her cigarette lighter on, eyed the flame. "So here's another thought. Why don't you go set your dick on fire and feed it to your cat."

"Lola, please..."

"Just get out."

"Look—honey—"

"Leave your key then get the fuck out, Philo. We're done."

She tossed her Zippo onto the granite top, put out her cigarette in the mug, and left the kitchen. At the end of the hall, she closed her bedroom door.

* * *

On his way home in his Jeep, he turned off his phone. Just how screwed up was he, not wanting to get too close? Not wanting emotional attachments, with women, men, kids, anyone, except maybe his father, now that his father was gone. And his cat.

Cats were resilient. Survivors. Which made a cat less likely to get croaked if it were in his company, nine lives and all, and less dependent on him. If, or more like when, his military past caught up with him, if he didn't get close to other people, other people wouldn't die. He wasn't screwed up, he was being practical. And being practical meant he'd miss out on some things, like healthy relationships.

He was getting maudlin about being maudlin. He chose an easier topic to stress about: the Lanakai fight.

Wally Lanakai said he'd let Philo select the fight venue. Earlier today, the mobster sent him a text to let him know he'd scoped out Philo's choice, the grain elevator.

Dangerous. Just like my fighter. I like it.

Location, location, location, convenient by air, land, and the Delaware River. Philo and the Blessid team would clean the grain elevator during the day, plus work other projects as required. Philo would personally head back to the silo at night to further prepare the place. It wouldn't take much. The bottom floor, where they'd hold the fight, was perfect, closed in from the elements and from prying eyes by heavy tarpaulins, and accessorized by jobsite lighting hanging from the ceiling. He'd begin prep shortly, to accommodate the anticipated small, select crowd of bloodthirsty fight fans who typically showed for these spectacles. Maybe fifty folks or so, there to watch two bare-fisted fools wail on each other for four minutes, five minutes tops, his goal, his intended outcome being him standing over a horizontal opponent, telling him he'd be better off if he didn't try to return to his feet. Also, as an expected outcome, and supremely important: two healthy lungs for Grace Blessid. Oh, and a fifty-thousand-dollar purse for him.

Two a.m. now, and the lateness of the hour might let him drift asleep more easily. His Jeep coasted down the back alley to the rear of his house and entered his short driveway. On the walk to the back door, he turned on his phone.

Messages. He scrolled through the numbers, listened to the first few words of each until he got to the call from Detective Ibáñez, the close-talker. A few of the words in her message made him take notice: "significant meat value." He replayed it, listening more intently the second time.

"*Rhea Ibáñez, Northeast Detectives. About that photo of the door at the aban-doned dealership. I have info I can share, but only in return for your feedback on a week-old crime scene the Sixth District is working. Significant meat value. Call me in the morning.*"

Her word selection was calloused and inappropriate as hell, but she'd sized him up correctly as someone who didn't wilt easily. The Sixth District wasn't hers, was downtown, encompassing Independence Mall, the Liberty Bell, and Old City.

Tough little fresh-faced bruiser, this detective was, with language that made her sound so...practical. He could use practical right about now. He'd call her back in the morning.

16

"Ibáñez, Northeast Detectives."

She related her request: Philo should meet her early afternoon in the Sixth District office on North Eleventh street in Old City. She'd take him to a crime scene remedied by another service, he'd see some pictures, then he'd tell her what he saw.

"If you're planning to eat lunch before we meet, Mr. Trout, don't."

* * *

Philo's next call before his trip downtown was to get a certain ball rolling, to coordinate it with his visit into the city with Detective Ibáñez. The good news was, the phone number he dialed, a landline, was still in service after fifteen years, but the bad news was it wasn't getting picked up, and it wasn't going to voicemail. After ten rings or so, his patience paid off.

"Hello," a male voice said, followed by a guttural, phlegmy clearing of throat. "Fargas here."

Still alive. Excellent. "Hump. It's Philo Trout. Long time no talk."

"I don't know no Philo nobody. I'm hanging up now."

Benito Fargas, father to Chuckie Fargas, Philo's former manager/promoter, may Chuckie rest in peace. Benito was "Hump" to people in the fight game. On the phone now, his grunting response sounded grumpier than a bear poked with a stick. One concern Philo had was, at Hump's age the denial of familiarity might not have been an act.

"No, Hump, wait. How about 'Buick' Temple? Remember him? Went about two-sixty? I kayoed him in fifteen seconds, Vogt Rec Center, Northeast Philly, early 2001. And Daniel Dorian Gray, two forty, thirty seconds, Saint Martin de Tours Church basement, New Hope. Or cruiserweight contender Oleander Clarke. Less than two minutes at the Saint Louis Armory, just before 9-11, before he turned pro—"

"Fine. So it's the prodigal Philo Trout. Quite a surprise, son, considering you're dead. You died in Turkey."

"Funny. I heard the same about you, but on a beach in Tahiti."

"Then someone didn't hear so good. I was on a bitch in Tijuana, heh-heh. Yeah, a real heart attack, that woman. How the hell are you, Philo?"

Chiding Hump Fargas for his insensitivities toward women would have been a waste of time, and lately, who was Philo to cast stones? He really should have stayed in touch after the fight fifteen years ago, felt super bad about it now. Hump lost his son twice because of it, the first when Chuckie bolted, the second time with no chance of a father-son reconciliation, considering Lanakai's people had found Chuckie first.

"I'm doing well, Hump. You?"

"I'm seventy-eight and I piss thirty times a day, but there's still some major lead down there. Doing my best to fuck myself dead, Philo. If I have my way, it'll still happen."

The stories about Hump and women, and him telling boxers to stay away from their girlfriends while training for fights, because having sex weakened an athlete's legs: Hump swore he personally started that infamous rumor, just so he could have all the women to himself.

"A favor, Hump," Philo said. "I've got an engagement in two weeks and I need somewhere to work out. A place with equipment where I can train, alone. Any suggestions?"

"Shit, man, you fighting again? Damn. Numero uno bare knuckler, making a comeback. Ha! 'I've got an engagement,' he says. What, your blue collar's all worn out, so now you talking like you're corporate? You're fucking killing me, Philo. 'An *engagement*'? Fucking funny."

"It's not a comeback, Hump. Relax. It's one fight."

"Well damn, no matter, you're in luck. I know a place. An old building near North Broad and West Glenwood, looking to make a comeback too. A gym. You'd be perfect for each other."

The cross streets sounded familiar, but Philo couldn't picture the place. "Again, Hump, not a comeback. Five minutes throwing some heavy hands, then I'll be back at my day job. I'll be in Center City later today. Give me a time we can get together."

* * *

Philo called Patrick to ask if he was busy this afternoon.

"I got tickets for a concert, sir."

"I've got some Saturday OT for you at a crime scene in Old City if you want it. You sure?"

"Um, I need to get to the concert, sir. Can you drop me off in time for the concert? If you can drop me off at the concert afterward, I can do it, sir."

"Where?"

"The Troc."

"I'll drop you off at the concert, Patrick," he said, staying with the theme.

"Great, sir. See you soon."

"Wait. How's Grace?" Grace was getting additional rest before she returned to work, but more rest wasn't going to be enough.

"She says she's fine, sir. Hank tells her she isn't." A pause. "Hank is right, sir."

"I think Hank is right too, Patrick. See you in a bit."

* * *

The Sixth District police were headquartered in a single-story red brick building on North Eleventh Street in the heart of Philly's Chinatown. It was walking distance from the Trocadero Theater, an opera house turned vaudeville joint turned stripper burlesque theater that eventually settled down in the eighties to become a small music venue, its long entertainment history making it yet another Philadelphia landmark on the National Historic Register. Philo double-parked their unmarked Blessid Trauma van, the company's small one, outside the cop station. Patrick slipped between the seats, moving from shotgun to rear. Detective Ibáñez climbed in to ride shotgun.

She was dressed for the weather in a cop hat with earmuffs, a zippered bomber jacket with a badge on her chest, gloves, and a Styrofoam cup of coffee carried above a black skirt and pumps. A thin valise occupied her non-coffee hand. Philo greeted her. "Detective."

"Mr. Trout." She turned in her seat and showed some on-the-job cop disdain for the rear passenger. "We won't need him. Nothing to clean up."

"He's got a good eye for detail," Philo said, the van reentering traffic. "Plus, he needed a ride. He'll be fine."

Patrick beamed. "Seeing Tassho Fearce today, ma'am, in concert. Tassho's at the Troc. Gonna see him there."

She faced forward, no acknowledgment of his exuberance, no remarks, no smile, only indifference, or what appeared to be. Or maybe she knew about this rap artist and was smart enough not to comment. Philo hadn't known who Tassho Fearce was until today, when he'd made the mistake of volunteering a listen on Patrick's earbuds on their ride here. He was treated to the most incendiary language he'd ever heard about cops and hos and drugs and guns. When young Patrick saw Philo's serious *what the fuck was that* face, he turned sheepish. "Sorry, sir. He's a nice man in person." Patrick tucked his earbuds back in.

Philo started his conversation with the detective with a patronizing comment. "Kids today and their music, right? Thug rap, promoting unhealthy minds and bodies in the disenfranchised for decades. Whaddya gonna do."

Ibáñez stayed professional, non-committal, and spoke past the sarcasm. "The crime scene is an address on Elfreth's Alley. Ten minutes tops without traffic. The concern is, bad as the scene was, it might *not* have been a mob hit." A coffee sip, then a grimace; she was less than thrilled with the cup's contents. "The coroner pegged the date and time of death as last Thursday. You're seeing it so you'll have a better frame of reference when I show you the photos before it was cleaned up. We want a second opinion."

"Sure. But why Blessid Trauma?"

"The car dealership slaughter. You kept us from missing a few things."

* * *

"Park here," she said, motioning at a space too close to a fire hydrant on Front Street, adjacent to Elfreth's Alley. "Any issue, I'll take care of it." She exited the van and started walking.

"Ready, chief?" Philo said to Patrick, who hadn't budged from his seat.

"No."

"*What?* C'mon, dude, we've got some things to look at in here. Just trying to help the cops."

"No."

"Patrick, what is it?"

"'*A great tourist place to visit,*'" he said, repeating someone else's words. "'*Beautiful old homes. Oldest street in America. 1702—*'"

Sounded like words from a brochure or a flyer, or maybe from a walking tour guide.

"Not going inside, sir, can't, unh-unh, not allowed, people live there."

"Okay, Patrick, calm down. You don't need to go inside if you don't want. Sit tight, I'll be back."

Philo caught up to the detective, already busy unsticking the door-size X made of yellow crime scene tape. She unlocked the door and they entered. "We're going downstairs," she said.

Descending carved stone steps to the lower level, Philo could smell the disinfectant and the enzyme cleaners. The basement was a stone and brick personal retreat that looked like an indoor grotto, an underground spring the only thing missing. An elevated hot tub sat in an alcove adjacent to the large empty room, the tub's padded cover off. No visual evidence of a biohazard event in this room, far as Philo could tell, but the lingering bleach odor indicated there'd recently been some aggressive cleaning either in here or nearby.

"Let me see the luminol impact," Philo said, jumping ahead.

"Or lack thereof," Detective Ibáñez said. She turned off the lights.

In the dark, there was no phosphorescent blue anywhere near the hot tub, which meant the sprayed luminol showed no evidence of an event, the walls and raised planked flooring clean of visible blood spatter. He leaned over for a peek inside the hot tub's dark, shadowy interior. No phosphorescent indigo there either.

"No indications of a blood event in here. Same thing with all of the floors above," she offered. "Follow me."

The smaller room next door was a sauna. When the detective opened the room's cedar door, the sauna's overhead light automatically turned on. She let Philo enter first.

Nice, Philo thought. A large sauna in this room, one room removed from a hot tub. A resort-style basement; incredible ambience. What a great house.

"Ready?" she asked.

"Go for it."

She closed the door and turned off the sauna's overhead light.

"Whoa," Philo said, wide-eyed.

Here was a ten-by-twelve cedar-paneled planetarium of blood splatter completely outed by phosphorescent indigo that overwhelmed the walls and left only portions of the room's surfaces uncompromised. After thirty or so seconds with the light off, the luminol's horrific show started fading.

She turned the light back on. "Now for the photos." She removed them from her valise, handed them to Philo. More than fifty forensics shots of the body and its pieces, its innards strewn across all surfaces in the sauna, on the bench and under it, and on the raised wooden floor, with sprays on the ceiling as well. Philo could have been convinced the body had exploded from the chest outward.

"I know what you're thinking; it looks like the body blew up. Not according to the medical examiner. Look at these individual marks on these organs."

Bite marks, and chunks of flesh torn from the thighs and the stomach, plus at least one chunk from a kidney, the missing part about the size of an adult mouth.

"No zombie wisecracks, Trout," the detective said, "but whoever did this, shall I say, is fairly fucked up."

"Huh," Philo said, shaking his overwhelmed head, still busy absorbing the photos. He raised them up in the light, piecing the room together with them. Yes, what he was looking at did show some major fucked-up-ness.

"I need more than a 'huh,' Trout. You see anything odd in here?"

What seemed odd was what he wasn't seeing. At the most recent organ-snatcher crime scene, someone with experience had performed the surgeries. But here, the organs in these shots didn't look cleanly severed from their cavities. They were ripped out à la a horror movie scene that actually could have featured, um, zombies.

"Overkill," he said.

"Ya think?"

"Seriously. Either someone extremely sick did this, or someone staged it to make it look that way. Might be hard to tell the difference. No matter, you do have a body, and you have organs from the body, so one question is, do you have them all?"

"Good thought. The answer is no. Per the coroner one internal organ, a kidney, wasn't here, and the second kidney had a bite-size chunk out of it. Maybe our perp, or perps, weren't as hungry as they first thought. All the other organs and body parts were strewn around here, in the sauna," she said, "tenderizing."

"The one organ missing, the kidney," Philo said, "happens to be the most expensive organ on the black market."

"Your point?"

Grace's skepticism—some of it had rubbed off on him. He'd researched organ trafficking when viewing public info about Dr. Andelmo, Patrick's trauma physician.

"If you assume it was someone with a lunatic zombie fetish," he said, "then whatever is missing doesn't mean squat. That person's nuts, and you'll catch up with him at some point. If you go with a staged scene assumption, then the missing kidney says they tried to make it look believable as a gruesome flesh-fest but got greedy staging it. What's one missing kidney? To forensics folks, maybe not much to care about, considering what else was in here. But to an organ trafficker, a kidney's worth two, maybe three hundred thousand bucks. Maybe their greed got the better of them. Then again, maybe someone did eat the fucking thing. How about active oxygen? Any traces of it?"

"No bleach, far as we could tell."

"Was there blood anywhere else in the house?"

"Ah, no."

"Does that seem right to you, considering the bloodbath in the sauna? Maybe the upper floors got super-cleaned with oxygenated bleach, and the sauna was the only mess left for you to find."

"A possibility."

"What about the victim?"

"He was the homeowner. Asian. Single. He had a housekeeper. The neighbors they interviewed felt she was undocumented. If the maid was involved...I don't need to tell you that undocumented aliens are good at making themselves scarce."

"She might be scarce for a different reason. She might be dead."

"Yes. We're looking for her."

The detective ushered Philo outside the sauna. "So here's the quid pro quo, Mr. Trout. About your red door at the car dealership: investigators decided it was the same door in the train suicide photo. We checked with the suicide's family. The man in the photo was the husband."

"No surprise there. Thanks."

"Here's the thing. The guy died weeks after an organ donation and before her suicide, from 'complications.' An organ donation he made, no doubt, for money. Although her family denied they received anything.

"I already knew what a kidney brings on the black market, Trout. The doctors get the two hundred grand. The donor husband probably got maybe five to ten thousand; a fortune to an immigrant. It's not too difficult to see what's happening here. Undocumented aliens are being exploited. Sometimes the exploitation kills them."

Detective Ibáñez, close talker that she was, suddenly pulled back. She misted up, something Philo didn't see coming, something he reckoned she wasn't capable of, hard-assed as she carried herself.

"I was born into that kind of community, Trout. Born in the States, but my parents weren't. I made my way out of the poverty, out of that hidden life. My parents didn't."

"Sorry to hear that, Detective."

"And I'm sorry I mentioned it. Let's move on. Time to wrap things up here. Anything else you can offer?"

He scanned the sauna again. "About these cedar pallets..."

The wood planks were in squared pallet configurations, four heavy cedar pallets fitted together to form the sauna floor. They could be lifted out of the way for cleaning underneath. "Is it clean under them, too?"

"Now it is. The blood and body effluence, it's all gone. Check it out. The 'before' is in the photos."

Philo did, more closely this time. Two sets of photos of the underlayment, a layer of a washable vinyl, then one of hardwood, then red brick. On the light-colored vinyl flooring under the pallets, the luminol showed where the bloody carnage had leaked through. With it, there was something written.

"What is it, Trout?"

Ho—lee—shit.

"I, ah..."

Block letters, on a space the size of a car window, in Sharpie-black against the tan vinyl. The first two rows of it:

THINK

HAWAIIAN

"Oh, that," she said. "Yeah. Two words that kept us from ruling this out as a mob hit. Another friggin' mob in Philly nowadays, supposedly from Hawaii. We saw this note at another crime scene, too. Just what the city needs, a mob war. Anything else?"

No, nope, nada, Philo thought. *Nothing I'm sharing.*

"Er, no, Detective. Nothing else."

The Sharpie message had two more rows to it. This was the part that had taken his breath away, and had kept him from volunteering anything else.

NOT

ALASKAN

"We haven't figured out what Alaska's got to do with this, if anything," the detective said, "other than to suggest these head cases might really be off-the-chart bizarros. You'll see what the media's doing with it later today. Headlines about cannibalism. Real bottom-feeders. Something comes to you later, Trout, let me know. Let's go. We're finished here."

17

Patrick was out of the van and standing at the foot of cobblestoned Elfreth's Alley, his shoulders hunched, his coat collar up, no gloves or hat, with earbuds a-jamming. His exposed phone hand shook in the sub-freezing temperature. Philo and Detective Ibáñez approached while she continued to chat Philo up. Hawaiian mob this, Asian mob that, your Satanics, your one-offs. Philo heard little of it, caught up in his own internal monologue fueled by the message in the crime scene floor's underlayment. They closed in on Patrick, who shifted his weight from foot to foot.

It was like Philo was seeing him for the first time.

He'd already bought into it. Hawaiian, not Alaskan. Not *Eskimo,* not even the politically correct Aleut, not Inuit. There was no longer a reason to make the distinction regarding anything Patrick wasn't. Someone, a person known to one of these mobs, noticed something about him; enough to make the assertion, to call out the obvious.

Patrick's Pat's Steaks saviors had declared Patrick an Eskimo. What the hell did blue-collar white guys from Philly know about indigenous peoples anyway? Typical insensitive white guy description: "That guy is black." Not African, not Caribbean, not South American, not Aboriginal. The nonwhite bucket to some white people was often all encompassing and imprecise, especially in a life or death situation, even when disrespect wasn't intended.

Seeing that pronouncement there, at so gruesome—so cannibalistic—a scene, had implications that invoked other considerations.

Meat value. Raw meat. Words that scared him on Patrick's behalf.

They reached the end of the block, the detective not slowing down. Philo beckoned to Patrick to fall in behind them as they turned the corner. To the detective, this man-boy was at best an afterthought, at worst invisible, a non-Caucasian non-person with his brain injury and amnesia. Her callousness was ironic, considering the revelation about her undocumented parents, and that her family was left to conduct their lives in the shadows, under the undocumented immigrant radar. Patrick wasn't far removed from the same marginalized existence.

Then again—

Ibáñez stopped short on the sidewalk, did an about-face. "Where are your gloves?" she asked Patrick.

"Dunno, ma'am. Home maybe."

"Here, take mine. They're too large for me. I'll get another pair at the station. In case you need them at your show."

"The concert's inside, ma'am."

"Take them anyway. And don't be practicing what that rapper preaches, okay? It's only an act. Cops are good people."

"Yes, ma'am. Thanks."

Detective Ibáñez—less hard-assed cop, more human being, doing some good here with Patrick. Philo was impressed.

"You have my card, right, Mr. Trout?"

"I do."

"Good. I want to hear from you if something else clicks."

"Will do, Detective."

"Now get me back to the Sixth."

* * *

Patrick climbed into the front seat after Detective Ibáñez exited. They watched her enter a back door to the police station, Patrick smitten both with his new gloves and the woman who gave them to him. "She's a nice person, sir. I like her."

"Me too." Philo had no opinion of her before, but he had one now. He fished in his pocket, found her card, then tucked it back away. Their van left the rear of the police station and merged into traffic. It was time to unload on Patrick; interrogate him about his crime scene manners.

"I wanted your help in there, bud. What was the problem?"

"That street, sir. I don't like it. I been there before. Two times."

A wee bit of a red flag. "Really? When?"

"First time was maybe before I got beat up and ended up in the hospital."

"You remember why you were there—what the occasion was?"

"*Step away from the doorbell,*" he said, mimicking a scolding voice, his finger raised. "*These houses are NOT open to the public.*"

"Tour guide?"

"Yeah."

"Anyone else with you?"

"Older people. A crowd. Don't know who, sir."

"So when was the second time?"

"Last Thursday night."

No—fucking *no*.

Thursday was the same day the medical examiners had estimated as date and time of death for the corpse the cops had found. Philo's wee garden-variety red flag morphed into a Times Square billboard with fireworks and a mushroom cloud chaser on New Year's Eve. "*Thursday?* You sure?"

"Yeah."

"Outside on the street, or inside the house?"

"Um..."

"Patrick, this is important. Inside or just outside?"

"Inside the house."

Kee-rist. "I don't fucking believe this. Why...How did you get in?"

"A lady with a suitcase went in first. She left the door unlocked. I peeked in. She didn't know I went in after her."

"This is *not* good, Patrick. Why in bloody hell would you go inside someone else's house?"

"Ummm...Here." Patrick leaned over by way of explanation and held up his phone to show a phone number. "A man called me, sir, said he heard about me, said there might be stuff inside that would tell me more about myself, before I was beat up. He said the house was for sale and I could go inside even though nobody was home."

Shit just got way too real. Philo screeched the van to a stop at a street corner and put the flashers on.

"The caller gave you the code for the real estate lockbox?"

"Yeah. But I didn't need it because of the lady with the suitcase."

Philo ran his hand through his rooster comb hair, his look pained. "Jesus, Patrick. Give it to me from the beginning. Now. All of it."

"But sir, I don't want to miss the concert—"

"You won't. Tell me everything."

* * *

Patrick had never sounded so coherent, so determined, a young man on a mission, that mission being a rapid-fire data dump that would get the van back in traffic ASAP, headed over to the Troc for the afternoon concert.

"...and she went downstairs, and I followed her and peeked in on her, and...Nope, she didn't see me, sir, she was too busy, and noisy...Power tools...Yeah, I touched stuff, some doorknobs, and I opened some envelopes...Because the man on the phone said the mail would have clues, but it didn't, sir, they were bills, all of it was bills."

"What happened next?"

His face got puffy, his dark eyes welled. "I sat on a sofa and cried, sir. I don't remember nothing after that. I woke up outside, waiting for the bus. I called the man back. He didn't answer. I went home."

He had dozed off then sleepwalked himself right out of the house, to the bus stop. Memory of being in the house but no memory of leaving it. One clusterfuck after another.

"Give me the phone number."

Philo dialed it, no answer, no voicemail. It would be a burner phone, a disposable, but he'd have no way of confirming this unless Patrick told the cops about his trespass, then they'd be able to run the number down. But telling the cops would be a mistake.

One glaring omission in Patrick's story. "Did you see the body in the sauna?"

"A body was in the hot tub, sir. I saw her lift it out. A little woman with big holes in her. That's all I saw, sir."

There it was, Philo's gut feeling explained. A second body, the mess addressed before the police arrived, no traces left behind. While inside the house, Patrick hadn't gotten as far as the sauna, the room next to the hot tub, where a slaughter had taken place. "Describe this woman for me."

"Asian. Two arms, two legs, a head, and a bunch of holes all over her body, sir."

"Okay, fine, but I meant the *other* woman. The one you followed into the house."

"She was tall and curvy, with dark brown hair, or maybe it was black, in a skirt with a short jacket. She was dressed like an airplane lady."

"You mean like a flight attendant?"

"Yeah, that's it, but she was a cleaner, sir, like me. She had the chemicals, the Tyvek, an electric saw, other stuff. Looked like me, too. Dark skin, black hair, but pretty. A pretty Eskimo lady."

A good place to mention Hawaii versus Alaska, but that would derail their discussion. "Eskimo's kind of a bad word, right, buddy?"

"Oh yeah. Right. Aleut. Sorry."

He squeezed Patrick's shoulder, a friendly, reassuring squeeze, still assessing the impact of this info. Patrick's observations about the woman's looks had sealed it. She was likely another Hawaiian, and the only person he could assign responsibility to for the message under the floor.

Philo needed to go after the craziness that was Patrick's trespassing snafu. "You entered a house where murders were committed. You were in there *before* the cops got there, and you don't remember leaving. You know what that means?"

"I'll be a suspect, sir."

"Bingo."

"But I didn't do nothing, sir. That's the truth, sir."

"They'll check for fingerprints, Patrick."

"The Eskimo lady probably cleaned them all up, sir."

"You can't be sure of that. And it doesn't matter what the truth is. It's what it looks like. This isn't good, Patrick."

"Sir?"

"What?"

"She had a gun."

Too much to process. Mob executions, then a mob cleaner who sanitized the scene for only one of the victims, eliminating traces of another execution; it was some kind of set-up. Then a cop forensics team, then a commercial crime scene cleaner to make the place presentable again, then Philo and Detective Ibáñez.

There'd be no volunteering of Patrick's trespass to the police. Maybe the evidence of his trespass actually *was* gone. Let them come to him.

Philo had more to discuss, like Hawaii versus Alaska, but screw it, he would let Patrick enjoy his concert. Plus, Philo was already late for a meeting with a pisser of an old friend, Hump Fargas, at a North Philadelphia address that was familiar to him, though he wasn't sure why.

A mess that could get messier. No matter; business as usual for now. People to see, places to go, and a fifty-thousand-dollar fight to train for.

"Let's get you over to the Troc in time for you to see your dope rapper buddy Lazlo make some noise. We can talk later."

"Tassho, sir. His name is Tassho Fearce. That would be great, sir. Thank you."

18

Kaipo poured the purple contents of her juicer into a large cup and sat at the counter in her kitchen. An afternoon pick-me-up before her next massage appointment. She clicked on the philly.com headline.

No Suspects Yet in Old City Cannibalism Homicide

Good; Ka Hui remained unidentified as a player. A strong nod to her cleanup work, although an unnamed source in the article did speculate about possible mob activity. It was also good news as a headline because after weeks of investigation, there'd been no mention of a second body.

On the bad news side, however, there was still Olivier.

She'd had only one other assignment since the car dealership snafu, and she remained wary of his longer-term intentions regarding her future as a contractor for Ka Hui, or, worse yet, her future as a living, breathing human being. He'd texted her overnight about her replacement pressure cooker, that it would be available in a few days.

Saturday eight pm in Bristol for the swap.

Can't tell a book without its cover.

She understood the fractured cliché. They would meet at a closed publishing warehouse on Radcliffe Street, where remaindered paperbacks with stripped covers intended for recycling still lay rotting years after its publisher who used it had ended its presence there. She'd go there prepared either way, would bring her passport, a large amount of cash, and firepower, plus the old pressure cooker, hedging that the meeting might actually be legit.

The second murder at the Elfreth's Alley house, the maid, had been collateral damage, but it had also been opportunistic. Another undocumented alien available for harvesting, the surgical team already on site.

Ka Hui's newest business model, from what she'd pieced together: illegal gaming that targeted high-rolling compulsives, the provision of unlimited credit, then Ka Hui's drop-the-hammer strong-armed tactics, as in to suddenly call the debt and suggest a way to work it off, "or else." Multiple doctors plus other professionals had fallen prey. The few who hadn't cooperated became gangland PSAs following their disappearances; examples of how not to act in the face of extortion. Blackmailed surgeons on site for one gig might gladly stick around for a piggybacked second gig if it helped pay off their debts sooner.

Also on her mind, Blessid Trauma Services and Patrick Stakes, the screaming, whirling-dervish, Hawaiian-war-dance-stomping amnesiac. Poor kid.

She sipped her juice, pondering the Blessid Trauma website on her screen. Some new testimonials about service, all good, plus notes mentioning Grace Blessid by name from various law enforcement types, encouraging her in her fight against her terminal lung disease. There'd been no updates to the page on the amnesiac. Kaipo's message inside the Elfreth's Alley sauna and the other crime scenes had apparently gone undelivered, or was misunderstood, or had been ignored. Plus, the website made no mention about the company being under new management. She'd do one more search online before she headed out for her appointment.

She mouthed the words while typing them: "New...owner... Blessid...Trauma..."

Mt. Airy Small Business Association News. Germantown's own Blessid Trauma Services was sold to Mr. Tristan Trout of Philadelphia, retired Navy...VA-Backed Business Loan Opportunities for Military Veterans...

"Let's try 'Tristan Trout,'" she said to herself, then entered a new search.

Three hundred seventy thousand search results. Aside from the one-liner about Blessid Trauma on the first page, the rest were mostly about fish.

19

Philo deposited Patrick in slushy curbside snow at the Troc Theater, then drove the van up Broad Street into North Philadelphia, on the lookout, per Hump's description, for a single building in the middle of a block empty of everything else but a gas station. The Amtrak train overpass loomed on the horizon, below an overcast sky. Was the building before the overpass or after? Hump had told him, but he couldn't remember.

What he did remember was the rest of Hump's over-the-top description: *"Clean, classy storefront that takes up a quarter of the block. Inside them walls, Philo, the glory of bygone days. The best years of Philly boxing, the sixties, the seventies. The doors will open again, my friend, you just watch. You say you don't know the address, well that's too bad, but I ain't gonna ruin a pisser of a surprise for you. Maybe someday* everyone *will know it.*

"So much heart inside that place, so much energy, and magic..."

On the right was a Speedway Gas station a hundred yards before the Amtrak overpass. Philo coasted past the gas pumps then slowed the van. "You have arrived at your destination," the GPS lady told him.

He stopped in a traffic lane with no one behind him, put on the van's flashers and stepped out. He craned his neck. Carved into the exterior between the first and the second stories, all caps: *JOE FRAZIER'S GYM.*

"No. Shit. *Ha!*"

The first story and a half had a fascia of stamped concrete free of graffiti, with tall front windows still intact from the building's last incarnation as a commercial storefront, and two plate-glass entrance doors. Recently pointed red brick continued above the concrete the rest of the way up, the building's third story windows cinder-blocked in and smartly finished with more concrete.

Hump appeared out of nowhere, hobbled up alongside him, a bit unsteady. He got shoulder-to-shoulder with Philo. "Whaddya think?"

Gimpier than Philo remembered him from fifteen years ago, Hump's cheeks still looked soft as a baby's ass. When most men his age were more wrinkle than face, the years hadn't cost Hump much from the chin up, still bright-eyed and cheerful, tan with a dust of rose, and skin that was pinchworthy. His hobbling, however, showed it was a different story from the waist down.

Philo leaned into a hug and a handshake. "Hump, you bastard, you should have said something. Smokin' Joe's Gym? This is great."

Here was the mecca for Philly boxers during Joe Frazier's reign as heavyweight champion and the years following his retirement from boxing. It fell on hard times after Frazier's passing in 2011 and closed, soon morphing into back-to-back furniture and mattress stores "with knockout prices." After neither store prospered, the building fell into decline and suffered a slow, shameful death. Local fighters, from Philly, upstate Pennsylvania and Jersey, even New York, fought for and earned its preservation as a historic landmark. In progress was publicity for more funding, to reopen it as a working gym and a permanent memorial to Smokin' Joe, all this info according to Hump.

"She's a real find, ain't she, this building? Getting her cleaned, all us volunteers...It's turned into a movement, Philo."

From the front, yes, it looked presentable, but the structure was a full block deep. "Sides and rear need some work," Hump said, "maybe need to slap on a few coats of paint. I just hope the dinero to get it all done shows up before I cash in my own chips, know what I'm saying? Move your van off the street and we'll go inside."

With the van parked, Hump unlocked the front door and shouldered it open. The floor was slippery as an ice-skating rink. "Watch your step, Philo, else you'll end up on your ass."

The place was a mess, crowded with rotting, waterlogged mattresses. The building's two most recent commercial busts had been late-night cable TV's advertisers North Philly's King of Mattresses, then the Mattress Maven, Mary Queen of Cots, also defunct, whose ad still appeared on the rooftop billboard. The damage came from a nearby water main that had burst two nights ago, below a fire hydrant used to fight a midnight blaze in the strip mall across the street. The mattress at the bottom of each pile was frozen solid to the floor, recent extreme temperatures and the level of flooding the causes. A few of the discarded mattress piles almost reached the ceiling.

"The businesses that used to be in here, those wall posters tell you, were run by a king first, then by a queen, and now the only royalty it's good for is"—Hump gave Philo a wait-for-it elbow while pointing at the tall mattress piles—"storybook princesses! The kind who don't want to feel no peas under their asses! Get it? Haw!"

Philo sniffed Hump's breath. Okay, so maybe he was a tad drunk. "Hump. Buddy. Tell me you didn't drive here."

"Hell no, I live near here now, around the corner. And no, I ain't drunk, if that's what you're thinking. Had one beer at lunch. I'm on some meds and just a little under the weather."

"You're weaving, dude. Under the weather with what?"

"ALS."

Lou Gehrig's disease. "What the fuck, Hump, why didn't you say something? I never would have had you—"

"Look—Philo—when I fess up to people about my condition, I don't get no action no more. No taking me out for cheesesteaks or a beer, no chess games in the park, no sex, no nothing. You show up, you tell me what you got planned, and now I'm feeling like a million bucks, like I'm gonna get to take a little heavy-hands ride with you like we did in the old days. So don't you be giving me no puppy-dog eyes and try to cut me out of this. I'm here to help you any way you'll let me. This old man needs this, so don't try to cut me out—"

"Fine. Calm down, Hump, I hear you. Sorry. It's all good."

"Great. Settled then. Oh. Got another surprise for you."

Hump cleared his throat, faced the door they came through, and projected his voice. "Miñoso! Come on in here, son."

A sepia-skinned man entered and quickly shut the door behind him. "Hiya, boss," he said. He put his hands in front of his mouth and blew into his fingers. "Is cold out there, boss," he added. "Is cold in here, too."

"Yeah, to tropical-blooded mutts like you just off the fucking boat it is. Get used to it, concho, there's plenty more cold where this came from."

Miñoso leaned into the old man's face, feigning upset. "Get used to these, viejo," he said, gripping his own junk, "all the women you ain't been getting with lately been keeping my pito warm, so how's about that?"

Hump grabbed the back of Miñoso's neck and surrounded him with a bear hug. "Wise guy. Don't mind us, Philo, we're in each other's shit every day. Philo, this is Miñoso. Miñoso, this is Philo, or 'campeón,' which is how you said you'd like to address him, right, Miñoso?"

"Si. The campeón. Sesenta y cuatro y nada, with puños de piedra."

Sixty-four and oh, the champ with the heavy hands.

With fifteen years in the military, Philo had learned his way around a few languages, Spanish one of them. Miñoso beamed, was close to genuflecting in Philo's presence. Philo might have even blushed a little. The two shook hands.

"Miñoso will spot you while you train, do some sparring. He can take a pretty good punch. Maybe not *your* punch, so we'll keep him head-geared up, but he's good for it."

"Hump." Philo beckoned him closer with his fingers. "Your guy's maybe five-eight, and he's lucky if he goes one fifty. How the hell—"

"Rocky Balboa and the chicken, Philo; you'll need to catch him first. The ring's upstairs, plus some bags and other equipment. And heaters. Let's go."

* * *

Another mess upstairs, this one more like the woman-haters clubhouse from *The Little Rascals*, with secondhand sofas and chairs and tables and exposed white brick the color of smoker's teeth, but the boxing equipment was there as advertised: a small ring, a heavy bag, a double-end striking bag, speed bags, and electric space heaters, with electricity. No Joe Frazier memorabilia other than one torn wall poster for "The Fight of the Century," Frazier–Ali #1, and a plastic replica of Frazier's Olympic gold medal affixed to a crooked plaque on the wall.

Philo approached the ring, climbed under the ropes, and got inside. He moved to a corner, leaning his back against it, then he lay his arms on the top ropes and took in his surroundings before he kneeled, pressing his hand against the blue canvas floor. It had some give to it and it dipped in the middle, no doubt a veteran of many rounds of sparring.

"Even got a nice bounce to it, Hump, but there's a problem."

"I know. No bouncy canvas where you'll be fighting. Solid concrete. Hell, no ring neither. Poor baby," he said in a whine, adding a pout to go with the sarcasm, "forcing you to train here, having to make do."

"All I'm saying is I'll need some training time in a space similar to the fight venue," as in something akin to the first floor of the old grain elevator.

"You haven't seen the third floor."

They reached the top of the steps, where the wind rattled the closed wooden door. Hump opened it for them.

"Welcome to Siberia, Rocky."

They stepped inside. This level had a hole in the roof in the far corner, the gray sky visible through it. A melting snow pile with runoff darkened the smooth floor.

"See that hole? Looks to be about the size of a large hot tub, don't it? That's because that's what used to be under it before the neighborhood scavengers broke in, cut out the skylight, and lifted the fucker out. Miñoso here—"

Miñoso averted his eyes, uncomfortable about the call out.

"—he was squatting up here, before I knew him. Got his clock cleaned the night they stole the tub, when he didn't move fast enough after the thieving pricks told him to clear out."

"Eliminé dos," Miñoso said, "with my fists."

"Right. He knocked two of them out. Problem was, there were more than two. They tied him up and beat him while they worked on lifting the tub out, left him for dead up here. I found him, took him to the ER, and then I told him he could stay with me. He wouldn't have none of it. He lives in a rooming house nearby, works odd jobs when he can."

"How old, Hump?" Philo whispered.

"What?"

"How old is he? And how did he get here?"

"I'd say he's maybe thirty-five. Just showed up, end of the summer. Landscaping work dried up in the 'burbs. Has some family around here somewhere, unless they left."

When Miñoso and Philo first shook hands, Philo saw what fueled the man's fire, the fear etched into his brown face, the gaunt eyes, the wiry body, the two missing lower teeth. This man, young man, child, whatever age he was, was used to adversity, but in this cold he would have died if he were still squatting up here, beaten to a pulp or not. And no way was he over thirty years old. Philo saw maybe twenty years or so in those frightened eyes, eyes like he'd seen in Iraq, Pakistan, Afghanistan, even South America, deeply inset on the faces of poverty-stricken orphans, all wishing for a chance at salvation, one that would never come. Environments like that added decades to a man's face.

"How old are you, Miñoso?" Philo asked, since Hump hadn't, and it seemed he didn't plan to.

"Twenty-two years."

The answer quieted Hump and Philo both for a moment. Just how many of these undocumented, worn out people were out there, Philo asked himself. His answer was too many. Not "too many" as in you're-not-welcome-here-you-fuckers, you-need-to-leave-our-beloved-country too many. No, it was too many as in these people were human beings trying to better their lot in life just like the rest of us, which meant they needed compassion, not reprimand. And here was crusty old Hump, burdened with ALS, trying to do good for one of them.

Hump started back up with Philo. "So here's the deal. I make you some keys, you let yourself in whenever you want for the next few weeks while you train. Miñoso here lives right around the corner, ready to spot you. Just call me and I'll send him over, and I won't be far behind. You get the urge to give him a few bucks he won't turn it down. How's that sound?"

The three men shook on it.

Back on the second floor where it was warmer, Philo hesitated at the door to the stairs, did an about-face, wanting a moment to absorb the energy, the determination, the will power of all those who'd toiled inside these hallowed, exposed brick walls in the name of so brutal yet revered a sport. Philadelphia and Joe Frazier were to boxing like Green Bay and Vince Lombardi were to football: classy champions in a bruising sport.

"I'll be back tonight seven-ish, to get in some work on the bags," Philo told Miñoso. "Will that work?"

"Si, campeón, I am liking that," Miñoso said.

20

Walking around money. That's what Wally Lanakai had tossed Philo when he exited his house after the break-in.

A showy gesture, like he was a benevolent mobster type with compassion for the little guy. The SOB had destroyed the bathroom skylight leaving a hole in his roof, and had busted through his front door. Two thousand bucks wasn't going to cut it. Ripping out the skylight and re-tarring the roof, that alone would be three, four grand at least. He took another pass at cleaning up the bathroom, the worst place in the house to have broken glass. He removed the tarp he'd tucked into the skylight, replacing it with plywood screwed into the ceiling from the inside. Soon as he drilled the last screw, he realized how dark this made it in there, the skylight the only natural light source.

Fuck this, he wanted another skylight. He'd replace the glass with something shatterproof and a bit heavier duty, then go for the iron bars. A cheaper solution, and letting the sunlight in would be better for human biorhythms, some shit like that. The front door was where he'd spend more money, maybe get something impenetrable but hell, who was he kidding, the front door wasn't the only way to breach the house. Sixteen windows front and back, upstairs and down, meant sixteen other ways for someone to get in and mess him up or his shit or both.

Regardless, he'd made his decision to live here and he wasn't going back on it. This was the last place his dad had lived, which made this the last chance he had to get their relationship right, even though he was the only one left to work on it.

"Six," he said to his cat, "your pop is heading into the city to the gym, to scrape off some rust. Sorry, but you need to stay in tonight. See you later, sweetums."

Meow.

* * *

Philo's messages to Patrick on the drive downtown, phone and text, went unanswered. New insights and a new territory to plumb for Patrick's identity—the Hawaiian Islands, for Christ sake. They had a lot to talk about. He visualized Patrick at this moment, nomadic amnesiac, on a SEPTA bus somewhere in the city, or on the Broad Street Subway, or on a trolley in Port Richmond, or maybe sleepwalking his way around Elkins Park.

Tomorrow. It would be tomorrow before they talked.

Philo selected a downloaded track on his phone and blasted it through his Jeep's audio system while navigating Philly's inner-city streets. The piece was a voice-over read by a movie-trailer-guy wannabe, the track from stop-motion video action shots featured in a Nat Geo film on fight science, the topic, "The One-Punch Knockout." The stills that accompanied the audio replayed in his head, with a beating heart providing the audio's pulsing, building background track.

Thump-thump, thump-thump...

"The one-punch KO sends the brain flying inside the skull, causing a chain reaction. The skull accelerates and decelerates rapidly, the brain recoiling toward the back of the head, causing trauma from the rear, then snapping back to the front of the skull, causing more trauma. This perfect flow of energy—this *kinetic linking*—travels through the puncher's entire body. The punch starts in the feet, the rear foot driving backward into the ground. The energy travels through the legs, into the hips, through the large muscles of the back, head, and shoulders, like the coiling and cracking of a whip. The whip snaps when the fist explodes against the target, and the kinetically linked energy is released. And yes, size does matter. The heavier and longer-limbed the puncher, the more dangerous the whiplash."

The thumping faded, was followed by more boxing tips, these including the science behind knocking out opponents in five minutes or less from an accumulation of blows. The beating heart returned, a new voice artist reading from a piece published in *Popular Mechanics* by journalist Marita Vera.

Thump-thump, thump-thump...

"Here's how it happens. The body contains dissolved sodium, potassium, and calcium, collectively known as electrolytes, which are responsible for conducting impulses along neurons. Every time a fighter receives a blow to a nerve, potassium leaves the cell and calcium rushes in, destabilizing the electrolytes, while the brain does all it can to keep these levels in balance. With each successive blow this balance is harder to maintain, and more and more energy must be spent in the process. When the body reaches the point where the damage outweighs the body's ability to repair itself..."

Thump-thump, thump-thump...

"...the brain shuts down to conserve enough energy to fix the injured neurons at a later point. In the words of Anthony Alessi, a neurologist and ringside physician for the Connecticut State Boxing Commission, 'After a brain injury, the heart must supply sufficient blood flow for the brain to repair itself. If the demand outweighs the supply, the brain shuts down and leads to a loss of consciousness.'"

The speaker's voice slowed for dramatic effect. "'That's when the ring doctor knows to end the match...'"

The heartbeat amplified, suffixed by a beeping hospital heart monitor.

Thump-thump-BEEP, thump-thump-BEEP...

"'...because if he lets the fighter continue...'"

THUMP, THUMP, BEEP...

"'...the fighter is going to die.'"

BEEEEEEEP.

* * *

Miñoso stood at the front door to the gym, a watch cap in Oakland Raiders black and silver pulled over his ears, a stitched-up hole near its crown. They shook hands, Philo taking measure of this young yet prematurely ancient man. "Miñoso. Hey."

"Campeón."

For Philo, the salutation was the equivalent of saluting a military superior while on a mission: if you want your lieutenant dead from sniper fire, you salute him. "No more of that 'champ' stuff, Miñoso," Philo said. "It's Philo from here on in, okay?"

"Is okay."

He handed Miñoso a greasy paper bag. "I brought you a cheesesteak. You need to put some meat on those bones. While I set up upstairs, you eat."

"Gracias."

Upstairs, Philo stuck bunches of small smiley-face stickers head-high on both sides of the heavy bag suspended from the ceiling, approximating where his opponent's temples would be at full height, then he did the same for the solar plexus shots. In his experience the punch that concussed the brain most frequently, and short-circuited the fighter's legs, was the hook to the temple. And the best shots to make a man lower his hands for those punches to the temple were punishing hits to the body. The info Philo had on Wally Lanakai's fighter was he was a six-four Hawaiian, two inches taller than Philo, and he carried a sculpted two hundred twenty pounds, with long arms and a strong chin.

While Miñoso chewed, Philo fished. "The guy's name is Tonka. No idea if it's a first name, last name, or nickname. Tonka. Ever heard of him?"

"Si."

"Where?"

"Kids juguetes. Toy camiones, excavadoras. Hijos de puta son indestructibles."

"I got the toy trucks and excavators part, Miñoso, but not the rest. Translate."

"Those Tonka toys, they are, how you say, indestructible. But I never hear of no fighter named Tonka." Miñoso eyed Philo's hands, his look skeptical. "No tape on your wrists, campeón...er, Philo?"

Philo pushed the heavy bag into a sway, circled it left to right and right to left, his punching against the bag slow, deliberate, up and down each side. "Taped hands? In this sport? Nah. Finish your cheesesteak, then hold this bag still so I can pound it."

"You are wearing Levi's. ¿Por qué?"

"Part of the charm of the sport, Miñoso, is fighting in the clothes that brought you here. I'm a jeans kind of guy."

"This fighter you fight, those etiquetas"—Miñoso pointed at the smiley stickers head-high on the bag; regardless of the heavy bag's back and forth swing, they remained at nearly the same height—"he no move his head up or down?"

"Yes, he'll move his head up and down. But when he's upright, that's where he'll be. After you put on the headgear, we go upstairs. You'll help me with the up-and-down part."

Upstairs, the snow on the floor in the corner had melted some but the room was still cold, the wind whipping through the hole in the roof. Hump had found an electric space heater and placed it up there earlier to take the edge off, but it wasn't much help, not much better than a pair of hand warmers. Fine, far as Philo was concerned, the grain elevator venue would fare the same unless the cold snap snapped. Miñoso bobbed and weaved in gray sweats and headgear in the center of the floor, but otherwise stayed flat-footed in front of him, stopping short of showing what he could do footwork-wise, "'cause gringos like you ain't be catching me if I did."

That, Philo figured, was Hump talking shit to him as his trainer, filling this young man with lightweight bullshit meant to show boxing ring generalship and an ability to score with flyswatter jabs and pattycake hooks. Things that didn't mean squat in a bare-knuckle fight. "Go ahead, Miñoso, move your bad ass around however you want to. Just make sure I get some bobbing and weaving along with it, bud."

Miñoso danced backward, forward, shadowboxed circles around a flat-footed Philo, his boxing gloves alternating between protecting both sides of his face and speed punching, with Philo taking something off his bare-knuckle punches each time he cornered him. Miñoso finally pulled up and dropped his arms to his side, pounding his padded forehead with a fist, yammering at Philo through his mouth guard: "You heet me like I am a girl! I am no girl! You catch me, you heet me!"

"Miñoso, this is our first sparring session. Calm down."

"HEET ME!" Miñoso pleaded, covering his temples with his gloved hands, and continuing his taunts, bobbing down, then up, then down again, then...

Miñoso awakened with his back on the cold, hard floor, Philo standing over him.

"Miñoso. You okay? Miñoso?"

Hump arrived alongside, his expression deadpan, Miñoso still laid out. "Mouthed off at you, didn't he?"

"Little bit. He wanted me to hit him harder."

"This was a bad idea, Philo, having him spar with you. He's giving up too much weight, but he begged me. The kid has a room in a row home where fifteen other immigrants live. He's living in poverty. He'll do anything for a buck."

"I hit him pretty good, Hump, stomach, arms, head shots. Men twice his size went down quicker. So if he's still game, I'm fine with it."

Miñoso spoke, still on his back, the words garbled, but Philo understood two of them, and what was being asked. "Los riñones?"

"No hits to the kidneys, Miñoso. All my punches were clean. You won't be pissing blood on my account. But next time we do it my way, a little slower and more deliberate, okay?"

"Si. Bueno. Gracias," he said, blinking his eyes clear and adding, still in Spanish, "I must check my gym bag for my other pants. I seem to have soiled these."

21

The warehouse was less than two blocks from the Delaware River in Bristol, a Philadelphia suburb. Convenient for an execution and watery disposal of a body, should this be what Olivier had in mind. Kaipo slowed her van as she passed the empty guard shack and drove to the rear of the warehouse. The parking lot sidled the building deep into the property, was large enough for forty or more tractor-trailers but now there were none, hadn't been any for nearly a decade. She parked outside the first loading dock, per Olivier's instructions. Her van's headlights brightened the graffiti-covered garage door.

Kaipo guided the pressure cooker down the ramp from her van, rolled it along like a piece of luggage, the cooker bouncing whenever it caught a pebble on the alligatored asphalt. Tonight she was particular with her personal appearance, going for friendly and unsuspicious: pink sneakers, a gray gym outfit under a warm parka, hair in a tight ponytail. Unthreatening and unassuming, because in her head...

She wasn't entirely convinced this wouldn't be an attempted hit just as easily as it could be the delivery of a replacement pressure cooker.

Also moving into her head was Patrick Stakes the amnesiac, and his display at the car dealership, with tall garage doors much like these here. She'd seen haka war dances before, once as a guest at a US Army change of command ceremony in Hawaii just before she left the Islands for the mainland. A group of soldiers in camo performed it, dramatic and serious, for their outgoing commander, its chest-beating, foot-stomping and flexing threatening and barbaric, visually and orally. Her head was full of haka now, the beat mounting as she walked onto a ramp that led to the dock, fueling her skepticism—her resolve—about this rendezvous with Olivier. She slowed, reached a pair of swinging doors next to the loading dock's overhead garages and rolled the cooker into them, testing to see if they were open; the doors separated. She unzipped her parka and inched the cooker forward into the warehouse, no complaints from anyone or thing on the other side. The swinging doors closed behind her.

Five hundred thousand square feet of three-story warehouse. She could see maybe the first fifty feet into its depths, courtesy of her flashlight. The general theme, no matter where she shined her light: pristine white, like she'd stumbled into a great hall in the afterlife. A nice touch if they wanted her dead. She rolled the cooker forward, her soft-soled sneakers squeaking on the shiny floor, and the cooker's squeaky wheels echoing; she stopped twenty feet in, did a visual sweep. Long yellow rectangles on the floor outlined where storage shelves once were, the rectangles disappearing into the recesses of the warehouse. Creepy. Her phone buzzed in her pocket; she read the text.

Follow the blue line toward the right wall.

Her flashlight soon outed her host in the far corner. His hands were clasped in front of him, and they also held a flashlight. It switched on and he turned it upward, so she could better see his face.

Olivier ʻŌpūnui. Bowl-cut black hair, long bangs, large, thin nose, long, clean-shaven face. Mid-length gray tweed coat, black fur collar, the ironed creases in his dark pants severe. Slender and delicate and always smartly dressed, he did not buck the stereotype: Olivier wasn't overtly gay, but he did prefer, exclusively, the company of men. In Hawaiian, ʻŌpūnui meant large-bellied or corpulent. Maybe that was somewhere in his ancestry, but it was not the case with him.

"Thank you for coming, Kaipo," he said. "Let me start by asking you about your sobriety. How are you doing?"

Small talk; Kaipo stayed wary. "I attend meetings when I can. But it's not good when the meetings turn to talk about missing and presumed dead dope dealers, mine in particular. No one knew his connection to me, thank goodness, but you need to stop doing that."

"Only you can know if Monte will be your last one," Olivier said. "You are staying sober, Kaipo, and that has been a good thing. Something we want to foster. Let's move to another topic. You are having doubts about Ka Hui's recent business direction."

A loaded comment. If she caved and said she was wrong to ask so many questions, he'd see that for what it was: patronization. She went with her real feelings. "Murdering innocent people for their organs is harsh, Olivier. Regardless—you made it clear it's not my call, and unless Ka Hui will let me out of my contract with no repercussions, I've decided I can live with that. Hopefully," her eyes drilled his, "you think I can live with it as well."

"Let you out of your contract with no repercussions? That's rich, Kaipo. Mr. Lanakai permitted one other associate to leave Ka Hui some time back. His business partner. That won't happen again. The repercussions were the direst of dire for the partner and his family. Not Mr. Lanakai's doing, mind you. Your employment with him is at will, Kaipo. At Wally's—er, Mr. Lanakai's—will, specifically."

Wally Lanakai. Olivier. There was something there, between them. Blind employee obedience, yes, but something more. A deep reverence; adoration. *Attraction.*

She surmised it was one-sided.

"Kaipo? Hello? Pay attention! *At. Will.* Your employment can be terminated at Mr. Lanakai's discretion only. Now, look behind you, please."

There'd been no footfalls, and she tensed as someone or something bumped against her back. She turned, pushed away, and drew her piece from its shoulder holster, quick, smooth, unflustered. She steadied the nine-millimeter at a bulky box on a handcart, the words *Commercial quality, with a stainless-steel tub and a 200-quart capacity* on cardboard just beyond the barrel. The box still had the shipping straps around it. Behind the box stood Icky Ikaika. Icky dropped the cart handle, raised his hands. "Fuck, Kaipo, hold up, relax. It's your new pressure cooker. Honest."

She stood frozen, her gun still raised.

Olivier chuckled, inserted his hand into his overcoat pocket. Kaipo snapped her gun in Olivier's direction. His hand reemerged with a minia-ture bronze-plated box. He settled it into his palm. "My, my, Kaipo, you are priceless when you get so serious." He flicked open the box's hinged lid. His snuff tobacco.

"We thought we'd surprise you with a brand new unit, not a hand-me-down. Such drama from you. Thank you, Mr. Ikaika, for delivering it yourself."

And with that came a snort and a sniffle-sniffle. The pinch of powdery black snuff disappeared up his nostrils. He brushed the remaining dust from his fingers, brushed his nose with his hand, repeated the process, ambivalent to her drawn gun.

She lowered her weapon and reluctantly re-holstered it. She released a breath she hadn't known she was holding.

Olivier's slender footfalls echoed on his pronounced advance toward her. "I have one more thing to discuss with you, Kaipo. Mr. Ikaika, why don't you load this new cooker into her van and let us chat alone, please? Thank you."

After Icky left, Olivier's officious demeanor returned. "About your message to the Blessids."

"My *what*?"

"Your message in that sauna. 'Think Hawaiian, not Alaskan.' That one."

How did Ka Hui—Olivier...Just how was it he knew?

"You are out of your element here, Kaipo. What is—and is not—known by certain parties needs to stay that way, including your knowledge about him, and his knowledge about you. Through a grievous misjudgment of someone's character on our part, the young man you were messaging now knows you exist. It is in your utmost interest to let that sleeping dog lie."

"How did you—?"

"Your—utmost—interest, Kaipo! Back off. Or next time, your apprehen-sion about meeting with me will be merited."

22

Philo paid for breakfast, brought it to the Blessid Trauma garage: bagels, a pork roll sandwich for Hank, coffees, and juice for Patrick. He pulled apart the bag with the bagels and let them tumble onto the break table in the office. After he dropped into a chair, he studied Patrick, busy with his OJ carton. Patrick sipped his juice, looked over the straw at Philo. "Sir? Something wrong, sir?"

"What would you say..." Philo started then hesitated. He searched for the right words, sheepish about having been less than aware of—blind to— this dark young man whose thick, tan skin had deserved more than a cursory pronouncement regarding his perceived ethnicity from a sandwich guy at a restaurant.

"What I mean is, Patrick, you, ah, you've got a guardian angel out there who helped me figure something out about you."

Philo locked eyes with Hank, grabbed a bagel, tore off a chunk. He began with an apology, his mouth full. "I tried calling the both of you last night but neither of you answered. So let me start by asking you, Hank, did you get Patrick's DNA test results back yet?"

"Nope. A few more weeks," Hank said, his look puzzled. "You're killing us here, Philo. Let's have it. What's going on?"

"When the DNA results come back," Philo said, unblinking, "they will show that Patrick's not an Eskimo."

"Aleut, sir, not Eskimo," Patrick said.

"Fine, right, whatever, Patrick, but you're neither. The results will show you're Hawaiian."

Patrick sat mesmerized. Hank showed his best *what the fuck* expression. "That's not even an ethnicity, Philo. Hawaiians are Polynesians. You know these results how?"

"I haven't seen them, I just know what they're going to show. Apparently some Philly mob person noticed it. And according to the cops, this Philly mob in particular is loaded with, odd as it sounds, Hawaiians."

Patrick choked on his bagel and orange juice. "Really?" He left his seat, wiped his mouth with his sleeve. "REALLY? I'm Hawaiian? I'm Hawaiian!"

Hank narrowed his eyes. "Philo, c'mon, how does some mobster know this? What mobster? How—?"

"Hank, I have no idea. What I do know is some criminal type took an interest in him. A mob cleaner-fixer type. Someone like us, but working for the other side."

Hank now learned about the message left on the sauna floor, and Philo explained the Philly police's concern that this new mob presence was from Hawaii. "The message was left for *us*, Hank, about Patrick. Who knows why the interest. Maybe it's a bad guy with a conscience, trying to do some good. Regardless, it's someone who knows something."

Patrick bounded around the room keying at his phone, doing internet searches. "Oahu. Maui. Kauai. Look at that. Volcanoes..."

"Still not buying it," Hank said. "Patrick, calm down, we really don't know much more than we already did."

"...luaus, leis..."

Philo had been skeptical, too, he said, but then he'd pieced it together. "Patrick—relax, dude. Sit please. I have a question for you; something I asked you before. Answer it for me again." He winked at Hank. "Your home state. When did it gain statehood?"

Patrick continued keying at his phone, didn't have to think, blurted an unfeeling response, one indelible, rote memory his traumatized brain never had trouble finding: "We became a state in 1959."

Hank nodded. "See, Philo, like I told you, Alaska."

Philo nodded. "Right. Alaska earned its statehood in 1959. But so did Hawaii." Philo, now on a roll: "Patrick, what was your dog's name?"

"Poy. Poy, sir."

Easier connection here, the Hawaiian food staple was poi, but then again—

"I did a search. *Poi,* Patrick, is—was—also a dog breed native to Hawaii. Could your dog have been a Hawaiian poi, not named Poy?"

"Yeah. No. Both, sir. That's it! He was a poi, and that's what I named him! Poy. With a *Y,* sir."

Poi dogs. Not actually a breed, more like the product of natural selection, and supposedly extinct. Also a food source to Hawaiians at one time, along with feral hogs. Fattened up like hogs, then eaten like them too. They were virtually wiped out last century, but Hawaiian shelters still ran across strays and wild dog packs whose existence second-guessed their rumored extinction.

"Christ, Philo, you and Wikipedia are just a fountain of circumstantial information."

"Fine, Hank, so you're not convinced, but this is looking like the real thing. I've got one more. You wanna hear it or not?"

"Look, I don't want Patrick's hopes raised only to have him get disappointed. We've had leads before; nothing ever worked out."

"I don't want that either. Patrick, you want to hear more?"

"Yeah."

"Then answer this. Who's your favorite rapper?"

"Tassho Fearce, sir! Saw him at the Troc yesterday. He was awesome."

"How long have you been following him?"

"Um, I don't know for sure, sir. Maybe I saw him as a teenager. Yeah, that's it, I saw him in person when I was a teenager."

"That means you saw him perform before the attack that put you in the coma three years ago. In Hawaii. Tassho Fearce is Native Hawaiian, never been to the mainland. His first tour outside Hawaii was this year."

Hank relented. The frontrunner for Patrick's ethnicity was now Polynesian, and his birthplace, Hawaii.

* * *

There were multiple trails to the grain elevator leading from the city streets rimming its perimeter, the only structure on this land parcel. The route they were taking was the most direct. The vehicle caravan—a truck with pressure-washing equipment with more psi than a fire hose, another truck with a mounted generator, and the Blessid Trauma Services step van— followed a white pickup, its route winding through a half mile or more of illegal dumping, boulder rubble, and dismembered concrete pylons veined with twisted steel reinforcing rods, scattered within thirty yards of the grain elevator.

The white pickup braked hard then stopped, kicking up dust. It idled, the two large rigs passing it to park as close to the building as they could, not far from a fire hydrant. Philo U-turned and arrived alongside the pickup, driver facing driver. The pickup's window powered down, cigar smoke billowing from its interior, the demolition site superintendent on the puffing side of it. The job boss was a bear of a guy with stained, chip-munk-like buckteeth. He pulled the cigar away from his mouth and dropped his cigar hand onto the pickup's windowsill.

"My guys will leave the keys and head back with me, Trout. We're late for happy hour. Do *not*, I repeat, do not do *anything* to the wood in the ceiling below the first floor. Don't scrub it, don't mist it, don't put any enzyme materials on it. After you guys finish cleaning belowdecks, we have people coming in to salvage it."

"Already in the contract," Philo said. "But what's the big deal? It's fucking wood."

"You'll know when you see it. It's like gold to carpenters. The wear patterns, grains pouring over it from the chutes, polishing it, some shit like that makes it valuable. It was in all the ceilings on each level, but scav-engers ripped the upper floors of it out. They stayed away from the pit; too nasty down there. Don't ruin the wood in the pit or it'll cost you your whole fee.

"My last bit of advice to you, Trout. Watch your step on those upper floors. I don't need any work stoppages, so don't do anything stupid like kill yourselves. Good luck."

* * *

Philo stood at the base of the crumbling building, Patrick and Hank alongside, Grace home with a private nurse. It took a lot for Hank to pull himself away, but she'd chased him out, made him go to work to take his mind off things. No Grace meant they needed an extra pair of hands. Joining them for the first time was Philo's boxing sparring partner Miñoso.

Why not Miñoso, Philo had asked himself, maybe help out the guy a little, let him make a few extra bucks? "The thing is," Philo had given Miñoso a speech, "you can't mention the fight. You're sworn to secrecy; es un secreto. There is no fight, understand?"

"Si. No fight."

They gathered around Philo. The main tower was six levels of poured concrete. The top three levels had, at one time, windows on all the walls, but they'd been blown out by repeated hits from a wrecking ball. The bottom three stories were shaped like tandem missile silos, the entire structure poking vertically from the empty flatland like a Canaveral launch pad, jutting out from land onto two stationary marine legs that extended over the Delaware.

"Hope you know what you're doing, Philo," Hank said.

"Looks scarier than it is. The demolition company strung lights on all the floors and cleaned out the debris. We need to sweep it for explosive material and combustibles, and check the cracks in the foundation and walls and iron welds where grain might have collected. Floors, walls, ceilings, everywhere. They want the demolition to be controlled. An implosion, not an explosion, to keep the building from toppling into the river."

"Any grain left would be like what, twenty years old now?" Hank said. "How's that still a problem?"

"All I know is, corn and other grains make grain dust, and grain dust is explosive. They can afford to be careful, so they're not taking any chances." He raised his voice. "Patrick. Put on your mask and help set up Miñoso with his. You'll both need to carry a bundle of rope. Six floors of dust and decay await us, gentlemen. We're gonna soak this bastard from the top down and scrub it clean."

They crouched to fit through chain-link fencing behind a black tarp pulled aside to expose the entrance to the ground floor, one of two entrances on either side of the rectangular tower. Inside the building the floor was debris-free, but its metal fixtures were corroded with rust, and four-by-four holes in the first floor exposed a dark pit underneath that, according to the job boss, was rumored to be home to dog-size rats. Rats here, regardless of size, meant there had been, maybe still was, a food source, likely some leftover twenty-year-old grain. Someone would need to drop into the pit to handle whatever was down there. The demolition company had no intention of doing so. "Rats are biohazards, far as I'm concerned," was how the demolition super put it to Philo. "And my opinion is the only one that counts. The pit's your responsibility."

The ground floor had no walls, only support columns reinforced with rusted iron rods, giving this level the appearance of an open-air parking garage. On the exterior, a multi-story black tarp flapped against the support columns, doing a poor job of protecting them from the elements. A one-person elevator anchored the floor with the crumpled vestiges of its manually operated, single-person cage sitting at ground level.

"Stairwell anywhere?" Hank asked.

Philo leaned inside a hollow cement tube that looked like one of the support columns. "Inside this column here. A spiral staircase. The steps aren't sturdy, so we'll go up one person at a time. Next level up is where the regular stairs begin."

Inside the corkscrew staircase the steps had separated from their railings, were tilted and rusted out in spots, some steps missing altogether. One by one they arrived on the second floor and crossed to the main set of metal stairs. Here the ironclad grain silos ended, the top of each section of the silo funneling out of sight into the floor above it. Parallel to the silo was a chain-driven vertical pulley that had once served as the guts of the grain elevating process, its chain now snapped, its buckets bashed and beaten, in some cases gone. Crosswinds whipped through large gashes in the walls, from wrecking balls handling some of the demolition chores in preparation for the implosion. They headed up the steps to the third floor, with time spent there and on each floor above it checking for electric outlets and junction boxes that hadn't been ripped out. Hank put a meter on each one, confirming none of the electric sources left behind were hot.

From the fifth floor up, tall openings that once held wood-framed glass windows were empty, with rusted bars across them to keep past and present occupants on the inside of the building.

Philo poked through a door onto the open-air rooftop. Bolted to the roof were oversize ductwork, dented red-orange metal platforms, and other steampunk-inspiring architecture. Next to the roof edge, he admired the view. Wow. One by one, his team joined him.

Such a sweeping panorama of the city. The Girard Point Bridge, the huge span where I-95 crossed the Schuylkill River. A view of the Philly pro sports arenas and the Sunoco gas tanks, plus large, building-size murals, and the rail yards, and mothballed US Navy ships. And something short of three hundred sixty degrees of graffiti on walls at street level, artist canvasses for inner-city youth, trailing off as they closed in on the Delaware River, behind where they stood. Incredible.

"Miñoso. Watch your step," Philo said.

Miñoso backpedaled from the edge and lifted his heel. He'd stepped in seagull poo. "¡Mierda!"

"Si, Miñoso, 'shit,'" Philo said, agreeing, "and if you slip it'll be more like a coupla hundred feet of 'ah fuck,' then a dip in the Delaware. Everyone seen enough? Good. Let's get to work."

The biggest issue for them could have been the temperature. At the moment, it hovered around thirty-five degrees, but that wouldn't keep the power-washing equipment and cleaning surfaces from freezing when the temperature dropped. The forecast, thankfully, was for daytime highs in the forties over the next week. A heat wave, relatively speaking.

"Patrick, you and Hank hang out on the floor below here, tie off the rope then toss an end out a window," Philo said. "Miñoso and I will head down to ground level and attach it to the hoses so you can raise them to that floor. We'll get all the work lights turned on and the pumps primed so we can start pressure cleaning this bitch. We've got a few hours before things start to freeze. Let's get moving."

23

Grace Blessid took a hit of oxygen and leaned forward in her lounge chair to get closer to the large screen TV. She seethed, her jaw muscles tightening. "You sonovabitchin' *bastard*."

"Missus Blessid, calm down please. Missus Blessid...!" The young home aide crossed the family room to the TV and was about to turn it off.

Grace yelled at the screen, then, in halting breaths, at the nurse. "You touch that button, Goldilocks, you're gone. *Move*."

Hank and Patrick weren't home yet, were still on the grain elevator job with Philo. The local nightly news on Grace's TV showed sound bites from a late afternoon press conference, where an attorney for Dr. Francisco Andelmo spoke outside a new urgent care facility in Philadelphia's Kensington section. Earlier today the district attorney's office announced the formation of a grand jury to determine if Dr. Andelmo and two other physicians would be summoned to answer charges of illegal organ trafficking and negligent homicide.

On the screen was a spliced video summary of the attorney's comments, one sound bite after another.

"Such an indignity. Doctor Andelmo and his associates are saviors and visionaries...

"This, folks, is a witch hunt. Evidence shows what the DA's office won't accept, or doesn't want the public to know, that this was not a crime perpetrated by doctors...

"There is a menace loose on our streets, and it goes by the name"—the defense attorney paused, milking the drama—"of cannibalism! The question is, does it come from psychosis caused by new, powerful synthetic drugs on the street, whose abuse fosters this ungodly, unconscionable hunger? Is it a ritualistic cult? Or could this be the work of a deranged loner, a sick and confused person who has a taste for human flesh? Whatever it is, it's certainly not the work of these benevolent doctors."

The court of public opinion. Andelmo's attorney lobbied it hard, condemning the grand jury formation. Not lost on Grace was his choice of venue for the press conference. Formerly an ice cream parlor, the closed restaurant was now an urgent care facility and free health care clinic, where according to his attorney "benevolent physicians like Dr. Andelmo have chosen to provide services to the disadvantaged public in an attempt to give back." Kensington was struggling, with the locals needing to fight the drug trade and gun violence demons every day. The new facility was a sign of neighborhood revitalization. At least this was how the attorney portrayed his client's investment there, with new, privately held urgent care facilities opening in other Philadelphia areas as well.

Grace grabbed her phone, called her husband, and filled him in with an earful.

"Andelmo's attorney's in the news, responding to the allegations. He's an idiot, Hank! He says it's cannibals. Cannibalism! Like there's a fucking epidemic! You just watch," she said, prophesying, "Andelmo knows Patrick's background. Just watch and see if he gets the authorities to point a finger at him. Bring Patrick home right now, honey, *please*..."

* * *

Philo, Miñoso, and Hank had worked their way down to floor number five, spraying, scrubbing then squeegeeing the slop into open slots in the walls of the ironclad silo, letting it drain to the floors below it, where the sludge collected. They'd address the dried residue later. Patrick tended to the water-pumper truck at ground level.

The view out the broken windows at night was vibrant, the cityscape a lifelike organism, pulsating with electricity capable of lighting up the darkest heart, but only if a person was in the mood. Hank, on the phone with Grace, rubbed his forehead while he listened. "Uh-huh, uh-huh..." Soon as she finished: "We'll leave now, honey. Patrick will be fine. See you in a bit."

"What's up?" Philo asked him.

"Andelmo might get indicted. His idiotic lawyer says the police should be looking for a roving cannibal." Hank smirked at the assumption, then his shoulders slumped. "I need to get Patrick home, Philo. Grace is worried."

Philo was, too. Hearing about the press conference, his blood pressure rose, the hairs on the back of his neck joining it.

Patrick—his trespass at Elfreth's Alley—this was so totally a setup, for reasons unknown, although now it might be making more sense. The trespass would remain their secret, Patrick and Philo's, something Philo reinforced before they left the jobsite. No confessions to Hank or Grace, and certainly not to the police. Not now, maybe never at all. As long as there was no proof he was there.

They packed up the step van, would leave the other vehicles behind for their return visit tomorrow for a full day's work at the site. The van warmed while they strapped themselves in.

Philo's phone buzzed against his thigh; an incoming text.

Hello Mr. Trout. Det. Ibáñez. Where can I find Patrick Stakes?

24

Pressure cookers. The Boston Marathon and other terror attacks had generated more scrutiny of them. Having a restaurant acquire one on Kaipo's behalf had been the M.O. in the past, eliminating any connection to her. Personal trainers and massage therapists had no use for industrial-size pressure cookers, but restaurants did.

Have new monster cooker, will travel.

She arrived at Welkinweir Estate, a 150-acre secluded oasis with an arboretum and an historic manse house overlooking a lake in Pottstown, Pennsylvania, an hour outside Philadelphia. An ecology-minded non-profit maintained the property's diverse wetlands and woodland habitats, and it also made a few bucks from the idyllic grounds, the property serving as a wedding venue during late spring and early fall. The estate would host the first wedding of its wedding season in May, less than two months away.

Olivier assured her the grounds would be empty on the weekend, no ecologists, no public. Kaipo circled the perimeter of the three-story stone farmhouse on foot and breathed in the chilly, early spring air. She descended a steep trail to the lake, needing to maintain her balance down the slope. It was easy to see the venue's attraction, so breathtaking, with panoramic views in multiple directions.

Kaipo returned from her trek to the lake and entered the farmhouse.

Olivier had related what happened, having witnessed it. Mr. Lanakai, divorced father of one, wanted the Welkinweir venue for his daughter's wedding, scheduled for October of next year. Unfortunately, the date his daughter wanted had already been booked. Olivier recounted the exchange for Kaipo's benefit.

"Unbook it," Mr. Lanakai told the wedding coordinator.

"Sorry, sir, no can do," the coordinator said, his rebuttal pleasant, adding a sympathetic smile. "A main line Philadelphia socialite family has that date. Maybe another date?"

"Unbook it," Mr. Lanakai repeated. "I'll make it worth your while, or I'll make you regret you didn't let me make it worth your while."

"That's good to know, sir, even funny, but no, marching in here and going all old-school mobster on me just won't cut it, so—"

The wedding coordinator's body lay eviscerated on the kitchen floor. White male, fifties, short gray hair, good-looking from the neck up. From the neck down, who could know, his throat slit, his disemboweled organs glopping up the kitchen tile, with Kaipo needing to steer clear of the stickiness. A tantrum kill, Olivier had termed it. Not meant to send a message, not meant to instill fear in the man's replacement, whoever that lucky person might be. And apparently with no interest in harvesting his internal organs either, considering they were all here, curing on the kitchen floor. No, Mr. Lanakai had simply produced an ancient Hawaiian, shark-toothed dagger he kept in a sheath under his jacket, performed the disembowelment, then cut the man's throat while Olivier watched. The 1750 farmhouse had its ghosts, a bronzed plaque noted inside its ballroom. The wedding coordinator was now queued up to join them.

Kaipo unclothed the body, gathered up the man's phone and his pocket calendar while eliminating anything that could place Wally Lanakai or his people at the scene. After twenty minutes of circular saw work trimming the body to size, she let the pressure cooker do its thing. She settled into a tall chair at the kitchen counter in her Tyvek suit. She retrieved her e-reader and read.

Olivier's admonishment about a certain third party resurfaced in her head: *"He knows you exist."*

Meaning Patrick Stakes, the war-dancing, crime-scene-cleaning gofer. A transplanted Hawaiian with brain damage. Regardless of whoever he might have been before, Mr. Stakes was a nobody now, even to himself. A biohazard jockey cleaning up sudden-death bodies. He was of no significance to her, and yet Kaipo's random act of kindness had somehow become a problem for Ka Hui. Listening to Olivier, she would face unpleasant repercussions if she didn't pay him mind. But why?

She set aside her e-reader and retrieved the Blessid Trauma website on her phone. She found the page dedicated to Patrick Stakes, chronicling the search for his identity. His face and his identifying info, height, weight, hair and skin color, the location where he was found, the hospital that treated him, his likes, dislikes, and hobbies, she studied it all. And there it was.

"I like riding the bus at night around Philadelphia. I know all the routes, all the stops."

The guy at the end of the street two weeks ago, watching her exit the Elfreth's Alley residence. Bitter cold, in the snow, in the wee hours of the morning, waiting for the bus, and watching her exit.

He'd seen her where she shouldn't have been, leaving a crime scene. So far there'd been no repercussions, for her or Ka Hui. In the past, circumstances like this called for a particular solution: eliminate the witness. This time the orders from Ka Hui were to back off. Why?

As if on cue, a text from Olivier, checking in.

Is it safe?

Her response text was she was still on site, there'd been no complications, the porridge was still cooking, and the kitchen could handle disposal of the waste with minimal difficulty.

Excellent. A bonus for you. An invitation to dinner this weekend from Mr. Lanakai. Details later.

Not what she wanted to hear. Wally Lanakai had made overtures like this before, the horny bastard. Problem was, saying no wasn't an option. She was still on site and could put off responding for a few hours, although this new beast of a pressure cooker was crushing it time-wise.

Back to Patrick Stakes. An innocent bystander; a lost soul worthy of a nudge that might help him learn his identity. Not that simple, she knew now. He was off limits per Ka Hui; an untouchable.

But this untouchable was someone who could identify her.

25

Philo approached the only cop he recognized in the squad room, Detective Ibáñez. "Where is Patrick Stakes?"

"He's being interrogated," she said. "Have a seat."

"I'll stand."

Philo was at the Sixth District police station, Old City, at seven a.m., the morning after Detective Ibáñez's text to him. Patrick was in an interrogation room with the precinct's detectives. The detective sipped coffee at an empty table, Philo hovering, irritated.

"I called you back, Detective. Then I texted you. I got no follow-up from either, heard nothing until your boys showed up at six this morning and scared the shit out of him and the Blessids. Grace Blessid is a sick woman. I would have brought Patrick in."

"People are brought in on our terms, not yours, Mr. Trout. He's now a person of interest."

"What investigation?"

"The Elfreth's Alley murder."

Fuck. "What makes him a person of interest?"

"I can't share that with you, Mr. Trout."

She didn't have to, but Philo knew. It was Dr. Andelmo and his cannibalism assertion. The police were likely running the theory down, probably got a set of fingerprints from Patrick for the asking this morning, then checked to see if they matched any prints taken from the site and bingo, they'd apparently found something, evidencing his trespass.

"I call bullshit, Detective. This was a divide-and-conquer thing this morning, so you'd have Patrick to yourselves. You guys know he's limited. You also know how sick Grace is, which meant he'd have no support down here after they brought him in."

"The Blessids called *you*, didn't they?" she said, her eyebrows tenting. No hair bun today for the detective, her dark hair gathered into a short ponytail that now listed starboard, with the tilt of her face. "That makes you the cavalry, right?"

"I was in the navy, Detective, but close enough. I called an attorney. He's on his way."

"Of course you did. Look, Mr. Trout, sit, have some coffee, relax. Far as I know, he hasn't been accused of anything."

"I don't get it," he said analyzing her, and still not sitting. "Why text me asking how to find him if they already knew where he was?"

"The text was premature on my part. They knew where he'd be, just weren't ready to make a move until today. My bad for contacting you."

She sipped, returned her takeout coffee to the table, her look sly, as in *you're not buying this, are you, and by the way, you shouldn't.*

Philo processed her answer and her body language—what the hell was she saying, and why was she sharing this? He sat.

"He's brain damaged, Detective. You guys are trained to get confessions, not necessarily the truth. Before they're done with him, they'll have him confessing to every fucking crime at every scene Blessid Trauma ever worked."

"Your prerogative to call an attorney, Mr. Trout, and you did, but I don't think they're going to charge him. Call it a hunch."

The door to the interrogation room opened. A detective exited first, then Patrick behind him, disoriented, then another detective. Philo hustled over. The first thing he noticed was Patrick wasn't cuffed.

"You're free to go, Mr. Stakes," a detective said. "Thank you for cooperating. Please stay where we can find you."

His arm around Patrick, Philo ushered him past Detective Ibáñez, still seated, her smug expression saying *see, told you.*

"Rear exit," she volunteered, thumbing them toward a door. "The media got a tip that an arrest in the Elfreth's Alley murder was imminent. They're out front. Seems the tip they got was wrong. Imagine that."

Philo guided Patrick, squeezing his shoulder. When they were out of the detective's earshot: "You want a cheesesteak? You look like you could use a cheesesteak."

"It's eight thirty in the morning, sir."

"Pat's is open twenty-four seven, right? I'm hungry. You?"

"I could eat, sir."

Outside the precinct, next to Philo's Jeep, Philo had one question for him. "So they were good with your explanation?"

"Yes, sir." Patrick cleared his throat, ready to orate.

"'*I went in the house,*'" tears rimmed his eyes, then came a subdued mewling. "'*I didn't see Philo or the detective. I sat in a chair to get warm, touched some stuff on the table next to me, just picked it up, some mail, I don't know why, sir. When I was warmed up enough I, ah, left to wait for Philo and the detective outside. They never knew I was in the house.*'"

"Perfect," Philo said, clapping his shoulder. "You did great, Patrick."

"Just a little white lie, sir, right? I didn't kill no one in that house, sir. Just a little white lie so people know I didn't do it, right, sir?"

"Exactly."

Patrick strapped himself into the passenger seat. Philo closed his car door for him, had him roll the window down. "Give me a minute, Patrick. I'll be right back."

Back inside the station, Philo found Detective Ibáñez speaking with the interrogating detectives. "I need a word with you, Detective."

"Over here," she said, pointing to a corner.

Philo started, his voice low. "Look, I'm a little lost here. The text you sent me last night," he lowered his voice even more, "I mean, this isn't even your jurisdiction. If I didn't know any better—"

"That's enough, Trout," she said, her hand up. "No more about it. Like I said, my bad."

Her text had made a difference. After it, and after getting nothing back from his response to her, Philo stayed at Patrick's place and coached him. By midnight Patrick had gotten his story straight, complete with the whimpering and the tears, believable because for Patrick, the emotion was real.

"I don't know what the hell just happened in there, but all I can say is you guys arrived at the right answer." He scoured the squad room. "And without his attorney present. A no-show. Last time I use him."

"Look. Chunks were torn out of the body," she said. "They asked Mr. Stakes to give them a sample of his bite. He cooperated. When the lab checks it out, I'm figuring his bite won't match. Plus, the other evidence that he was in the house—"

"Fingerprints."

"I'm not at liberty to confirm or deny that. But his story on how that evidence got there now has corroboration as being plausible."

This took Philo aback. "*Corroboration?* This still isn't working for me. What corroboration, by whom?"

"The timeline all fits, the door left open, you and I in the house downstairs, busy reviewing the scene, not knowing if anyone else wandered in..."

"Yeah, sure, I agree, all plausible, but who's corroborating it?"

"Me."

Philo blinked hard at her, speechless.

"Don't act so surprised, Mr. Trout. It could have happened just the way he said it did." Her close-talker persona returned, staring him down again from her disadvantaged height, like when they'd first met, but this time it was so he'd hear her speaking in a lower voice. "Although we know it didn't. How did this evidence get in the house? A question for another day. Something we want to ask him, but without an attorney present."

"The attorney never showed. Why not ask him today?"

"Yes and no. He did show, just had trouble getting past the desk sergeant. Seems whatever held him up got straightened out soon as you guys left, out the back door. What are the chances of that timing? Pretty wild, right?"

What was he hearing? Something bigger going on here? "Right. Wild."

"They want Mr. Stakes back, Trout. They need to know when he left that evidence, and under what circumstances. Someone from the Sixth will call to arrange it."

No shit. The cops had decided the cannibalism claim was a setup, with Patrick the mark.

"One more thing. No one needs to know about my text to you. Someone might think it was to give Mr. Stakes a heads-up so he could prepare for the interrogation, know what I mean?"

26

Front and center in the Blessids' living room, Grace was in a hospital bed, a red and white Phillies bandana tied around her head.

"Why— the *FUCK*—didn't you tell me, Philo?"

Between her gulps of oxygen and the fire she was breathing, Philo worried her face might ignite.

Patrick tried to take the bullet. "Ma'am, it's my fault, see—"

"Quiet, Patrick, I'll get to you in a minute. But *you*, Philo..."

She took chest-size swallows of air from the tank through a plastic mask. After three or four tokes she ripped the mask away from her mouth, still fuming, then lifted the cannula tubing up from her neck and reinserted it in her nostrils like she was going to snort it whole.

"I thought we had a good thing going here, Philo. A decent, respectful working arrangement. And now (*cough*) you've got Patrick (*cough*) lying to the cops?"

"But it was just a white lie, ma'am," Patrick said.

"Patrick, QUIET!"

Grace coughed and sputtered, her face a throbbing, deepening shade of purple; Hank found a bottle of water for her. She grabbed it, sucked some of it down, then tossed the bottle back at her husband. "I want to hear from *you, Philo, now.*"

"Then you need to calm down, Grace, otherwise, we're not talking."

"Philo, goddamn it!" Grace's ample chest inflated to the max then slowed its heaving when she didn't get her way, her breathing settling into a low wheeze, then a controlled purr, then eventually approached normal; the flush in her cheeks subsided. While she calmed, Philo grabbed an armchair and sat.

He explained. "What went on with the police—what Patrick told them —it was the only way, Grace."

"Pardon me for fucking up your victory lap with the cops, Philo, but that's just bullshit." The cannula tubing was out of her nose again, followed by an oxygen mask munch. "Patrick doesn't—need *(cough)*—to lie. He never went near that place!"

"Grace, chill, honey," Hank pleaded. "You'll stroke out."

"Shut up, Hank!"

No one moved. She continued to fight for air, gulping, wheezing, more gulping, repeat, until, finally, she was purring again.

Philo waited her out, her calm returning. Her struggle for breath subsided, her air intake normalized. He'd need to drop the bomb now.

"The problem, Grace, sorry to say, is that he did go near that place. Sometime after the slaughter and before the police arrived. He compromised the crime scene, and the cops found out about it. That's why they were interested in him. Except now, after he provided them with an explanation, it looks like they aren't. At least not as a suspect. Crisis averted."

Philo launched into it, confessed everything he and Patrick had kept from them, the reason for Patrick's trespass, the fingerprints, the woman he saw, his sleepwalking, the white lie. Grace, nearing tears now at the revelations, dropped back against her pillow, pissed and exhausted.

"You should have trusted me, Philo, damn it," she said.

"It was never a question of trust, Grace, it was a question of how you'd react, and your condition; your temper."

"All right, fine, I get it, but don't pull that shit again. Now that we sold the business, Patrick's all we've got, right, Hank, honey?"

"Yes, sweetie, yes. Try to relax."

She started to drift off then rallied. Her eyes heavy-lidded, she reached for Patrick, patted his hand. "So you sleepwalk, Patrick?"

"Yes, ma'am, sometimes. Maybe. Not much. A little."

"I never knew." Done with him, she suggested he go back to his place. After he left, she swiveled her head. "Philo."

"Yes, ma'am?"

"Something about the cop interrogation doesn't sound right."

"Yes, ma'am. Can't put one past you, can we, ma'am?"

She held out against her exhaustion, listened as Philo explained his take on Patrick's visit with the police, that Detective Ibáñez hinted the cops believed the crime scene was a setup, an attempt at redirecting attention from what these doctors were doing to get body parts for the black market. Which made the next discussion Philo needed to have with her as duplicitous as it would be difficult. And to top it off, Philo would need to shade the truth with her yet again because Wally Lanakai had gotten back to him. There was a plan, but she'd hear nothing about Wally's part in it, or the bare-knuckles fight, scheduled for three Saturdays from now.

Instead she heard about regional military organ transplant lists, and how a military medical tribunal had reviewed her records. How she'd been found acceptable as a transplant recipient sponsored by navy veteran Philo, and sooner rather than later because of her dire condition, and about how they'd work toward making it happen when an acceptable donor became available.

"In other words," she said, "we're waiting for someone to die. An organ donor who is a veteran."

"Won't work any other way, Grace."

"Hank, doll," she reached over, patted her husband's hand, "you get with Philo and ask all the appropriate questions for me. I need a nap."

"Will do, honey."

"And Philo?"

"Yes, Grace?"

"You better not be fucking with me. If I find out anything's funny about this, I promise I'll wake the fuck up on the operating table and walk out before I let the transplants happen."

She nodded off. Hank covered her with a blanket, resettled her bandana and kissed her on the cheek, lingering close to her a moment, watching her sleep.

Philo could see this more clearly now; Hank would be no trouble when he told him the truth. He thumbed Hank in the direction of the door. "We need to talk."

Hank heard the parts that were real and the parts that had been bullshit. Regardless of the inauthenticity, the scam became an easy sell. Hank wanted her to get relief, wanted, needed her to live, and he didn't care how. Philo answered his questions.

"What is this 'regional military transplant list'?"

The list was bullshit. There was no such thing.

"Her records were reviewed by a military medical tribunal?"

Nope. No such tribunal.

"The lungs will come from where, then?"

The black market. Or "red market," if the name made Hank feel any better, which was what journalists had coined as an identifier for economic transactions related to the human body. Black market or red, Hank said he flat-out didn't care.

"There could be no leap-frogging other deserving recipients on a list. This is important to Grace."

True fact, there wouldn't be, considering there was only one potential recipient on this particular list: Grace.

"We'll need a doctor's name, his credentials, and we'll need to meet him."

A name and creds were doable. Arranging a meeting would be a little dicey. Philo would get on that.

"Where would the surgery be?"

A sterile operating theater inside a TBD urgent care facility, somewhere in Center City. The facility would be fully equipped, including a heart-lung machine; that was the promise. They wouldn't know the location until the last minute. She might need to go to where the donor was for the organ hand-off rather than the reverse.

"Any guess how soon two lungs would be available?"

A quid-pro-quo deal was in progress. Its consummation would be after Philo provided a certain reciprocating service. Three weeks at the earliest, pending someone dying.

"Cost?"

A bartered transaction. Zip, zero, not one fucking dime, from them or from Philo. Her health insurance would need to cover her aftercare.

Philo opened up. "You guys have been troopers during this transition, Hank, especially Grace, ignoring how ornery she can get. I owe her, and I owe you."

The front door to the house whooshed open and closed, the home health aide letting herself into the vestibule. Hank and Philo needed to close out the discussion. He ushered Philo into the kitchen. "Tell me about this 'bartered transaction.'"

Philo decided a little truth wouldn't hurt. "Ever hear of Philo Beddoe, fictional movie character?"

"Can't place him. Maybe."

"Look him up. Bare-knuckles boxing. Clint Eastwood character. In three weeks that will be me, earning some extra cash the same way. The organs were tossed in to make me close the deal."

"Tossed in? What the hell, Philo, this needs to be real. No screwing around here. It needs to be professionally done, with real doctors, and nurses, and in a safe environment. This is my Grace we're talking about."

"It will be, Hank. This red market activity goes on every day, whether we like it or not. So the question is, can you sell this arrangement to her?"

Hank watched the aide enter the living room. They heard her rouse Grace from her nap to have her take some meds, also heard Grace fight through the agony of simply trying to catch a breath.

"Yes," Hank said. "Fuckin'-a, I can sell it."

27

Patrick got the call from the Sixth District detectives when he and Philo were heading to a small job, an apartment over a store in Philadelphia's Glenwood section, within walking distance of Frazier's Gym and Hump's neighborhood. Patrick ended the detective's call with "Sure, sir. After work today. Bye."

In the van were Patrick and Philo only, Hank taking a breather, Grace taking a breather also, but in her case a poor choice of words. Miñoso was to be a late addition, Hump to send him along to the apartment address. The job was a crime scene cleanout after a decomp had already been removed. They arrived at a detached building with a shuttered bodega on the first floor, the building in a horrible state of disrepair. The job would be a slam dunk, four or five hours tops.

The van idled. "This new visit with the detectives, you'll need to tell them everything, Patrick, so they can piece things together. They're trying to build a case."

"I know, sir. No white lie, sir. The truth, sir." In particular, the truth about the call luring him to the Elfreth's Alley house, plus the burner phone number it came from; about the body in the hot tub, and the woman —"the airplane lady"—who entered the house before him.

The police wouldn't have him retract his other statement; it gave him a cop-corroborated reason for his prints being there. For them, what Patrick would offer would be new territory. Leads they could run down, to help move the case in the direction it needed to go: illegal organ harvesting and trafficking, not roving cannibalism.

An Asian woman left a storefront across the street from where they parked and met them out front of the bodega. "I call you. I am landlord. Follow me."

The second-floor apartment had a first-floor entrance facing the street, a single door next to the bodega storefront. The door opened to a narrow stairway; she filled them in on their way up the steps.

"One body found in kitchen. Cops take him away Monday, won't clean up, say not their problem, give me your name. How long dead, don't know. He was new tenant, three weeks only. Tây ban nha," she said, paused, caught herself. "How you say, was Spanish. No, Latino. Nice man. Not like crazy man other tenant who had gun. Crazy man left fast, no pay rent." At the top of the stairs she waved her hand in front of her nose. "Place stinks. Dead body. Horrible." Inside the upstairs door, she flipped a switch for the lights.

The apartment was filled with cheap, trash-day-confiscated furniture sitting on throw rugs atop worn wooden floors. In the kitchenette, a fridge, a hotplate, a microwave, and a small table and chairs.

"Leave appliances, clean everything else out, take it away. Another new tenant moving into apartment next week." She threw her hands up. "No time for this. Send me bill. Bye." After she about-faced, she retraced her steps downstairs and out the front door.

Philo walked the apartment. A sitting room, kitchenette, and bedroom, five hundred square feet plus or minus. Torn couch, a listing futon in the bedroom. Broom clean except for a few dead roaches. Peeling wallpaper, with water stains on the ceiling in the small parlor, the room damp with a mold smell, plus the death odor, maybe more. Patrick produced his phone in the sitting room and started taking snapshots, for "before" and "after" job validation. Philo stood in front of the kitchenette, absorbing the scene.

Blood stains covered the linoleum floor behind the kitchen table, between the table and the white refrigerator. There was a blood splat on the fridge itself, against the top door, the one for the freezer, a puncture there too, the blood dripping south, all the way to the floor. He opened the refrigerator door. No exit hole on the inside. With the door closed he shined a flashlight inside the puncture. Gray matter clung to the jagged edge. No slug fragment in there, far as he could tell.

On the hotplate sat a small pot with a handle, food caked inside. Near the edge of the kitchen table was a lone cereal bowl. In it, a porridge, maybe oatmeal, hardened, some of its tan color retained, but now it was mostly black. A spoon jutted from the bowl's center, anchored in the brick-like mixture like a sword in a stone.

For Philo, a memory trigger from the other side of the world. An unattended bowl and spoon; the blood-spattered carnage of an Afghan family he'd helped extinguish. His heart pounded, his head sweeping side to side on instinct, looking for automatic weapons that could be here, had to be here, were always here. In Afghanistan, yes, they were there in the room where the terrorist family had been executed, but here, no, nada, no weapons, only the days-old bowl of oatmeal and a spoon and blood and gray matter.

A cleansing breath evened him out, helped him embrace the calm so he could process the before and after of the crime scene. The short victim had stood up from the table, faced an intruder head on, and was blown away.

"Patrick," he called. "Over here. Get a picture of this bowl for me, please."

Planked kitchen table, cereal bowl, spoon standing at attention, and desiccated oatmeal. Not a photo with any marketing value for the website. Worthy more so, and perhaps with no other value, for a study of the human condition.

Oatmeal with Spoon: A Still Life, Before the Annihilation.

Click went Patrick's phone camera.

* * *

In the alley behind the store's basement, the pieces were piling up pending a biohazardous furniture cleanup Philo would arrange for later. The red hazmat bags they'd filled with enzyme-soaked rags would leave with them in the truck when they were finished. Patrick winged the last piece of the broken futon atop the pile, where it landed just short of the bodega's rear window. They were nearly finished, and could now set up an ozone machine to eliminate the odors in the apartment.

Patrick removed his mask, stretched himself upward on his toes to inspect the glass of the window he nearly shattered with his futon toss. "Black windows, sir. See 'em?"

"Yes. The store's empty, the basement probably is, too. Painted windows keep the curious away."

"Just like at the car dealership, sir."

"Patrick— relax, bud. Not every abandoned property in Philly is hiding organ traffickers. People sometimes paint or whitewash them while they're doing remodeling. Less of a street audience that way."

"They also paint them when they're meth labs, sir."

A possibility in this neighborhood. Philo's experience cleaning meth labs was exactly zero, no occasions so far during the transition of the business. Curious, he tried the rear door to the basement, then circled around to the bodega's front door at street level, confirming they were both locked.

"I'll get a meth test kit from the truck, sir. We can test the apartment. Won't take long, sir."

Upstairs, Patrick shook the glass ampule from the kit and mixed the chemical reagent. The liquid changed color, from clear to amber. "Ready to test some room samples, sir."

They wiped the surfaces around the apartment with the collection sample papers, the walls, window frames, and around light switches and doorknobs, separate papers for each wiped space. After the samples were collected, Patrick removed the cap from the dropper end of the ampule.

"What color are we looking for, Patrick?"

"Blue means meth, sir."

He dripped the reagent onto each paper. After five minutes, every paper showed a powder blue, some fainter than the others, but blue nevertheless. The place was contaminated, but that could happen from one occurrence, one person smoking one pipe in the area, just one time. "We should take one more sample, sir."

Patrick crouched next to a duct embedded in the hardwood floor for the forced hot air system, the furnace in the basement. He removed the grate. He leaned closer to the opening.

"Smell this, sir."

The air duct emitted a strong, breathtaking odor, from solvent or paint thinner or ammonia, or a cat's litter box on steroids. After a swipe inside the duct with a collection paper, multiple drops of the chemical reagent, and the five-minute wait—

Royal blue. The deepest, royal-est blue of the bunch. "Meth lab downstairs, sir, in the basement."

The apartment execution: there was nothing of value here; dingy walls with ripped 1970s wallpaper; second-hand furniture; not even a portable TV or stereo equipment. Why execute a Latino man living so dismal an existence, in a space that provided little more than shelter from the elements?

Noise, on the stairs. Footsteps, ascending them in a hurry, and far from quiet. Philo gestured at Patrick with a raised finger to his mouth. He tiptoed to the closed door, reached inside his Tyvek suit, and withdrew his Sig from a shoulder holster. The footsteps arrived on the top step.

The door handle jiggled, then the person spoke through the door. "Tío? Tío Diego?" He pushed through with no attempt at minimizing his entrance.

Philo slammed the intruder's face against the wall, stuck the Sig in his ear then eased up. "Miñoso?"

"Si, Campeón, si! Owww—"

Miñoso unstuck his face from the wall, but Philo kept the rest of him pressed against it. "Why—?"

"Mi tío Diego—where is my uncle Diego?"

The prior tenant, Philo soon learned. Not the "crazy man who had gun" tenant, but rather the one whose blood and gray matter they had just scrubbed off the floor and flushed out of the puncture wound in the fridge door. Miñoso wept as he paced the empty apartment, inconsolable.

No, Uncle Diego never used meth, Miñoso said. Si, he was poor, in Philly only three months, in the US only six months in total, but his dishwasher's wages gave him enough to rent his own place, dismal as it was. It was a roof over his head and little else.

"His family, my family, beggars…"

Families in poverty, eking out their existences in Mexico. His uncle was sending them money. "Yo también," he said, meaning Miñoso had sent money also, when he could. He slid down the wall and sat, sobbing into his hands.

Just another meth operation and the fallout surrounding it, in yet another sorry-ass part of the city. Wrong place, wrong time for Miñoso's uncle, apparently one tenant removed from the gunman's real target, the "crazy man." Miñoso wanted to see the body. Philo retrieved his wallet, fished out Detective Ibáñez's card and called her.

"I'll bring my friend in but he's undocumented, Detective. I want you to guarantee his safety. No funny business."

"You're handing us a meth lab," she said. "We like that. You have my word he'll be fine."

Philo gave up on having them do any work together at the grain elevator today. "We need to go now, Miñoso. The detective will get you into the morgue."

Miñoso pondered his fingers, turned his palms up, pondered his hands.

"Miñoso. Dude. Let's go. Detective Ibáñez will be waiting."

But Miñoso wasn't finished praying and pleading under his breath, questioning himself, "How do I get you home to Mexico, my dearest uncle," all of it in Spanish. Ramblings, from the suddenly bereaved; Philo paid little attention. He ushered Patrick to the door, had to wait on Miñoso, still sitting on the floor. "Miñoso. Please."

Miñoso stood, raised his chin like the strong man he'd need to be, continued talking to himself with a new resolve. "El cuerpo de Miñoso, la selección de Miñoso."

Miñoso's body, Miñoso's choice.

"I will get you home, uncle."

28

Miñoso, as next of kin, identified his uncle's body. Detective Ibáñez made the morgue visit happen, then excused herself, Miñoso leaving with her, short-circuiting anything that could have remotely mimicked an ambush because of his non-citizenship. Philo's next stop was downtown without Miñoso, to deliver Patrick to the Sixth District detectives, not as a suspect but as a bona fide witness offering information about what he saw during his Elfreth's Alley crime scene trespass.

While Patrick did more fessing up, Philo hung outside the interrogation room. The TV in the squad room showed a news replay of the Philadelphia District Attorney's grand jury announcement regarding organ trafficking suspects Dr. Andelmo and friends; Philo had missed it as live breaking news. ADA Lola Pfizer, Philo's former main squeeze, stood behind the DA. Philo liked DA Herm Dennison, a holdover metrosexual, despite his affinity for expensive suits and his cozy relationship with Philadelphia's garment industry. Lola on screen with him meant she was also on the team handling the case.

DA Dennison's remarks, speaking into the camera: "We continue to pursue illegal organ trafficking allegations regarding Dr. Francisco Andelmo. Religious cults, lone attackers—they're not in our sights at the moment. Depending on the grand jury's findings and the police department's continuing investigation, this could change. We want the truth, and we will follow all leads that will surface it. That's all I've got. Thank you."

* * *

"They're after the airline lady with the suitcase, Philo, sir."

"No surprise there, bud. She could be key."

Patrick's info dump to the cops was finished for the time being. He alternated between ringing his hands and rubbing the dent in his head while Philo drove him home. Today as a workday was a no-go for him, Philo decided; the kid was too nervous. But Philo's plans for himself would take him into the late hours.

"Sir, you think I could have done any of this?"

"Done what?"

"You know, hurt anyone, sir? The police explained what was at the scene, and..."

Bulls. Patrick was a person of interest, an informant of sorts, but no one could know how this info might ricochet around his impaired head and cause unintended outcomes, like misguided guilt. They'd decided no attorney was needed for the interview, but maybe a shrink should have been in there with him instead, or even now.

"No, Patrick, it wasn't you."

"But I sleepwalk—"

"You were there because someone tricked you into going there."

"Yeah, sir, but maybe some other time..."

"Patrick, listen to me, it's not you. It's the work of more than one person. The other time you were on that street it was as a tourist, before you got mugged. You were set up because Andelmo knows your background, even has your phone number. Even the cops don't think it was you."

A block away from Patrick's Germantown apartment. "Maybe they're wrong, sir."

"Enough, Patrick. My head hurts."

"Mine too, sir." More rubbing. "I don't want to hurt no one else, sir."

"Patrick, please. You haven't hurt anyone. I'm more concerned someone might want to hurt you."

Then Philo found himself thinking the unthinkable. Guns. Maybe Patrick should have one. But that would be crazy.

Philo's last words to him, the Jeep in Patrick's driveway now: "Get some rest. We've got a busy day tomorrow."

* * *

Philo phoned Lola. She picked up after one ring. "ADA Pfizer."

The quick answer surprised him. Maybe she'd deleted his number from her address book and didn't know it was him. Then again, maybe she had a slight case of buyer's remorse or lover's regret or whatever the hell it was called, and she just hadn't been able to bring herself to let go. In the latter scenario, he surmised she was waiting eagerly for his call, and would act quickly to answer it, which she had.

"Lola. Hi, babe. How you—?"

"Go fuck yourself, Philo. Lose my number." *Click.*

Scenario clarified.

After the call, the text he sent her wrote itself. When she read it, she would explode. He now didn't give a shit.

I'll be visiting Andelmo to straighten his ass out about Patrick Stakes. My call to you was a courtesy. Have a nice day.

His phone rang.

"Hi, Lola. What a surprise."

"Listen, Philo, stay the hell away from Andelmo. We're building a case. Do NOT intimidate him—"

"Nice to hear your voice, counselor. Look, that prick's attorney is trying to drag a certain someone into his little organ-munching circle-jerk, and soon he'll have that very impressionable someone believing he's responsible for all those organ harvesting murders. So, counselor, the answer is no, your request is denied."

"Philo, I swear to God, if you screw up this case, I'll personally sic a fucking badger on that limp dick of yours, you understand? You'll be a sworn enemy of the DA's office. Blessid Trauma will be fucking history. Philo, you listening? Philo?"

"Still denied. Great to hear from you, counselor." *Click.*

He pocketed his phone, did a quick neck and shoulder stretch to loosen himself up from his seat in the waiting room at Dr. Andelmo's practice, then he stood. Calling her from the doctor's office gave Lola no time to send any police to intercept him. She'd call the doctor's defense attorney about Philo's threat, then maybe she'd send a few of Philly's finest to the office ASAP to protect him. Regardless, either response would be too late.

Fuck waiting in this waiting room; fuck all of it. A phone call could alert the bastard. Time to move.

Philo bypassed the admitting desk, ignored two protesting records clerks, and pushed through a door into a hallway. At the end of the hall he found a room with the doctor's name on the door and a sliding sign that said *Consultation in progress*. He opened the door unannounced and closed it behind him.

Seated across from Dr. Andelmo at a resplendent mahogany desk was a stylish, fiftyish-year-old Latino woman with bold red hair and too much makeup.

"Ma'am, sorry to impose, but would you give the doctor and I a moment please?"

"Doctor! Who is theese, theese..." Her displeasure at the interruption dissipated, her head back, her eyes running up and down Philo, rugged and tall in his tight jeans. "...Theese handsome chico, who is being so rude—"

The doctor was quick on the uptake. "I'm sorry, señora. It appears I need to provide an emergency consultation." He rose, pushed himself away from his desk. "A nurse practitioner will make you comfortable in another room. Gracias."

Andelmo escorted her to the door. When the door closed, Philo instantly eliminated the distance between them.

"You conniving little prick. You set Patrick Stakes up."

Andelmo said nothing, remained calm, unblinking. Too calm. Something pushed up into Philo's groin, under his balls, and he half expected he'd be asked to cough.

"It is a stun gun, Mr. Trout, and my hand is on the button. Back away, or you will find yourself on the floor pissing and shitting your pants. Security will be here any minute."

Philo saw no security presence on his way in and considered the threat bullshit, and as of yet, no high voltage had arced into his scrotum. Andelmo was bluffing. Philo had time to react.

"And pointed at your dick, Doctor, is a nine-millimeter with a hair trigger. Hand over whatever it is you're pressing against my balls, or that loosened bowel movement you're about to have and the colon that delivers it will be embedded in the wall studs behind you."

Philo's eyes got a little bigger when he accepted the doc's weapon and held it up for observation. No shit, a real stun gun. He pressed the button and watched the electricity arc. *ZZZap.*

"Jeez, Doc, this looks like it would have really hurt," he said. He tossed in onto a loveseat, re-holstered his Sig, then pressed a finger into Andelmo's chest for emphasis.

"This is a warning about the bullshit your attorney is feeding the media on roving cannibals. If *any* of it causes Patrick Stakes *any* trouble whatsoever, either with the police, or the media, or if Patrick has so much as one fucking nightmare about your wild-ass allegations, you better hope for a conviction and jail time, otherwise it'll be worse when I catch up with you. Comprende?"

A buff, capped-teeth, smiling Andelmo stood his ground. "Back off, Mr. Trout. Patrick Stakes made statements about his odd tendencies; they are a part of his medical records, and nurses will attest to them. I'm sure he will attest to them also. All my attorney would have to do is prove to a jury that someone—*one* person—might have acted in a cannibalistic way at that site, and there would be reasonable doubt regarding the charges. As there should be, because it is innocent—*I'm* innocent—until proven guilty."

Footsteps, more like heavy strides, pounded down the hallway, advancing toward the office. They emboldened the doctor. "My guess is the police also know Patrick was there, at that crime scene. He is a menace who is one bad memory away from a suicide. He was quite capable of that gruesome murder."

Philo ripped Andelmo out of the chair with a hand to his throat and shoved him back against the wall. "*You* put him there. *Your* phone call sent him to that house on Elfreth's Alley."

The door flew open. Philo was oh for two, having guessed wrong about both Andelmo's stun gun and security personnel. Within seconds, multiple hands dropped onto all parts of his body, with four burly dudes and one stun gun turning him into electrified modeling clay. They zip-tied cuffs on him, relieved him of his Sig, emptied its clip of bullets, and deposited him on the street outside the office like the glorified bar bouncers they probably were. But then, to his surprise, they cut off the plastic zip-tie cuffs.

"Here's your gun, Trout," the guy who emptied the clip said, tossing the Sig against Philo's chest. "Let me make something clear. You need to stay away from the doctor, no matter how pleasing it might be for you to do otherwise. He's ours to worry about. *Ours*. Stay. Away."

Eskimos, Philo decided. No, Aleuts. No, no, not Aleuts, Hawaiians. Which meant they were probably mob guys, not glorified bouncers. They had let the stun gun do its job but hadn't also tried to tune him up, with no punches thrown before, during, or after they cuffed him. His only bruising came from the stun gun. And they returned his weapon.

Unsteady, his brain still fuzzy, he mulled their words.

"He's ours to worry about..."

These guys, they were Andelmo's bodyguards, but they were doing more than protecting him. They were watching him.

29

Philo's Jeep bounced and dipped across the rutted serpentine trail that led to the grain elevator. Tonight Philo was solo, his team busy, Hank with Grace, Patrick at another concert, Miñoso in mourning. He would concentrate on the first-floor space, where the fight would be held.

He arrived on site, hopped out, and uncovered one of the gas-powered generators. A few pulls of the cord and the unit sputtered to life, coughing itself into a low, throbbing purr. The hanging jobsite lighting on the ground floor flickered on, slits and rips and a few poked holes in the tarp making the lighting visible from the outside, but only barely. He found the separation in the tarp and inside it the separation in the chain-link fencing. The entrance would need to be taller and wider, room enough for maybe three or more people abreast to exit quickly if necessary, without lowering their heads. An easy fix with bolt cutters, something he'd get to later. He slipped inside.

A rat scurried from behind a column and disappeared into a four-by-four foot hole in the floor, one of a few such holes encircled by traffic cones and yellow caution tape. Grain dust and the other slop they pressure-washed from the building's six stories had settled into the subterranean space, would continue to settle there as they finished cleaning all the floors, to eventually dry out before the building's scheduled implosion. After they finished the power-wash above ground, they'd drop a ladder down there. Patrick and Miñoso would spray and shop-vac the basement space, staying away from the wood-inlaid ceiling.

The weather had changed, from winter's brutal cold to a spring chill. The hanging tarps would lessen the wind and whatever cold was left, and keep some of the audience's body heat inside. It would also minimize the beacon effect of the building's jobsite lighting.

For fight night there'd be standing room only outside the sticky-tape square he planned to lay down as a fight space outline, a bit larger than a boxing ring. Inside the square would be room enough for him and his opponent to maneuver, to play their chess game of parry and retreat.

Philo removed his heavy coat, then his shirts. Stripped to the waist, his holstered gun was exposed, sitting just above his ass. He blew into his hands then took his solid two hundred ten pounds for a spin, working up a sweat, the floor dusty but uncluttered, pedaling backward and forward, sticking and jabbing, his shadow-boxing giving him a feel for what the fight space would be, and the epitome of every out-of-the-way venue he'd ever boxed in. Raw, unadorned, barbaric. Never comfortable, never pampering, never welcoming, and yet he'd felt at home in all of these spaces just like he did now in this one, because he was doing what he loved. Twenty minutes later, out of breath and sweat dripping, he toweled off, covered up, and returned to the business of scrubbing the walls of the accumulated grain dust, to ready it for a Wally Lanakai walk-through.

30

The limo driver buzzed her apartment from the first-floor lobby at eight-fifteen p.m. The car was punctual, ready to take Kaipo to the Borgata in Atlantic City, Mr. Lanakai's treat, with him planning to meet her there. It would be a treat for him only; for her, an awkward evening awaited.

She grabbed her wrap, threw it around herself and her tasteful evening dress—classy, not sexy—grabbed her coat and her overnight bag. The casino had a room reserved for her, in her name only, a single, as in for one occupant, not two, just like Mr. Lanakai had promised her.

Time to get this grope-fest over with, she told herself.

* * *

"We have someone joining us tonight, Kaipo."

Mr. Lanakai led Kaipo to the bar inside the Borgata's Bobby Flay Steak House. Leaning over a drink, something that was clear and carbonated with a lime twist, seltzer maybe, Mr. Lanakai's other guest soon acknowledged their approach by disengaging himself from his bar stool. The process took a moment, in deference to the man's superior height.

"Kaipo Mawpaw, this is Tonka Omanopa."

She had to raise her head an unusual distance for the introduction, but it was worth it.

"Hello, Ms. Mawpaw," he said, his smile wide. "Glad to meet you."

Good teeth. Moussed black curls atop high and tight sideburns, with a dimpled Hawaiian face she could only describe as beautiful. Beneath it were square shoulders, an open collar, a tailored suit jacket that grabbed at over-size biceps and a large chest, and a tapered waist. An imposing physique.

And those teeth. Not just good teeth, great teeth.

"You too, Mr. Omanopa," was as much as she could manage.

"'Tonka.' Please."

"Yes. Of course you are," she said.

Mr. Lanakai chuckled, shook his head. "I know, Kaipo, I know, he's gorgeous. He's also very loyal. To me. Let's get to our seats."

* * *

She stirred her drink, seated in the front row just below the ropes at one of the corners, Mr. Lanakai next to her, Tonka on his other side. Young Mr. Omanopa studied a boxing ring that was now getting busy with the main event.

"Ever hear of bare-knuckle boxing, Kaipo?" Mr. Lanakai said. "Not mixed martial arts or UFC." He gestured with his eyes at the ring looming so close above them. "And not pro boxing like this. Bare knuckles is boxing without the big puffy gloves. No taped-up, gloved hands. No timed rounds. The fight ends only after one of the fighters gets counted out or can't or won't continue. Mano a mano. I bankroll Tonka here. He's undefeated in thirty-four bare-knuckle fights. He is a spectacle to behold."

"I've heard of it," she said. "It's like cockfighting and dogfighting. Animal abuse. I despise them both. No offense, Mr. Omanopa."

"None taken," the young fighter said. "Again, 'Tonka.'"

"Lately he's heard 'champ' more than anything else," Mr. Lanakai said. "So how do you like these seats, Kaipo?"

Yes, they were good, Kaipo said, first row, next to the ring, almost within arm's length. Mr. Lanakai bragged on what else he had planned for the evening: bankroll her gambling plus take her to a late show at the casino. After that, "We'll see where the evening takes us."

As long as it ended with her back in her hotel room by herself, which could prove difficult after all this fuss. She decided on a topic she knew he'd be less than thrilled to discuss, with her not wanting to score points, rather looking more to distance herself. "Wally—may I call you Wally?"

"Yes, Kaipo, yes, of course. Good. Finally, you are relaxed. 'Mr. Lanakai' is so formal."

Calling him by his first name didn't mean to her what it meant to him. Regardless, she'd fan his flames of false hope while trading on his interest.

"Yes. Something has been bothering me lately, Wally."

The bell rang for round one. Wally leaned over while she spoke, ostensibly to better the crowd noise that had increased now that the fight had started, the two boxers circling each other in the ring. Wally's arm dropped onto the back of her seat then onto her shoulder, the move about as subtle as date night at the movies in middle school.

"This new business model," she said, nonplussed, raising her voice, "the one Olivier says leverages cheap, disposable raw materials, it seems sooo—"

The punishment began above them, a mismatch in the heavyweight division, a young, white, East Coast stud on his way up the ranks, wailing on a black tomato can from Chicago with a losing record, there to be slaughtered, to pad the stud's resume. The older fighter backed into the ropes to weather the early onslaught, the stud's repeated left and right hooks keeping his opponent in the corner just above them. Two minutes into the first round and already the older fighter had trouble defending himself. Sweat, and splatters of spit and blood, sprayed the ringside patrons repeatedly, Kaipo's incomplete comment hanging out there, totally eclipsed by the savagery above them. Her wrap protected some of her outfit but there was nothing to protect her face, yet she barely flinched at the pounding in progress above her. The bell ending the round stopped the beating; the blood-soaked older boxer wobbled to his corner. She turned to Wally knowing how intimidating she looked but making no attempt to minimize it, the bloody distortions an exclamation point. She completed her comment.

"Yes, your new interest seems so opportunistic, and barbaric." Blood spatter dotted her face, her neck, was in her hair. In retrospect, Tyvek rather than Talbot's would have been a better fashion choice tonight. "The new business you've sent my way—it's bothersome. It involves desperate, innocent people."

Wally's jaw remained open, dazed by Kaipo's deadpan expression underneath the spattered blood, including no acknowledgment of the gore. He retracted his arm from behind her to dab at himself with a hanky. Behind them a Lanakai lackey also produced a hanky and began patting Wally's suit jacket.

"Get the fuck off me," he said, brushing away his assistant's hand. Wally's focus was stern now, directed at Kaipo. He squared his jaw.

"Listen closely, Kaipo. These people are roaches, feeding off the fat of America's mainland—Mexican and South American roaches coming north illegally, looking for handouts. We're simply tidying up the place a bit now that our country has grown a pair and has the stomach for it, and we're making some money while we do it." He gestured to the flunky behind him. "Find her a towel. You need to clean yourself up, Kaipo; you look like Carrie at the prom. And let's get one thing straight. Tonight you don't talk about what I do for my living, and I won't talk about what you do for yours."

Kaipo let the reprimand simmer. Round two started, a replay of round one but in a different corner, Tonka more vocal when the action moved in front of him, working himself up. At the end of the round a ring doctor examined the bloodied fighter. The doctor's headshake ended the bout, the East Coast stud a victor by technical knockout.

They all stood to leave the small arena. "My apology, Kaipo, for the lecture, and for appearing so repulsed at your appearance. I'd forgotten about your tolerance for this sort of thing. Which brings me to my next question. How would you like to be my guest at a bare-knuckles fight I'm promoting?"

Not a chance, she thought. "Look, Wally"—she hadn't even the remotest interest in seeing one, not even if she were accompanied by someone she liked—"that sounds exciting, but—"

"It's next Saturday night, back in Philly. The amazing Tonka here fights a man who's knocked out more than sixty fighters but has never been knocked down once. Two undefeated knockout artists throwing hands, out by the Navy Yard. The cops will be looking the other way. It'll be quite a rush."

Tonka's sparkling teeth flashed, betraying his pleasure at hearing Wally talk him up.

"Please say you'll come, miss. I'll be fighting the best fighter out there," Tonka said, all bust-your-buttons like, "not counting me, of course. He's an old guy from Philly. What's his name again, Mr. Lanakai?"

"Tristan Trout. Prefers 'Philo.' And he's not that old, Tonka. Show some respect by at least remembering his name."

"Sure, Mr. Lanakai, sure. Come see my next knockout victim, Mr. Tristan Philo Trout, miss."

She now had an additional question. "Is he the same Tristan Trout who owns Blessid Trauma, the crime scene cleaning business?"

"Why yes he is, Kaipo," Wally said.

Her no became a yes.

31

Less than a week away from the fight, floors two through six of the grain elevator were now fully scrubbed and vacuumed, the first floor presentable enough to show Wally Lanakai. Philo and his guests left their respective vehicles, flashlights on, and congregated amid the rubble, all lights aimed at the ragged, cave-like entrance to the building while they talked.

"About this property," Wally said, eyeing the unpaved serpentine trail behind them, "was the trail we took the only way here?"

"No. There are multiple trails in and out. Easy all-points dispersal, in case, you know, cops. It'll be fine."

The four crunched their way over tamped stone and dirt and around debris to enter the building. Philo's guests followed him in single file, Wally between the two beefy oddjobs, the same ones who came with him to intimidate Philo at his home. Once inside, Philo led them to the squared space that would become the boxing ring, its perimeter defined not by ropes but rather by fluorescent yellow sticky tape affixed to the floor.

Oddjob Number 1 spoke. "What's under that plywood?" He gestured twice in succession with a raised chin at the two far corners, where wood scraps covered openings that dropped into the space under the floor.

"An underground pit. The slime we sprayed off the building's walls and floors settled in it. Not pretty down there. Looks like decaying oatmeal."

"Good," Oddjob Number 2 said, snickering, a larger version of Number 1. "Something for you to eat when Tonka gets through with you."

Philo slapped his knee then burst into a mock laugh that he severed with a glare. "That's good, fat boy. How about I drop a ladder down there for you so you can get a closer look? I hear it tastes like poi. You'd probably like it. I know the other rats do."

Both oddjobs started forward, their fists clenched.

"Kulikuli!" a stern Wally said, demanding their silence. The two men stood down. Wally straightened his tie. "We've had a friendly arrangement so far, Trout. I get the fight I want, you get what you want. Lose the insults. A confrontation here does no one any good."

"Then muzzle your goons, or we might not make it that far."

"They'll behave," Wally said. "Starting now. What else needs to be done?"

"We're still cleaning out the space below us. My guys will be here tomorrow, scrubbing then vacuuming up whatever the hell is down there."

"What's above this floor?"

"Five empty levels, ready for the implosion. Still a few weeks away."

Philo led Wally around the perimeter. Wally wandered to the far end of the floor, Philo following, the hanging black tarp just outside their reach. Here, the rusted iron safety bars between the columns connected them horizontally along this side of the building, the tarp pushing in like heavy drapes in the wind.

"What's outside here?" Wally asked.

Philo retrieved a pocketknife and cut out a flap head-high. He used a discarded metal rod to lift the flap so they could see outside, into the night. "The Camden skyline."

Across the river, Camden's city lights flickered, shimmering off the calm of the water separating the two cities. "Directly below this side of the building"—he and Wally leaned over and looked down, the sound of lapping water against pilings thirty feet below providing the only hint, the dark revealing little—"is the Delaware."

* * *

They returned to their cars. Wally explained the fight's financials.

"So we have no misunderstanding"—Wally nodded in Oddjob Number 1's direction— "my associate here will hold the purse. I'm doing this for your own protection, Trout, considering what happened at our last fight. This part of the arrangement is non-negotiable."

"Go for it, Wally. It's your money. For now." This way, if the money disappeared, Philo wouldn't be held responsible. No need having more crazies with guns and grudges and long memories after his ass.

"Good. Wonderful. So let me share some news with you. I've increased the purse to seventy-five grand. I'm feeling benevolent toward my fighter. Tonka ships out next week, to one of your old haunts, Afghanistan. I want him and his family to know how much I appreciate his patriotism."

Philo ignored the bias toward the fight's presumed outcome, instead addressed what he just learned. "So he's in the military."

"A newly minted Ranger. Special forces. After the fight maybe you guys can swap stories. The increased purse also reflects late betting my organization is holding on the fight. You apparently made some enemies overseas. The Middle East, Afghanistan and Pakistan."

Wally paused to let that sink in for Philo. "I took the bets," Wally added, "but trust me when I say I wish you no harm from any nefarious forces, before or after the fight. During the fight, heh, a different story, of course. I might add that you're a seven-to-one underdog. In case you want to lay any money on yourself."

"The seventy-five-grand purse will be enough," Philo said. "Tell me about the rest of our agreement. The transplants?"

"Ah yes, the two lungs." Wally looked north, at twinkling city lights on the horizon. "The logistics are worked out. The surgery will be at a new emergency care walk-in facility in Old City that my doctors will shut down for a night; they own the place. We'll have an ambulance pick her up, they'll get an I-V started and make her relaxed and comfortable. She'll think she's on the surgery floor of a major hospital."

Philo wasn't convinced. "She needs to be sure this is the real deal, Wally. That the organs are coming from a legitimate donor, not the black market. When they pick her up and transport her into the operating room, no matter how out of it they think she is, there can be no mention of the surgery being anything other than one hundred percent above-board and on the books. The doctors, the nurses, the facility—you can*not* fuck this up, or she'll try to stop it."

Wally puffed up, got chest-to-chest with Philo. "Hear me good, Trout. I owe you nothing—not one fucking thing—other than guaranteeing the purse and the two lungs, and a best effort in relocating them to your friend's diseased chest, but I went one better.

"My guys worked out her post-op care; it'll be at an accredited hospital. One of my doctors is the chief administrator; he'll get her admitted. Who can resist a patient in need of medical care, hmm? The professionals I have at my disposal—with gambling debts, med school loans, drug addictions, hefty divorce settlements—they all owe me. They're paid handsomely under the table, no taxes, and no chance of malpractice suits. They're top notch, including the Latino ones with south-of-the-border credentials, who are our face to the Hispanic base."

Philo heard *Hispanic*; on went a light bulb. "Andelmo. You've got Andelmo. That bastard's facing an indictment."

"Dr. Andelmo is an excellent transplant surgeon whose reputation has, unfortunately for all of us, taken a hit lately. He's highly respected in the Latino community. But lucky for me he does have a significant gambling problem. I will betray no other confidences."

"No. Not Andelmo. Get someone else to do the surgery. She'd never forgive me."

"I'll take your request under advisement, Trout, and get you the name of a different doctor to pass along to her if needed, but it's not your call, now is it? Let's move on. I have your friend's husband's name and his phone number. He needs to stay on call the night of the fight, and he should expect a message from a Mr. Smith. We'll begin prepping her organ donor shortly thereafter."

"These are lungs," Philo said, puzzled. "We're talking about someone who'd need to be dead or on his deathbed at that point. How fucking far *is* your reach?"

"If I say the organs will be ready, they will be ready, soon as your friend's anesthetized head hits the pillow. And just before your unconscious head hits the floor."

"You can't know when two lungs—" Philo stopped himself. "Christ, you ruthless fucks. You're preselecting innocent donors and croaking them."

"You insult me, Trout. If I didn't need you to stand in front of my fighter on Saturday night and take a beating, I'd have my guys take you apart right here. Let me be clear about this business. I deliver on my promises. Recruiters, transporters, hospital and clinic staff...These transplants happen every day, with middlemen, buyers, even banks that store the organs. I pay my donors what I say I'm going to pay them, then I send them home alive. We might, occasionally, have a problem finding appropriate donors to fill orders. When that happens we get aggressive, but only with someone who deserves it. The deaths you learned about during those transplant surgeries weren't planned, they were simply unfortunate.

"You should focus your concern on your friend, the recipient. I'm happy to say our doctors haven't lost a transplant recipient on the table yet. See you Saturday, Trout."

32

Kaipo and Mr. Lanakai—Wally—didn't have sex that night, in Atlantic City or elsewhere. Dinner, the boxing match, gambling...Wally made a late-night pitch, but she'd helped him remain a gentleman by intimating that their next date, the bare-knuckles fight, might get him what he wanted. In the past week he'd sent her flowers twice.

An admission to herself: Wally Lanakai, older, powerful mob godfather, successful businessman, wasn't doing it for her, but his fighter Tonka Omanopa might.

She'd gone through the motions during her first appointment today, a massage, her client the divorced wife of an insurance exec. She finished up, was now at her second appointment in, as coincidence would have it, the same Center City high-rise—the first appointment's ex-husband's separate digs. Some personal training with him in his home gym, then a deep muscle massage.

Bare asses, oftentimes bare tops, and occasional peeks at bare genitals: she'd gotten offers from both sexes for certain intimacies, had declined them all, because she knew bedding a client ultimately meant losing a client. And in the high-end client circles she inhabited, word traveled fast, and large chunks of business could disappear as quickly as two thumbs could key a text or post a picture.

She kneaded the ex-husband's lower back, his bare buttocks covered by a towel.

Her mind wandered, to Tonka. What did he look like under that tight suit? No doubt spectacular, top, middle, bottom...

"Ah, miss?"

The voice startled her. It was her client, sprawled on his stomach beneath her open-legged straddle as she worked his lower back. "Yes? What is it?"

He lifted himself to an elbow, raising his head from the face cushion. "You seem to be, how do I put it, grinding a bit against my butt. I'm flattered, but like we agreed, let's keep this professional, shall we?"

"Oh. Sorry. My mind is, er, elsewhere, sir. So sorry."

"No problem," he said, smiling. He tucked his face back into the cushion. "Whoever he is, he's a lucky guy."

Her interests in seeing the Saturday night fight, when being honest with herself, were, in order of importance: One, Tonka. She hadn't been with a man that way in some time, would like to get to know him better. He'd awakened an appetite, had gotten her motor going.

Two, the Blessid Trauma owner Philo Trout, now truly a curiosity. Crime scene cleaner by day, pseudo–Fight Club participant by night. Another man with a secret. Maybe they could talk shop.

Three, the Hawaiian kid Patrick Stakes. No idea if young Mr. Stakes would be in attendance at the fight, but her intuition said he might. Someone on the outside, an innocent bystander who was a witness to her true avocation. Not a healthy situation, for Kaipo or for him.

Dead last was Wally Lanakai. Poor, heart-struck Wally, a middle-aged mobster who remained patient with Kaipo's coyness. The man held her financial wellbeing in his hands; her connection to well-to-do clients like Mr. Insurance Executive here. Adding to this was his organization's continued interest in her sobriety, except to date they'd had a too protective, too over-the-top way of showing it.

While she packed up, she addressed her massage client. "You were a perfect gentleman today, sir, and I apologize again for where my mind was earlier."

"No apologies needed. You did a fantastic job. I'll pass that along, nothing more, to people I know. And to people who know you."

Meaning star-crossed Wally, still not much more than an afterthought romantically, yet more dangerous than the other three fight-night interests combined.

33

Friday morning at sun up the Blessid Trauma step van arrived at the foot of the grain elevator, the building appearing older and closer to death to Philo today, almost pleading with him to please put it out of its misery. Its demise would happen soon enough. Next week at this time, it would be gone.

Patrick and Miñoso pushed open the van's rear doors and climbed out, hazmated in blue from the neck down, their masks and head gear in their hands. The two crime scene astronauts moved slowly, deliberately, readying themselves for their trek into the belly of the beast, this time for more than recon. Philo got out of the van and climbed into his blue bio-suit while he spoke. His guys started unloading their equipment.

"We have one job, and one job only today, gentlemen, with overflow into tomorrow morning if we need it. After we finish cleaning out the hole, this job is done, fini, adios, this eyesore all set for its sendoff next week. Let's finish early enough today so we can crack open some cold ones this afternoon and celebrate."

The "hole" was the pit below the first floor. The Blessid team needed to scrub the pit's walls, vacuum up the remaining moisture and grain, then shovel out the few inches of silt-laden sediment the internal mini-ecosystem had survived on for decades.

Patrick, his mask off, his crime-scene game face on, lifted an institu-

tional-size shop vac onto a wheeled cart, then returned to the van for additional supplies. Miñoso picked up a second shop vac and put it on the cart,
next to the first. Miñoso addressed Philo.

"Boss?"

"'Sup, Miñoso?"

"You still have work for me tomorrow night here too, yes?"

The fight. Miñoso was playing coy around Patrick. As far as Philo knew,
Miñoso had kept his word, with no mention of any such event to anyone.
"Sure do. There a problem?"

"Si, señor, yes. I cannot make it."

"Why? What's going on?"

"My uncle, Tío Diego, his cuerpo—body—tomorrow night I must make
the final payment so I can send him and his things home to Mexico. I am
sorry, Señor Philo, but I cannot help you tomorrow. Please forgive me."

"You can't get your uncle and his stuff squared away some other night?"

"No, Señor Philo. Is necessary tomorrow night."

Well, this was a fine kettle of fish. "Sorry to hear that, Miñoso. I was
counting on you."

But in reality, no one could be of help to him tomorrow night. In bare-
knuckles boxing there were no corner men, no cut men. No ring corners,
period, where stools could be slapped down onto the canvas for a fighter to
rest between rounds, because there was no canvas and there were no
rounds. Once the fight started, it would go until one man was unable to
continue, over with one punch or with a flurry of them. No gate, all side
bets, and one promoter who collected bets via the underground, same as
running numbers. Word of mouth, email, twitter, even wire transfers to
overseas accounts. The fighters themselves didn't care how the money was
made, only that there was a winner-take-all purse that was worth the
effort.

Patrick spoke up. "Sir, I can do it."

Something, a knowing glance, passed between Patrick and Miñoso.
"You have a fight tomorrow night, sir," Patrick said. "I can be here for it."

So much for secrecy. Philo scowled. "Miñoso, damn it, I told you—"

"Not his fault, sir," Patrick said. "You and Miñoso been training at Joe
Frazier's Gym after work. I seen you both there a coupla nights, from the

bus. I forget stuff, but I'm not stupid. I asked him about it. He didn't want you to be at the fight without friends, so he told me."

The one friend Philo wanted to attend more than anyone was Hump Fargas, but he was in a bad way. His ALS had limited his participation during Philo and Miñoso's time at the gym, his appearance at the fight out of the question; Miñoso would have been a good surrogate. Such had been the plan.

Damn it; Philo would still try to control what he could. "You do *not* tell Grace about the fight, Patrick. Do we have a deal?"

"Not telling nobody, sir. Deal."

Cold and crude and dungeon-like, the forty-by-forty footprint inside the grain elevator below ground level smelled as ripe as the fish stands and seafood restaurants at the South Philly Italian market in August. Patrick stood at the bottom of an aluminum extension ladder in heavy-duty work boots. He switched on a twelve-volt lantern, one of six Philo had tossed him.

"Sir?'

"You, Patrick?"

"It's beautiful, sir."

"How's that, Patrick?"

"The wood in the ceiling, sir. It's like, really cool."

"So I've heard."

Reclaimed grain silo wood, forty square feet of it, layered most of the ceiling, a mosaic of inlaid planks and timbers salvaged from the Tidewater Company's ill-fated other local grain elevator and screwed into place here. A nostalgia thing for the company, plus it was valuable. When doing the bid Philo thought the ceiling was a morbid way to commemorate the grain company's black eye of sixty years past, then he learned it was worth some coin when his cleaning contract was adjusted to reflect that no harm come to it. A Philly architect won the bid for the wood. It would be removed next week, after they made the pit more inhabitable.

"Kind of looks like jellyfish got caught up in it while it cured, huh, Patrick?"

"Yeah."

The wear patterns stretching across the grayed planks were captivating, smooth and naturally polished by the grain with subtle, swirling indentations and slight discolorations in the worn wood, the patterns spreading in all directions like wheat waving in the wind. After Philo learned of the contract change, it took less imagination to see the wood's charm.

"We stay away from the ceiling, fellas, got that? Do *not* clean the ceiling."

Patrick left the lantern near the ladder, headed into a corner where he'd place another lantern on the moldy floor, then did likewise with the others. He called up the ladder to Philo.

"Need another lantern, sir." Lantern number six hadn't cooperated, would not switch on, was either defective or the battery was toast. Philo tossed him a replacement, then a few extras.

"It's not too bad down here, sir," Patrick hollered from another corner. "'Bout the same as before. Soon as the lanterns went on, everything on the floor scattered. Except the dead stuff. Don't know where the live ones went, sir."

Philo got into a crouch and returned the holler. "Be careful, Patrick. Survival of the fittest, son. Stomp first, ask questions later."

Miñoso and Philo lowered one shop vac on a flat piece of plywood with ropes, then the second. Next came shovels, push brooms, scrubbing brushes, bottles of detergent, a box of red hazmat bags and a pair of snake-grabber tongs, plus a tensioned-top wooden box to contain any live prey they'd need to capture. Miñoso climbed down into the pit to join Patrick.

This was heavy, sweaty, arm-weary work, their power-washing and scrubbing removing decades of dust that, once disturbed, formed a mist head-high around them that also floated into the shafts of sunlight the opening to the floor above provided, their filtering masks earning their keep against it. After hours of tedious, sloppy work, with more than a hundred buckets of dirt and dust destined for the trash truck, and a rat bite that ripped Patrick's Tyvek suit above his ankle, the space was soon scrubbed raw top to bottom, the ceiling off-limits. No moisture, no debris, no leftover grain.

"No more food source for that rat, Patrick," Philo said once they were topside, "other than you guys. Did the bite break the skin?"

"A mouthful of Tyvek and sock only, sir."

The three men were exhausted. They reloaded the van, Philo checking off each item and tool as they returned it. "Shop vac one, shop vac two. Broom one, broom two. Lantern, lantern...how many lanterns, Patrick?"

"Seven. No, eight, sir. Eight."

"You sure?"

"...six, seven, eight. Eight, sir. We have eight."

"Eight's a good number then. Get back up here so we can drink some beer. I'm giving us the rest of the afternoon off."

They sipped their beers outside on beach chairs. Miñoso, teary-eyed, clinked a bottle with Philo. "Señor Philo, it has been an honor helping you train for your fight. Please, señor, to take care of yourself."

It wasn't only what he said, it was how he said it, with a hint of *don't ever forget me.*

"Miñoso, this better not be the last I see of you. There's more work if you want it."

"Si, Philo. If I survive what I must do to get Uncle Diego home and return to the US, we shall see. Gracias, for everything."

34

At ten thirty p.m. on fight night, the view from the third floor of the grain elevator showed nothing moving on the buckled wasteland that stretched a half mile in three directions. Adjacent to and south of the building, the fourth direction, it was all Delaware River. A single length of jobsite lighting shone dull against the ceiling, enough light to find one's way to and from the stairs. Two metal rods drilled into the cinder-blocked window frame separated Philo from a thirty-foot drop into the river. He stood shadowboxing in front of the empty window, the alcove deeply inset. His hooded sweatshirt covered half his face and hung loosely over his upper torso. Underneath, a snug camouflage tee was tucked into worn jeans— "the clothes that brought him here"—the jeans too long for his six-two frame, their pant legs bunched up against his black Nikes.

He sucked in the crisp night air, exhaled it with each thrown combination. The temperature was in the mid-forties and forecasted to stay there overnight.

Feel the punch. Start it in your heels, let the energy gather as it travels up through your calves, your thighs, your chest...

This was the calm before the storm, and Philo used it to work up a sweat. Patrick exited the spiral stairs and crossed the room. Philo continued throwing his fists with bad intentions.

"The two generators outside are on now, sir."

"Thanks, Patrick."

"You look good, sir. Glad I'm here for this, sir."

Obliging cops had decided to fight crime elsewhere in this district tonight, except for the few who Wally said would be in attendance. Outside of Patrick, the only people Philo expected to see from his side of the fight equation were drunks he knew from the local Northeast Philly bars. If they showed, they'd be surprised to learn the guy who'd been buying them shots for weeks so they could drink to the fight that would showcase a favorite son—someone none of them knew personally—was actually one of the combatants. Philo expected four or five of these barflies to attend, maybe a few Center City drinkers as well. The rest of the spectators would be cheering for the other side.

A pair of headlights entered the serpentine trail, bobbing in and out of sight behind the junk piles before the vehicle, a taxi, circled in close to the front of the condemned building. The rear door opened and someone stumbled out, hitting the dirt hard but landing on his hands and knees. A cab driver with a turban hustled to the guy's side, helped him stand, and brushed him off while the man paid his fare. This was something you didn't see every day, Philo thought: a cabbie helping a drunk to his feet.

Hold on. It wasn't a drunk.

Philo flew down the stairs, was at ground level and outside the building in seconds, loping up to the taxi. He tucked a twenty into the cabbie's hand, something that took the hack by surprise.

"Already collected the fare," the Sikh cabbie said.

"I know. Just wait a minute. He's not staying."

Philo draped his arm around the taxi passenger. "Hump. You're sick, dude. I appreciate your enthusiasm, I really do, but you need to get right the hell back into this cab."

"Ain't gonna happen, Philo. No way I'm gonna miss this. Just get me inside and I'll be fine."

"Hump—"

"Find me a chair and a beer, not necessarily in that order." Hump looked skyward, at the clear, cloudless cosmos packed with black and white magnificence in what appeared to be almost equal portions. A starry, starry night. "A night this beautiful, watching a sport I love—I've died and gone to heaven. I ain't leaving unless it's on a stretcher. Now, if you'll excuse me, beer and a chair."

Philo turned to speak to the cabbie, his arm still around Hump. "You can go, he's going to stay awhile. Keep the money."

Philo introduced Patrick to Hump, then directed Patrick to grab the cooler from the unmarked Blessid Trauma Econoline and follow them inside. "No chairs in here, Hump, you should know that, but Patrick's got a cooler full of beer you can sit on. Covers you on both counts."

The two of them navigated the uneven terrain into the building, Patrick following. Philo peeked past Patrick at headlights in the distance twisting their way across the landscape. Other fight spectators were starting to arrive.

* * *

"Rough out here, boss," the driver said. It was a little past eleven p.m. "Your suspension's taking a beating."

"The biggest illegal bare-knuckle fight ever arranged," Wally said from the back seat, "and you're worried about my SUV. It's a fucking Range Rover. They'll be using these things when we get to Mars. Shut up and try to miss one or two of the potholes. Excuse my profanity, Kaipo."

The man murdered people for a living and here he was worried about her virgin ears; comical, Kaipo thought. Wally, Kaipo, and Tonka, belted in across the SUV's rear bench seat, gripped their armrests as the all-terrain tires crested and fell. Fanning out from the building were thirty-plus parked cars and motorcycles plus a few airport limos. Wally beamed, thrilled at the turnout.

At the building entrance the shotgun passenger, the other half of Wally's bodyguard muscle, hustled out to remove a traffic cone for their reserved parking directly in front; they were arriving fashionably late. Kaipo accepted Wally's extended hand as she climbed out, looking smart and curvy in tight jeans and wearing flats. Tonka exited the other rear door.

"What's on the other side of the building, boss?" Tonka said, stretching.

"The Delaware River."

"Cool. You know if he swims?"

"Who?"

"Trout."

"He was in the navy, Tonka, so I imagine yes. Why?"

"Probably doesn't matter. If he ends up in the water, he'll already be unconscious." He eyed Kaipo, puffed out his chest a little. "Don't worry, Kaipo, I'll rescue him."

Kaipo's attraction to him was waning; cocky guys didn't usually do it for her. Still, the man was a gorgeous physical specimen, and that counted for something. Regardless—

"If you don't pull him out," she said, "I will. No one needs to die here tonight, right, Wally?"

"Philo's got a mouth on him but sure, why not, no one needs to die. Tonka, remember, this is boxing, not UFC, and certainly not an execution. It'll be the Queen's rules for the most part. Just knock him out so we can all relax and go home early. Let's get inside."

* * *

The gas generators thrummed outside the hollowed shell of a building that was once a grain elevator. Inside, Hump had his ass planted on his beer cooler seat while he held court with a semicircle of new friends in what Philo considered his corner of the floor, just inside the breezy tarp. These new friends were serious drinkers who had left their bar haunts earlier than usual tonight, to see the fight. Philo gestured for them to make him a path; the small group parted. He sat next to Hump on the cooler.

"Miñoso here yet?" Hump asked.

"Miñoso bailed," Philo said, pushing his hood off his head. He ran his hand through his sweaty rooster-comb hair. "Something about shipping his uncle's body."

"Not sure how he'll manage that. He has no money."

"What can I say. That's the reason he gave me."

"He also tell you he's quitting boxing? Told me that today."

A surprise to Philo. "The kid's good, Hump, got some real skills, and he can take a punch. You should try to talk him out of it."

"His mind's made up; he said he's done. Doesn't wanna chance any more kidney shots. You ready to go, Champ?"

"I believe I am, Hump. I'm feeling good."

"Great. Not hung over or nothing? These boys here said you been getting them all liquored up lately up there in the Northeast, listening to them talk about the fight. Hope you ain't been drinking or carousing during training."

"Broke up with my girlfriend. I've had a beer here and there, but my serious drinking money went to these guys," he said, a thumb in their direction, jonesing for a partisan response. Heads bobbed and cheeky smiles emerged, punctuated with multiple raised beers and thank-yous and woots.

"Truth is, Hump, the adrenaline rush from the hype—I've missed it. With them all talking about how their local phenom barnstormed the country years ago, laying guys out, I loved hearing about it. I loved being their champ, their kid from the neighborhood. I also got to hear the old timers talk about..." he paused, composed himself, "how proud the old man was of him, the kid getting it done back then, no gangs, no involvement with any bad actors, no crime. Like I said, a good kid back then, his dad real proud of him."

"Damn straight he was a good kid."

"Until he turned twenty-one."

"Philo—"

"Women, drugs, cars. Burglaries, beat-downs, gambling, and scams. The old man kicked him out. Then the old man died. He never saw his son with his life turned around."

"Look, Philo—"

"Hear me out, Hump. When I went bad, Chuckie followed. It wasn't the other way around like everyone thought. That last fight...taking the purse was my idea, not Chuckie's. The plan was for him to bolt with the money while I stayed local, for a while at least, no one the wiser. But like Mike Tyson said, everyone has a plan until they get punched in the face. When 9-11 hit and my old man died, nothing mattered anymore.

"This kid"—Philo gulped in air, breathing out the sentimentality—"he still seeks absolution. He's got a steamer trunk full of the old man's things from dubya-dubya-two, from when his father joined the navy same age as he did.

"I finally got past the trunk's medals and the flag and the Pearl Harbor news clippings, and my old man's navy officer whites. Checked the whole damn thing out. Painful as hell, because I didn't find any forgiveness in there, only common ground: war, and hate, and violence.

"I'm so sorry you lost Chuckie, Hump. Sorry I put him up to it. Sorry I was a shit and let him take all the blame. Sorry for all of it."

"You finished? Do I get to talk now?" Hump dropped a hand onto Philo's shoulder and squeezed. "I knew all that shit, Philo. I knew it wasn't my Chuckie's idea. Chuckie wasn't smart enough; it had to be you. And I was tickled pink as a pussy hearing afterward that you had enlisted. It was the only way out of that fight scam alive, me praying for you every night, hoping you'd stay that way after your deployment.

"So now, *right* now, this kid needs to forgive himself. And if he wants to get this old man's absolution, he needs to get violent and knock one more fucker out." Hump nonchalanted a head-point. "That one, over there."

On the other side of the floor, Wally Lanakai and the tall, put-together dude who had Hump's interest entered the room together, as did an attractive raven-haired woman on Wally's arm.

Patrick, also in jeans and a hoodie, waded through the crowd. He arrived alongside Hump and Philo, then pointed back across the room. "That's her, sir."

Philo squinted at the woman with Wally, then at Patrick, not understanding.

"The airline lady, sir. The cleaner. Over there, with those guys, sir."

Philo was now curious. "How about that. I best go introduce myself."

He threaded his way through the spectators, the room quieting, then going fully silent when he arrived.

"Wally," he said, "you're late." He looked sideways at the dude who'd entered with him. "Having trouble getting your guy to show, so you brought this guy instead?"

"That's funny, Trout, really. Hilarious. So finally, our day of reckoning," Wally said after their quick handshake. He dropped a hand onto his fighter's shoulder, had to stretch a little to do it, and said, beaming, "Mr. Trout, I want you to meet—"

"Hello, miss." Philo ignored Wally, instead extended a hand to the woman. "I'm Philo Trout. A pleasure to meet you. You are?"

"None of your goddamn business is who she is, cabin boy," Wally's fighter said, stepping up.

"Wasn't talking to you, sport, I was talking to the lady here. Your name, miss?"

Philo already knew her dark secret; what he wanted was her identity. Pissing off Wally's fighter was simply the icing.

She didn't respond, didn't flinch, didn't even blink, instead stayed completely deadpan during their eye contact. Very smart. But her exchanged stare said *yes, I'm who you think I am, the one who outed Patrick's ethnicity.*

The reaction he wasn't prepared for was Wally's, so quick to show his gun in a holster tucked into his waist. "Back—the hell—off, Trout. She's with me is all you need to know." Wally remained all flash and no draw, but his two goblins reacted, bookending Philo; Wally waved them off.

"It's better if we stay on script and you meet my fighter now, before he tries to take your head off where you stand." Wally composed himself for the greeting. "Philo Trout, this is Tonka Omanopa."

Philo sized Tonka up, impressed but trying not to show it. "Army, right?"

"Rangers."

This, right here, was the part that had always taken the most out of Philo, faking niceties to his opponents. "A proud group deserving of respect. I thank you for your service."

There. Being nice wasn't so bad. Then again, hell, maybe a little jab between Armed Services wouldn't hurt. "Semper fi, Ranger."

Tonka's eyes narrowed. "That's the Marines, bozo."

"Right. Sorry," Philo said, smiling, his patience fading. "All you SEAL wannabes look alike."

Tonka erupted, his chest inflating under a jacket he discarded in Wally's face. He lurched, was stopped by a husky black man with a bouncer's physique who inserted himself between them. "Calm down, fella, he's just fucking with you," the peacekeeper said, his hand on Tonka's chest. "You'll get your chance in a minute."

Wally introduced the bouncer-type as the referee for their match, a guy big enough to get the job done. He separated the two men and directed the crowd to move behind the yellow tape on the floor.

The standing-room crowd swelled, larger than expected. The first floor of the grain elevator space was warming up, starting to rock in anticipation.

Philo motioned to the ref. "I need a moment with Mr. Lanakai."

Wally nodded his okay, waved Philo forward.

"Tell me the where and the when of our other arrangement," Philo said.

"Her surgery's at a walk-in facility in Old City, fifteen minutes from here. A new place; won't open for a few weeks." He leaned in. "She's already there getting prepped. No issues, Trout, she's in good hands. Take care of your end of the deal here and it's all good. After the first punch"—he removed his phone from his jacket and gestured with it—"surgery will begin."

"Fine. Who's got the purse?"

"You mean Tonka's pay for the night? Heh. No worries, it's secure. Nice little stunt, the semper fi comment. Tonka's pissed."

"Yeah, well, what the hell. Some fights are lost before the bell rings. Your boy's gotta learn the head games, too."

Wally smiled. "You're not such a bad guy, Philo. You ever want to continue this craziness after tonight, let me know. Tonka could use someone to spar with."

"I doubt he'll want it to be me," Philo said. "I'll always be his 'and one.'"

"His 'and one?' Sorry, what's an 'and one'?"

"It's something else he'll need to get used to after tonight, Wally. Whatever wins he racks up the rest of his bare-knuckling days, after tonight they'll always be followed by 'and one.' His only loss—to me. Now if you'll excuse me, I'm heading to my corner so we can get this exhibition started."

Philo arrived alongside Hump, who was quick to comment. "Tell me, we the only ones in here without guns?"

"Guess I didn't think that one through, Hump. Mine's in the van."

Philo stripped down to his camo tee shirt, jeans and sneakers. Thirty feet away Tonka stood square-shouldered in high-top boxing shoes and sweatpants, bronzed and bare from the waist up, looking young and fresh as a poi-fed baby, if babies had twenty-inch biceps and iron abs and multiple tattoos.

"He took off his shirt," Hump said.

"And your point is what, Hump?"

"Christ, look how big he is. You gotta take your shirt off too, Philo. Show him you're not intimidated."

"I'm not, and I won't. He's only ten pounds bigger than me. You've seen me fight guys bigger than him before."

Hump shook his head, then feebly shook Philo's hand. "That was fifteen years ago. And all ten of those pounds are in his arms. Protect yourself, Philo. Oh, and try not to suck."

"Appreciate the vote of confidence, Hump."

"Sir?"

"What is it, Patrick?"

"Don't hurt him too bad, sir."

Philo wrapped his hand around the back of Patrick's neck and pulled him into an embrace, the two of them forehead-to-forehead. "Thanks, Patrick. If it can be helped, bud, I won't hurt him. But one of us might get his wits scrambled tonight. I just want to make sure it isn't me."

"Gentlemen," the referee called, "over here please. A few words, then we'll get started."

Tonka went for the tough-guy stare at his shorter opponent while the ref spoke. Philo countered with his less serious and inconvenienced, smirky malcontent face. Mind games, always. Many in the crowd had their phones raised, filming the exchange, would keep them raised throughout the fight. Bare-knuckle boxing and YouTube, fast friends for years.

"No rounds, gentlemen, therefore no bell. The rest of the Queen's rules apply. I tell you to break your clinch, you break it. The fight goes for as long as you can both continue. Let's get started."

The next instruction was something Philo had heard sixty-four times before, a bare-knuckle boxing directive as familiar to him as the pro boxing catchphrase *"Let's get ready to rum-bullll—"*

"Fellas," the ref said, "bring your toes to the line."

35

Olivier's first call dispatched a private ambulance. His second call was to Hank.

"Mr. Blessid? Mr. Smith. A donor's been identified. They'll do some tests to make sure there's a match. Your wife needs to be ready in ten minutes."

Hank grabbed Grace's portable oxygen and her suitcase. "Grace, there's a donor, honey. Time to go to the hospital."

"Where?" she said, dropping her tired frame into her wheelchair.

"Old City."

"What's the donor's name?"

They were past discussing the arrangement's particulars. Hank had trampled through her objections one night over a dinner Grace couldn't eat. She was too weak physically and emotionally to argue, and yet they'd continued playing their roles, Hank the adoring subservient husband, Grace the indignant, self-righteous wife. But as the end drew near, she relaxed her stand, willing to trust her husband. She wanted the name of the donor for one reason: as a Catholic, it was so she could pray for this person's soul.

"Not available yet, honey, but I'll get a name soon."

"Thank you, doll."

"Love you so much, Grace."

"Back at you, loverboy."

Once Hank and Grace were in the ambulance, an attendant started her drip.

* * *

A nurse handed Dr. Andelmo his phone, so he could take a call. "Yes...? Thank you." He handed the phone back and addressed his team. "It is a go."

The facility was the entire first floor of an Old City low-rise, its prior life a low-income dental clinic, the waiting room converted for tonight only into an operating room complete with a heart-lung machine. The team would need to work all night; the procedure could take up to twelve hours. Ka Hui had promised Dr. Andelmo that after tonight, his gambling debt would be settled in its totality. Not that they were giving him any real choice.

The doctor hovered over his mildly sedated patient, addressing his team of four nurses, anesthesiologist, and two other surgeons, one his gambling buddy Dr. Barry Heinzman. "We now wait for her donor's prep." He searched the faces of the people standing inside the glassed-in reception area, then spoke to them, raising his voice. "We'll strap her in and ready her for general anesthesia. Let me know when the donor gets here."

Mr. Smith tapped on the glass separating the waiting room from the medical team. "The donor's here, Doctor," he said, projecting his voice. "The organs will be available shortly."

As an onlooker, Hank listened alongside Mr. Smith, nervously observing his supine wife surrounded by this group of medical professionals who, he'd accepted, were each beholden to a group of clandestine mobsters. This didn't make them bad doctors and nurses, just bad gamblers, maybe guilty of other victimless sins as well. Mr. Smith had a few cautionary words for Hank, delivered while Mr. Smith took repeated tobacco dust hits from his snuffbox.

"What you are about to witness—this massive medical endeavor, and the professionals it will take to execute it, all assembled here before you—

none of this can *ever* be divulged to anyone under any circumstance. You must agree to comply. Otherwise, Mr. Blessid, we will find you, and your wife, and render this procedure moot. Do you understand?"

"I'm on board," Hank said, "and I'm grateful. Just get it done."

A nurse closed a Velcro cuff around Grace's left wrist. They moved to her other arm and laid it straight so they could press it into place inside the second cuff. She suddenly pulled away from their grip and clamped her hand onto the surgeon's wrist.

Hank stiffened, took a step toward the door to the operating room. Mr. Smith grabbed his forearm. "Sterile environment, Mr. Blessid, you can't go in there."

"My wife—she needs more sedation..."

Grace's shaking hand moved to Dr. Andelmo's shoulder, gripping his scrubs and pulling him down, closer to her face. She snagged his mask in her groping fingers and yanked it off.

"An-mel-mo?" she said, slurring her syllables. "You're that crooked doctor. Hank! HANK—"

Hank shook loose from Mr. Smith but was quickly subdued, held against a wall by a large man while he continued to struggle. Mr. Smith spoke to him in a soothing tone: "Please, Mr. Blessid, relax. It's okay, we're on it, it's under control."

Hank watched from behind the cajoling Mr. Smith as another doctor leaned in to listen to Grace, calming her with a gentle hand to her shoulder while the anesthesiologist tinkered with her drip. The hovering doctor straightened up and exchanged words with Dr. Andelmo. Andelmo glared, turning his bluster away from the patient to settle on Mr. Smith, behind the glass. Mr. Smith shrugged; it was not the vote of confidence the doctor wanted. Andelmo slammed his scalpel onto the tray, rattling other instruments, then stormed out of the operating room. Additional calming words from the second doctor got Grace's attention, settling her.

Mr. Smith wrested Hank from the men restraining him. "I will need to have a word with Dr. Andelmo, then I do need to leave. A different doctor will perform the surgery. If you behave, you can stay in this room and watch. My colleague here will keep you company."

* * *

Tonka Omanopa, twenty-five, was taller, darker, and prettier than Philo, and no doubt a favorite with the ladies. But akin to Philo he was also blessed with a long reach and large, quick hands, and rumored per Wally to have a facial structure of muscle and bone tough enough to survive a gorilla swinging a two-by-four.

They circled each other in the middle of the floor, fists raised, the crowd quiet, as keen to their movements as each fighter was to the other's, both flatfooted and with no bounce; a precursor to a slugfest. A slugfest wasn't Philo's game. He relied on crippling body blows leveraging snapping punches with pinpoint accuracy to the temple or the chin.

Tonka waded in, started loading up and releasing. Straight rights to the cheek and chin that Philo slipped, left and right hooks to his forearms and biceps, some blows glancing, others connecting. The kid could punch; Philo couldn't let his head or chest be on the receiving end of any of it. Philo opened his hands, started blocking the shots with his palms, standard bare-knuckles defense, did some back-pedaling...

Tonka lowered his head and bent himself at the waist, tucking his chin inside his big fists, his face now waist-high, his temples protected, the top of his head exposed while standing directly in front of Philo, an invitation for Philo to—

Go ahead, straight-arm a few shots, right at the top of my head here, on the button, I dare you.

It was enticing, his beautiful moussed curls right there in front of him, waiting for Philo to club him into submission, except there was nothing but skull underneath, pure bone, and skull shots in bare-knuckles boxing produced broken fingers.

"Straighten the fuck up, asshole," Philo said, pulling back.

Tonka smiled from underneath, started to rise, then sprang forward with a left hook that whizzed by Philo's chin. Philo stepped in quickly and released a fisted uppercut square on the chin that lifted Tonka off the floor. No mouth guard meant a mouthful of blood and, more often than not, an unconscious opponent.

"Ouch," Tonka said, smiling, and spit out some blood. He moved back in front of Philo.

Fuck, Philo thought, *that shot—it could have dropped a hippo...*

Then, three minutes into the bout, after a flurry of heavy hands by them both, Philo's breath suddenly left him, his chest air emptied by a Tonka punch to the solar plexus, followed by an overhand right he never saw. Philo kissed the cold, hard, cement floor.

* * *

Hank, behind glass, keyed on Grace's breathing while watching the doctors put her under. Her next shallow breath didn't come, was replaced by a shudder; Hank lurched at the window. The anesthesiologist gestured for him to settle down. He focused on his patient again then gave Hank a thumbs-up: *you wife's fine, she's now in dreamland.*

* * *

A first time for everything: the shot to the chest stole Philo's breath, a phantom right hand had dropped him. The partisan crowd erupted, bouncing, hooting, and pumping their fists. From Philo's vantage point, his cheek against the cold floor, the spectator pandemonium was of little consequence save for puffs of dust coaxed from the pit underneath by the weight of maybe sixty bouncing, boisterous fight fans, the particles rising through a seam in the concrete.

"...six, seven, EIGHT," the ref called. Philo got to a knee then to his feet, the ref moving into his face, finishing the count with "and...up at nine. What's your name, son?"

His breath was back but he was light-headed. "Joe Frazier." His lips danced with the words, he was delighted he'd said them, oh how witty he was, the count still resonating in his fuzzy head, *"six, seven, eight, and up at nine..."*

"No fucking around, son. Tell me your name or it's over."

...eight maids a milking...

...nine ladies dancing...

"Philo Trout."

...eight days a week, nine angry men...

...nine lives...

"That's better. You good to go, Philo Trout?"

Nine lanterns, one more than eight.

There'd been nine lanterns in the pit, not eight, damn it—

Fuck.

"Start it back up, ref, we need to get this thing over fast."

"Whatever you say, son." The ref held out his fist to draw the two fighters together. When they knuckle-bumped, the ref retreated. "Ready, box!"

Philo's new urgency, in his head now: his conversation with Patrick yesterday. Six lanterns had gone into the pit—all with twelve-volt batteries —but one hadn't worked. Philo tossed down a few more—three, not two, he was sure now, for a total of nine. Only eight came back up.

The space was rocking, its audience clamoring for the knockout. Tonka waded in then teed off with shots to the chest, the arms, ribs, Philo taking the blows, covering up, Tonka getting arm weary, Philo eyeing the open seam in the floor every chance he got.

More dust rose from the pit—for fuck's sake, how had they missed this...?

Philo's fist connected, channeling Smokin' Joe Frazier with a left hook to his opponent's cheek, rocking him. Tonka's knees buckled, shook his head like a neighing horse, clearing out the cotton. Tonka moved back inside, whaled on Philo again, Philo covering up—

He knew now. The wooden inlaids a few feet below them, embedded in the pit's ceiling: the grain-polished wood, forty by forty of it awaiting recla-mation, with wormholes, knots and grooves. Places for old grain to cake up and eventually turn to dust particles, jostled loose by a raucous crowd on its feet on the floor above it, the particles going airborne. Not a problem as long as there wasn't an energy source, as in no electrostatic discharge, no open flame, no friction.

And no lantern, damn it, because even a battery-operated lantern was capable of producing a spark.

...Below them, corn, barley, wheat, none of it left to eat, all scrubbed away and vacuumed up. Their teeth gnawed, gnashed, bit, crunched—the rats were hungry, desperate, chomping on anything that wasn't dirt or concrete or wood. Green plastic, clear plastic—a lantern—*crunch-crunch-crunch*—because something edible might be inside. Inside, instead, was a bulb, the bulb attached to a socket, and the socket wired to the terminals of a battery. The teeth clamped on to and ripped at the wire insulation the bare wires touched, creating a spark amid the dust. The rat squealed when the fur on his face ignited...

Philo and Tonka straddled a narrow gap in the floor, a breathing floor joint, the two men hunched over, trading short left and right hooks. A swirl of air swept past their ankles on its way to getting sucked into the gap —*pfttt-t-t*—the audience feeling it too, their short collective gasp quieting the room for a beat. Backfilling the gasp fueled by the buffeting air, Philo had a sinking feeling that all was about to be lost.

And it would be, right after the shockwave.

Pfttt-t-t...

BOOM.

The belowdecks blast expanded like a depth charge, blowing the plywood pieces and cinder blocks off the holes in the open-air first floor. A fireball found the small elevator shaft and geysered upward, rocketing through to the second floor then whooshing upward to the third. The crowd panicked and pushed away from it, scattering in all directions into the cold night through seams in the hanging tarps, heading to safety outside, to their cars...

Tonka and Philo lowered their fists and held up, distracted, chaos surrounding them. The fire geyser burned its brightest and quickly extinguished itself, but the damage was done. Fissures in the columns from the explosion climbed to the floors above, the corner nearest the two fighters shuddering on its two marine legs under the pier, shaking loose chunks of building already compromised by the wrecking ball. A cement corner column collapsed, and the Camden skyline was suddenly visible from the elevator shaft outward, jagged building chunks raining down on the outside, bad as an earthquake. Philo, now in survival mode, was on autopilot—

Get out now, that way, past the shaft, onto the pier.

"Patrick! Hump!" He'd drag them out with him if he could find them among the screaming, panicked audience. He scanned the crowd—

One of the massive marine pilings supporting the pier snapped under-neath, with chunked concrete, rusted iron, and stone crumpling and slip-ping on a slant into the river, Philo sliding into the ice-cold water with it. Above him a grain silo calved like a glacier in slow motion, cascading along the water's edge before sliding in, Philo swimming hard, trying to escape the vortex. A second corner separated, tilting at its base then giving way like a felled tree—timmm-*berrr*! Twenty feet away while Philo tread water, someone splashed helplessly in the tilting silo's path.

No, fuck no...

"Hump!" Philo called. The second concrete silo gathered momentum on its way down, Hump's eyes getting bigger, watching it descend on top of him.

"Hump! SWIM!"

The felled silo displaced Hump and the ton of water where he'd been, pushing tidally outward. *"HUMP!"*

Five seconds passed, ten, Philo still treading water, frantic, spinning in all directions. Thirty seconds. When Hump didn't resurface Philo dove into the murk, spent two chest-burning minutes searching underwater in the swirling muck, reaching river bottom, a long shot, had to try—

No Hump. Waves continued oscillating from the collapse, greeting Philo when he surfaced. On one wave, a dead body. Wrong. The guy was alive, but he was dazed and floating.

Tonka.

Philo cupped Tonka's chin, kicked fiercely away from debris still pummeling the water around them, the pier and the river under assault by one side of the grain elevator now folding in on itself. Tonka gurgled, regaining his wits as they reached a second pier thirty yards upriver. Philo pushed Tonka into a ladder, Tonka wrapping his arms around it and climb-ing, Philo following. Atop the platform Tonka doubled over and heaved, the two men shivering. The wobbling bare knuckler finished coughing up water, said "Thanks, bro," then stutter-stepped into squaring his feet and shook off the shiver. He raised his hands, showing his fists again. "You ready to go? Let's finish this."

Philo, hands on knees, peered up at him. "You crazy? No, I'm not ready to go. Look around you. Fight's over."

"Don't be a pussy, Navy boy. A little water don't bother us Rangers," Tonka said, coughing again. "You don't finish, you lose. A technical knockout," he pointed at the dock adjacent to the collapsed pier, "with witnesses."

Philo rebuffed him, turned away. "Not gonna happen, assho—"

Tonka threw a sucker-punch combination to Philo's chin from behind, then finished with a loaded overhand right that caught Philo's cheek flush, dropping him.

"You're right, it's not gonna happen," Tonka shouted. "TKOs suck! Get the fuck up. My record's going to thirty-five and oh, all knockouts, right—fucking—now, brotha."

Philo grimaced, pushed himself up from the pier's concrete, onto a knee.

Tonka bounced on his feet in front of him. "Comin' at you, old man."

What Philo knew now: his opponent's hardest punch couldn't put him away. Philo stood, summoned himself, ready to deliver two hundred ten pounds of coiled rage with one heavy-handed punch that Tonka was going to walk into. Kinetic linking, leverage, electrolytes, neurons, and beast mode—all of it was a go. Brotha.

He planted his right foot, pushed off against it, a full extension of his right leg, back, shoulder and arm muscles, energy moving from the platform up through his body and springing out his overhand right, its torqued release exploding against Tonka's temple. The bare-knuckle punch stunned the advancing Tonka into a standing knockout, priming him for an uppercut to the chin that lifted him off his feet. Tonka thudded onto his back on the concrete pier and didn't get up.

Philo stood over his sixty-fifth KO, rubbing his knuckles. "Now you're thirty-four and *one*, bitch. We SEALS like the water, too."

In the distance, sirens gathered.

Philo scanned the river's edge while haggard-faced survivors wandered through the smoke and the haze of what was left of the grain elevator. Wally Lanakai, disheveled and leaning heavily against one of his bodyguards, stood at the edge of the dock, a witness to the knockout. Philo searched other wandering faces, looking, calling for Patrick, getting no response.

Behind him on the ladder, amid fits of coughing and gasping, a woman climbed out of the river: the unnamed mob cleaner who'd been on Wally's arm during the fight. Climbing out behind her, and now silhouetted against the reflected Camden skyline, was Patrick. Patrick called to his boss. "Philo, sir! You're safe!"

"You're bleeding, son," he said, examining a gash over Patrick's ear. "Hell, that looks bad."

"I've had worse, sir. I found Kaipo in the water, and I woke her up, sir."

Kaipo? Patrick was now on a first-name basis with his crime-cleaner-slash-airline person. "Glad to see you made it, miss. Let's get off this pier and figure our way into some blankets."

"Mr. Trout," she said. "Wait."

Her eyes drilled his. "Out there, in the water, your friend finding me floating, reviving me..." she said, shivering. "It was a weak moment. A person says things..."

"A near death experience. Been there."

"Yes. But you both need to forget my name—need to forget I exist, forget what I do—soon as this is over. For your own good."

"Works for me," Philo said, less than concerned about it, "but I'll need the same courtesy. You, and Wally, and this guy"—he chin-pointed at Tonka, who was starting to come around from the knockout—"you guys need to distance yourselves from this, and me. Far as we're all concerned, this was an industrial accident."

She eyed the collapsed grain silo, one half of it in the river, the other standing, the dust on land still spreading. "Tall order, Mr. Trout, but I get it. Tonight didn't happen, for any of us."

Philo turned his attention to the end of the pier, where a hobbling Wally approached, still hanging onto one of his goons. "Yo, Wally!" Philo called. "Your guys bring any blankets?"

A fireboat was underway upriver, paralleling the shoreline and closing in, its searchlight blazing. The beam swept the area of the collapsed pier and the gurgling black river next to it.

"I'm so sorry, Hump," Philo said to glistening tar-water still rippling from the silo collapse. "I love you, man."

36

Philo and Patrick hustled, more like stumble-rushed, back to their unmarked Blessid Trauma van fast as their battered bodies allowed them.

Philo stripped and toweled off, threw on clean jeans and a tee he'd retrieved from the van's interior. Patrick was commando, shivering inside a heavy Tyvek top and pants, nothing else for him to change into, with a biohazard hood that hid a gauze pad on his bloodied head. Wally's Range Rover roared up and fishtailed to a stop alongside, kicking up dirt and dust that swirled in the SUV's taillights.

"Stay in the van, Patrick, it'll warm up. Be right back."

The SUV's rear window powered down, exposing Wally in the back seat along with Kaipo, drying out in Wally's overcoat. Tonka, up front and riding shotgun in name only, slept under icepacks to his temple and chin. On the horizon, headlights navigated the long, serpentine dirt trail leading to where they were, on the grain elevator's doorstep.

"Here's the purse," Wally said, tossing a gym bag out the window. It landed at Philo's feet. "You want to count it, you do it on your own time. We're leaving before the unwanted company arrives."

"What about the action from my bet?"

"Heard about that. We'll settle that up later. Gotta go."

A five-hundred-dollar bet, at seven-to-one odds. "Give the thirty-five hundred to Tonka. Tell him he needs to come back alive so he can spend it. He does that, maybe I give him a rematch."

The Range Rover spun out, and like the other shell-shocked fans in attendance, the SUV found one of the overland paths that spider-webbed away from the building rubble, slipping around law enforcement and the other cavalry-like vehicles arriving now.

Far as he could tell, all the fight fans were gone, or at least their vehicles were. Philo wouldn't run. He needed to deal with, needed to fix this apocalyptic fuck-up, one that he and his team had facilitated; needed to give it the right spin with the authorities. This was, after all, a building scheduled for implosion, and Blessid Trauma had been here preparing it for that outcome. Dealing with the collapse *now* made more sense; he had a reason to be here.

Police cars, one fire truck, a fireboat, one EMT vehicle. The back half of the building was gone, the part that reached out over the river, leaving an open-dollhouse-like reveal into the building's front half from the waterfront side. The explosion had stayed in the pit, the fire flashing up the open elevator shaft only once before it ran out of explosive material, nowhere near the same magnitude as the grain silo fire of '56. When a fire marshal spotted him, Philo had already costumed himself head to toe in Tyvek, to sell his presence here better.

The fireman chatted him up. "You witness this?" A cop fell in with the fireman, then another, all of them keenly interested in his account.

"Philo Trout, Blessid Trauma Services, Captain. We were finishing up for the night, my employee and I, still getting the building ready. It comes down in a few days." He spoke through his mask, not proud of the way he looked, split lips, cut forehead, and an eye that was closing up. "Seems that part of the building had its own timetable. Something in the basement exploded. I think one of my guys might have left a lantern down there that could have sparked up some of the old grain dust. Whatever it was, before we knew it, ba-*boom*, half the building was in the river."

"Anyone else here with you we need to go looking for?"

"Only other person here is my employee, in the van, both of us on the job—"

And Hump. What about Hump?

"Wait. There was someone else, out on the dock."

He would hate himself for doing this, for not according Hump, a dear friend, the respect of identifying him.

"No idea why the guy was here. Some midnight fishing for catfish maybe?"

...I'm so sorry, Hump. So, so sorry...

"Okay, thanks, we'll look for him." The captain shined a flashlight on him in his mask, checking his face out from different angles. "Hell, it looks like you got pretty banged up. You need medical attention, Mr. Trout. Let me get an EMT—"

"I'm headed to the hospital already, to get myself checked out. You need anything else, follow up with me later. Gotta go."

Philo watched the emergency response from his rearview mirror, his van negotiating the pocked acreage as he calmly navigated his exit from the property. A news helicopter circled the site, shooting footage of the building, the rubble, the river. Things could have been worse, way worse, many more dead than just one.

If—when—Hump's body was found, they would investigate and draw their own conclusions. But the truth was there'd been no foul play, just someone in the wrong place at the wrong time. An industrial accident; sure, why not. He'd need to add it to the list of gruesome mission outcomes and collateral damage he had to live with every day.

But this list—it was too long. Lovable, harmless, ladies' man Hump Fargas. This one would take a toll.

The van entered traffic. "Fifteen minutes to Grace," he said to Patrick.

37

The large interior vestibule of the former dental office could have used more potted plants, less Hawaiian muscle. Two sumo-size guards stood in their way. Philo dropped his sweatshirt hood to his shoulders so his battered, post-fight face would be visible, enough ID, he figured, along with his name, to gain his and Patrick's admission. He figured right.

"Heard what happened, Mr. Trout," one of the big men at the entrance said. "You're on the list, but your hardware isn't. Raise your arms, the both of you."

After the painful frisk and Philo's weapon confiscation they were led into the dental clinic turned urgent care turned temporary lung transplant venue. It was there they found Hank on the office side of the reception area, riveted to the glass, observing the surgery in progress inside the makeshift operating room. After brief hugs and backslaps, Hank gawked at Philo and Patrick, both eyesores, then returned to his vigil observing Grace, Philo and Patrick alongside him. Grace was five hours into the planned six-to-twelve-hour transplant, still attached to a heart-lung machine.

"Too late for me to say this, Philo," Hank said, "but I'm worried this is too much of a Hail Mary for her."

Philo squeezed his shoulder. "No alternative, Hank. It was either this or watch her die. A no-brainer in my book."

"But this place, it's no better than a third-world infirmary. Who are these people?"

"Best guerilla surgery personnel mob money can buy, to my thinking. Part of the deal. They'll get the job done."

Hank eyed Philo's purpling face. "A deal made with the devil," he said. "You're a mess. And you won?"

"He knocked him out, Hank, sir," Patrick said, beaming, "after they climbed out of the river."

"Wait, what? The *river?*"

"Yeah. After the grain elevator collapsed," Patrick said.

"What?" Hank squinted at them both.

"Yeah. The explosion did it," Patrick said. "Took out the corner silo, and the pier, almost killed us, sir..."

"What the fuck, Philo? This all true? The building exploded?"

"Pretty much. Something in the pit set it off. Half the grain elevator collapsed; the half we were in."

People scattering on land and dock from the collapse no doubt suffered cuts, bruises and broken bones, Philo said. The few who slid into the river nearly drowned, Philo and Patrick among them. They pulled themselves out, along with a few others. All except one.

"I watched Hump drown," Philo said, swallowing hard, "went down after him, couldn't find him. Sweet old Hump..."

"Dude. So sorry, Philo," Hank said.

"Yeah. That one, it's, ah..." he felt his mouth and eyes moisten, gulped it all back, "it's gonna leave a mark. Let's concentrate on Grace. How's she doing?"

All eyes returned to the patient and the doctors and nurses hovering over her.

"Leave it to Grace," Hank said. "She was awake long enough to see Andelmo scrub in. She had a fit. They pulled him off the team, replaced him with another doctor, Barry something."

"Heinzman. He and Andelmo, both part of the same practice. Best corrupt docs money can buy. Makes you wonder if there's anyone out there practicing medicine who isn't dirty."

Behind them, a grunt from their deep-voiced babysitter, quiet until now.

Philo had met him before; he was one of the goons who broke into his house with Wally. "You're a piece of work, Trout. Mr. Lanakai didn't have to do any of this. Show some respect."

Much as Philo wanted to cram the guy's ball sack into his mouth for all his posing, the dude was right. And at four a.m. after an extremely difficult night, everyone's nerves were shot.

"My apologies. My bad. We're grateful he's keeping his promise. When he gets here, I'll tell him myself. He on his way?"

"He has business elsewhere."

"How about Mr. Smith?" Hank asked. "Where's he?"

"None of your fucking business. Not here."

And we're back.

All eyes returned to the operating room and Grace again. The doctors and nurses stayed focused, leaning in, light glinting off their microgoggles and scalpels, a flurry of hands and stainless steel surgical instruments snipping, stretching, dabbing, fusing, and wiring. The new lungs were in, but from what the observers could tell they weren't yet functioning because she was still attached to the heart-lung machine.

Philo scanned his surroundings, checking out the doors to the side of this room, which led to the recesses of the facility. "Her organ donor—is the body here, too?" Philo asked Hank.

"I figured yeah, but now I don't know." Hank eyed their thug babysitter again then spoke softly to Philo. "These black-market organs, Philo—they're doing donor surgeries somewhere else tonight, en masse. I heard one of the docs talking about it. But for any of them to be double-lung donors, that would be suicide. Or murder."

"It would at that," Philo said. "One crisis at a time, Hank."

Patrick leaned in. "I know where, sir," he whispered to Philo.

"You know where what, Patrick?"

Patrick over-dramatized his whisper: *"I know where they're doing those operations, sir."*

"Okay, Patrick, but it's not our problem right now. Let's just stay focused on Grace pulling through here, okay?"

"You betcha, sir, but they're not gonna kill him, are they, sir?"

"Kill who?"

"Miñoso. He told me he's selling his kidney. So his uncle Diego's body can get shipped home. They won't kill him, will they?"

Philo thumbed Patrick out of the room, toward a rest room in the hall. Once inside he scolded him for staying quiet about Miñoso until now.

"Tell me where he is, Patrick."

38

The unmarked Blessid Trauma van sped north on I-95 at five a.m., on its way to a Bristol warehouse, the pre-dawn traffic sparse once it passed the northeast Philadelphia exits. Philo needed to check his guns, didn't hesitate doing it, his hands leaving the steering wheel, his knee and thigh doing the steering now. He examined each gun at seventy miles an hour, the one the bouncer returned to him and the one he would strap to his ankle. The post-op thank-you he'd proposed to give Wally, should he be where Philo was headed, might now need to look and sound a bit different if it involved springing Miñoso.

His headache was a motherfucker, multiple-concussion grade, and his ribs were bruised big time. Tonka had hurt him more than he realized, and now, with no adrenaline other than what came from his anxiety, the impact of those brutal punches took more of a toll. He popped more Advil, washing the pills down with gulps from a can of Mountain Dew.

It would be an easy extraction when he found Miñoso, he told himself; easy-peasy. All that was needed was cash money to talk him out of the surgery, and now he had seventy-five grand of it. Getting inside the warehouse and getting access to him...that would be the issue.

He left I-95 and followed his GPS, took a ride alongside the wide expanse of the Delaware River, this side Bristol, the other side Burlington,

New Jersey. It creeped him out, so close to the river again, so soon after watching his friend Hump hug a snapped pier piling downstream, on his way to his death in the murk. He made a hard left away from the water, forcing the GPS lady to announce a revised route. A minute later he arrived at his destination two blocks inland, a repurposed warehouse with a sign the size of a small billboard occupying a chunk of the front lawn. *Opening Summer: Keystone Distribution Services. Now Hiring.* He coasted past an empty guard shack, circled around to the back of the warehouse, where a large parking lot faced a loading dock. The lot was busy with cars, SUVs, and a number of what looked like 1970s pizza delivery pickups. A fucking convention.

The delivery trucks occupied all the spots up and down the loading dock except one. He grabbed it. A garage door opened, at the far end of the dock. Three people with picnic coolers hustled out and deposited them in the rear of three trucks. No, check that, they were seafood delivery pickup trucks, refrigerated.

This had to be the place.

Okay, how to get in?

* * *

"I have you here with me, Kaipo," Olivier said, "so we can kill two birds."

Wally's overcoat was draped around her shoulders again, warming her. Under the coat she was in nurse's scrubs, the only dry clothes available. Olivier sat across from her, not close, a good ten feet away, the two of them inside one of the warehouse's former glass-enclosed break rooms, seated in cheap chrome-plated office chairs left behind when the warehouse closed. A string of utilitarian work lights crisscrossed the ceiling. She dried her black hair with a towel, rubbing vigorously, fresh from a locker room shower with leftover hand-pump soap that had almost rid herself of the Delaware River stink.

Killing the first of the birds, per Olivier, was medical attention for Wally, Kaipo and Tonka. Their driver had stormed up I-95 to the Bristol warehouse, to where multiple doctors and nurses were performing tonight's marathon donor surgeries. Wally was injured from the building collapse, his shoulder dislocated, his scalp lacerated, and he had a concussion. A doctor gave him meds then popped his shoulder back into place and stitched him up. Tonka was on an I-V drip, brained and bloodied and on a gurney somewhere in the recesses of the warehouse. Kaipo had declined medical attention, needing only a shower and dry clothes.

Bird number two, of Olivier's doing: It was urgent that Kaipo meet with him. Company business.

"Sorry," she said, her hair starting to frizz, "but unless you plan on putting me to work after the surgeries are finished, I have no idea why we're talking." She eyed the stark, dusty break room surroundings. "And in case you haven't noticed, I'm a bit short on the equipment I'd need to get any work done here."

"Wally wanted you checked out by the doctors," Olivier said. "And in case *you* haven't noticed, Kaipo, you've made a significant impression on him. As far as putting you to work—tonight's surgeries have gone very well —perfectly, as a matter of fact. There are a few left in the queue but they're simple kidney procedures; we're expecting no issues. Whatever else might happen, to whomever"—his smile turned pained, bordering on bizarre— "can wait until you're ready to deal with it. It seems Wally has made his mind up about grooming you for a different, more personal role. It's a role I wanted, Kaipo, and this is why I'm meeting with you now."

A role I wanted? Wally Lanakai had the hots, but those hots were for her, not Olivier. What was happening?

"Where's Wally?" she asked, apprehensive.

"He's in la-la land from the meds. I had his bodyguard drive him home." Olivier crossed his long, thin legs, then picked some non-existent lint off the razor-sharp creases of his pants. "I told him you were given a lift home already, and that seemed to satisfy him."

She stood, officially spooked. She was shoved back down into the chair by two men she hadn't heard enter the room.

"Stay seated, Kaipo, please, and try to relax." Olivier banished the men with a dismissive wave, then stood and paced, dipping his fingers into his snuffbox. After inhaling his second pinch he unbuttoned his long leather overcoat, was deliberate about it, then he swept it open like a well-dressed Western lawman might, revealing a holstered handgun on his hip. He slipped the gun out of its holster and sat again, crossing his legs while settling the gun on his lap, his eyes intense. In them, she sensed angst... despair...sadness.

"I've accepted Wally's choice, painful as it is, and will be, for me in particular, Kaipo," Olivier said. "But I also need to explain something to you."

* * *

Philo knocked at the door on the loading dock, a steel entrance portal between two of the tall garages. When the door opened he got all gosh-golly chatty with the white face that appeared. "Hey. How's it going. I'm here to pick up, ah, you know, one of the, um..."

An act. What should he label Miñoso? A donor? Say the wrong thing, it would all go south in seconds.

"...to pick up someone who's, ah..."

"A donor," the youngish blond guy said, all smiling and gym-suited and broad-shouldered, no doubt a former high school jock turned goon. The door opened wider. "Sure thing, come on in."

Strong Philly accent, the *come on* coming out as *ka-MAWN*. Philo entered, the blond jock leaning back out the door to check behind him, confirming he was the only person out there. He snapped the door shut, the turn of the lock echoing.

"Wait over there," he said, pointing at the interior of the garage, "I'll get someone."

Philo took three wary steps in the direction suggested, overheard Blondie whisper into a mouthpiece, knew immediately this was a problem, it had been too easy, wasn't frisked, hadn't had to give a name, or mention who he was after

Philo spun, delivered an upturned palm under Blondie's nose, his head snapping back, blood gushing from both nostrils, the raised nightstick in Blondie's hand pinwheeling to the floor, its bounce reverberating. Philo and his bruised ribs slipped behind him and put him in a sleeper hold, would snap his neck if he had to, certainly didn't want to, maybe wouldn't need to, then—

"Let him go, douchebag," a disembodied voice said, "and move away from him, *now*."

One thug down, bloody and unconscious, but a second one had his handgun raised, exiting the darkness from the depths of the garage. The gun's laser sight found Philo's forehead.

* * *

"We have a problem, Kaipo," Olivier said. "We, as in you and me both."

"Nothing that releasing me won't fix," she said, "before you do something stupid."

"Oh, hush. It's too late for that. Three years too late. For you, and for me. You are disgusted by Wally's new 'business plan.' You want out; your conscience can't stomach poor, innocent people being maimed or murdered for wealthy people to live longer lives; you want to return to a normal life. So admirable, Kaipo, that you now have a conscience; cue a slow clap. Except your status with Ka Hui is about to dramatically change. You are being promoted from contractor to family member, whether you, or I, like it or not. It will come across as an offer of wine and roses and love and lofty pedestals, but it will really be an 'or else' proposition.

"The only do-over Wally Lanakai ever allowed was three years ago, and it backfired. Another principal in the business—one of Ka Hui's founders when we were on the Island—was, truth be told, my brother. Not family to Wally, but the closest thing to it: his teenage friend from the slums. The Feds and local law enforcement destroyed our business on the Islands, put most of the principals in prison. Wally served eight years, my brother Denholm ten. When Wally was released, he had a vision: resurrect the business in a big city on the mainland. He did, and here we are."

"Olivier," Kaipo said, impatient, "let me help you with this. I already knew about Wally and his 'vision.' He brought me here, remember?"

"Yes, of course you knew. Wally cleaned you up, probably saved your life. But you know nothing about my dead brother and his family. Even though you've, sort of, met their murderers."

Olivier lifted the gun from his lap, admired it, a silver-plated long-barreled revolver befitting his flamboyance. When he returned it to his lap, this time he kept his hand on the gun's grip, and his finger on the trigger.

"See, Denholm came to the mainland too, after his release from prison, but he abdicated his partnership in the business. He told Wally, ' 'A'ohe mea hou aku.' Short version, 'No more.' Wally agreed, but under one condition: Denholm had to release all his holdings *and* his people, plus had to agree to a non-compete, or else. Wally let him keep his cash, but otherwise he needed to start over, in this wonderful City of Brotherly Love. Ha! *Brotherly* Love.' My kind of place, heh-heh. Denholm had no intention of competing, but he did have one condition of his own: Wally must never recruit—never allow—Denholm's son to join the life.

"Your first mainland cleaning job, Kaipo? The punks. who attacked my brother and his wife in a robbery, leaving them to die on the dirty, frozen streets of South Philadelphia. Denholm was no wallflower. He'd resisted and was gunned down. Him and his wife. Wally had their bodies sent back to the Islands for an honorable burial."

Kaipo recalled these punks, or at least what was left of them, when she did the cleanups. Four teenagers—two black, two Latino, all decapitated, not a head left among them after Wally's people found them. And one without a pinky finger, now that she recalled.

"Wally had their heads delivered to their families on Christmas Eve," Olivier said.

He smiled, his laugh giddy. The laugh turned upside down; he swiped at a tearing eye.

"To remember my brother, to relive this tragedy—it's one of a number of things that have depressed me lately. His son, my nephew—I won't name him—survived the attack, apparently wandered off after being severely beaten. We found him at a hospital, but he disappeared before we could retrieve him, gone to the streets, and was rediscovered only lately, when you outted him. Yes, he survived the attack physically, but his identity, the family surname, him knowing who he was, did not."

By any other name, Patrick Stakes.

"Wally chooses to be an honorable man in this oftentimes dishonorable life, Kaipo. He will keep his promise to my brother. And he will not suffer anyone who defies him. *Anyone.* You seem hell-bent on helping my nephew understand who he is, but he can never know. Are you on board with this, Kaipo?"

He lifted the revolver from his lap and laid it on his bony knee, his hold on the grip visibly tightening, but the end of the large barrel was now facing her.

"Yes," she said, the gun a strong argument. "He'll never know, least not on my account."

"Excellent. That is a relief."

Olivier's jaw tightened, fighting his emotions, his mouth and eyes moistening. "Wally is a good man, Kaipo. An incredibly benevolent, beautiful, lovely, talented man. But sadly, and to close out our discussion, his newest choice—you, as his intimate—is one I'm afraid I can't accept."

His hand twitched, the gun leaving his knee, him leveling it at her.

Kaipo pushed herself up from her chair, froze, her mind spinning. Ten feet from the door, ten feet to him, which should it be, fight or flight—

"Olivier, no, don't do this, I'll disappear..."

"You leaving won't matter, Kaipo. It's you who he wants, loves, not someone with a body filling up with tumors. I ask that you please be respectful when you clean this one up."

He turned the gun around, stuck the barrel to his temple and squeezed the trigger. The other side of his head splattered against an abandoned candy machine and the white wall next to it.

* * *

The blond jock jerked his head up, was conscious again, but now his forehead wore the red laser dot meant for Philo. Philo grimaced while he tucked and rolled, let the semi-automatic gunfire slice through Blondie's head, his gray matter and hair and blood and bone fragments spraying the back of Philo's shoulders.

Stop rolling, ankle gun, go to a knee, draw, owww, point, SHOOT—

Pfttt, pfttt, two slugs, head and chest, dropped the punk with the gun into a rumpled pile. Philo advanced stealthily past the shooter, was wobbly now, his handgun sweeping the darkness until he found a door. He peeked on its other side, entered and remained in the shadows, his eyesight drawn immediately to the far corner of the warehouse brightened by kettledrum lights hanging on rigid tethers from a metal framework ceiling.

From this distance he counted four men in scrubs, two of them in microgoggles, the number of nurses tripling that, and six thug-types on the unlit perimeter. On gurneys under the lights were two patients, their surgeries in progress, the surgeons and nurses hovering, murmuring. Also on gurneys in the dim lighting that skirted the area were four more patients with drips attached but no staff attending them. Closer to the operating theater, one patient lay on a gurney, also unattended.

Philo had to decide, the group of four or the single person—how to get close without being seen—

A gun went off in another corner, interrupting his decision. Everyone jumped, a few nurses squealing, all eyes focusing on a room to Philo's far right, a string of hanging job lights illuminating its interior. In it were two seated figures, one teetering sideways from the gunshot until it dropped out of Philo's view.

Someone else's problem. He needed to find Miñoso, needed to take advantage of the distraction. Multiple thugs scrambled to that corner of the building and entered the room, their guns drawn.

Time to move. He decided on the group of four gurneys. He leaned over one, then another, whispering between them—"Miñoso? You here? Miñoso?"

A lolling head grimaced with pain, another snored. Donor patients, all post-procedure, none of them Miñoso. Over there, closer in to the surgery in progress, was the single gurney. He arrived alongside.

"Miñoso?"

"¿Qué? Si. Si! Miñoso! Campeón?"

"Yes, and still campeón. You and I are leaving. Now."

"No, I need the money, Philo. I cannot go—"

"I have the money. Plenty of it in cash, from the fight."

"You are a púrpura mess, Philo. You speak the truth? You won the money?"

"Si, I won the money. I can cover your uncle's burial expenses. Let's go."

"Mi ropa—"

Philo reached under the gurney, retrieved his clothes. "Put on your pants. Then we're outta here."

They backed away from the surgery staging area, turned and began walking briskly. The morning sun made its claim, illuminating the ceiling through the second-story glass, the sunrise slowly working its way down the walls, in search of the floor. It was then Philo realized how white the warehouse interior was, the ceiling, the walls, the floor, except for one corner, the one with the surgeries, the floor there smeared red.

A perimeter nurse with a picnic-size cooler quick-stepped away from the group, handing off the cooler to a Hawaiian twenty-something. The kid hustled past them to the same door Philo had used on his way in, two dead bodies awaiting the kid on the other side. Philo pointed Miñoso to another door, one that would take them past the glass-enclosed room where there'd been the gunshot, that space now swarming with husky Hawaiians, their guns drawn and looking for something to shoot.

They strode silently past, nearing the exit, Philo's hand on his gun inside his jacket pocket, not taking his eyes off the gunshot's aftermath and the men gawking at it. A headshot at close range, an execution or a suicide, he couldn't tell, but seated across from the dead guy on the floor was a woman with dark, frizzy hair, her scrubs disheveled. Philo pushed Miñoso ahead, through the steel door, took one last look into the room with the dead guy in it to confirm: Kaipo, the mob's cleaner, was the other person.

He held up his exit, paralyzed, watching the guys with the guns crowd her, wave their hands demanding answers. Grimacing, Philo eased the gun from his pocket, his ribs convincing him that one or more of them were broken.

Kaipo saw him through the glass, recognized him, saw his indecision, his temptation. Her headshake at him was furtive but steely-eyed, the message *Don't interfere, get out,* plus *Don't worry, we're good, you and me,* all conveyed in one long, grim look. Philo and Miñoso squeezed out the back door and were gone.

39

The van stopped at the curb, the morning sun glorious, an hour past sunrise, its brilliance glinting off the train tracks and the broken glass in the lot next to Joe Frazier's Gym.

Philo stuffed rolls of tens and twenties into the greasy Burger King bag late of their fast food breakfasts. "Fifteen grand, Miñoso, that should do it."

"It is too much, Philo Campeón. I cannot take it."

"Yes, you can. Some for getting your uncle's remains to Mexico, some for you personally. You deserve it, for all your help."

"Praise Jesucristo, Philo Campeón. I will pray for Hump tonight, tomorrow, and every night after. And for you too, mi amigo."

"That's a lot of praying, Miñoso, but hell, I'm sure we both need it. And don't forget, if—when—you come back, you have a job."

"Si, Philo Campeón, si. Muchas gracias." Miñoso took Philo's hands in his, raised and kissed them. Philo's face twisted, the pain to his ribs excruciating.

"Señor Philo, you need el médico—"

"I hear ya, and I'll handle that shortly. Go on, get out. And have a safe trip, bud."

Philo pulled away from the curb and rounded a corner, out of sight from where he'd dropped off his passenger. He cradled his side and pulled over so he could call Hank from the van to check on Grace. Hank answered, said the marathon surgery was finished.

"And?" Philo prompted.

"She's alive, breathing on her own, but she's still unconscious. This Heinzman guy says he's getting her admitted somewhere. How the hell he's able to manage that I have no idea, but they're letting her in."

"Part of the deal, Hank. He's chief administrator at Pennsylvania Hospital. That where they're taking her?"

"Yes. We'll be there in about an hour. These fucking guys—" Hank started choking up. "I don't know what to think right about now. My wife is alive because of them, and you. I owe you my life, too, because, see, without Grace—"

"Knock that shit off, Hank." Philo pulled the van back into traffic, a one-handed effort, his destination the same hospital, his ribs throbbing again, goddamn it. "You've got Patrick to worry about too, remember? How's he doing?"

"On cloud nine now that Grace is out of surgery."

"What changed her mind?"

"About the surgery? I still don't know. She flipped out while she was on the table, wanted it stopped, then some whispered assurance from one of the doctors shut her up, made her giddy, actually. She was good to go after they switched surgeons. That, and an adjustment to her anesthesia. The doc wouldn't tell me what he told her; something about the donor. Right about now I don't care. You good to talk with someone else?"

"Put him on."

"Philo, sir! Did you find Miñoso?"

There'd be no mention about the warehouse rescue fiasco: who lived, who died, who might have broken ribs, and who had probably decided to completely rethink her Hawaiian-mob, crime-scene-cleaning avocation. Philo would give him the short answer.

"He's safe, Patrick. My guess is he's packing for his trip to Mexico right now, to deliver his uncle's body."

"But Philo, sir, does he still have his, um, you know—"

"Both his kidneys, Patrick, yes, he still has them, and the rest of his body parts, too. It's all good, bud."

Patrick's voice perked up. "Got some news, sir! Hank says the DNA test proves I'm Hawaiian, sir. Er, wait, no. Polynesian. Yeah, that's it, I've got Polynesian DNA. Same as Hawaiians. Cool, right, sir?"

"Very cool, Patrick. Tell you what. We'll plan a trip, my treat, after Grace gets back on her feet. Hawaii. The four of us. Look, I gotta go. I'll find you guys at the hospital."

Philo ended the call, was fading fast. It would be a half-hour ride in traffic to Pennsylvania Hospital, but his plan of driving himself there was starting to look like a bad idea. The fuck if these lanes on Broad Street didn't look like they were moving, wiggling, like snakes...

His ringtone. His phone. Where was his phone...?

"Hello?" he said, concentrating, his vision blurred, his elbow tucked against his ribs, his hand draped over the steering wheel.

"Detective Rhea Ibáñez, Mr. Trout. I'm at the Sixth today. I've got some news for you about Dr. Andelmo. A press conference..."

It all sounded so nice, lightheaded as he felt, and after he told her where he was—only because she seemed extra concerned that he didn't sound so good and had asked his location—he promptly fainted, his van jumping a curb, crossing an empty sidewalk, and plowing into a Wawa storefront near Philly City Hall.

40

The double doors to the urgent care facility opened into an alley. Kaipo sat in her van, was showered and dressed, but still drained. She watched what she hoped would be the last piece of medical equipment exit the building, two men in scrubs pushing it. The heart-lung machine could have passed for a stainless-steel hotdog cart after a busy day on the street.

She'd been told it would be one body, an organ donor who hadn't survived.

The men in scrubs lifted the heart-lung unit into a cargo van advertising a nineteen-ninety-five-a-day rate and the image of a bucking bronco trampling Wyoming's state motto, *Equal Rights*; had they really thought that one through? The scrubs guys closed the rear doors. The truck exited the alley.

She could barely see straight. The fight, the building collapse, the dip in the river. Wally was awake now and recovering, directing his mob business traffic from somewhere, doing damage control after Olivier's suicide. But there'd been no rest for her. She was on the job here because she needed to be per texts from Icky Ikaika that came with Wally's apologies.

Mr. Lanakai will take care of Olivier and be respectful about it. Already got someone lined up to fill in for you. But this other one needs your attention, to close out the deal with Trout. Get it done. Find a couch or a bed while it cooks, get some sleep.

Philo Trout. Patrick Stakes, or whatever his name was. Glad to have made your acquaintances, fellas. Good luck with the rest of your lives.

Icky's follow-up text:

Two weeks in Paris for you. You and Mr. Lanakai. He has something he needs to discuss. Text me when you're done.

She scrolled through her phone, busying herself while she waited for the guys in scrubs to tell her she could enter the facility. A news headline popped up on a philly.com link:

Grand Jury Delivers Indictment for Illegal Organ Trafficking

Not a good outcome for Ka Hui. She clicked through to read the story, lingering on each of the photos. One indictment so far, Dr. Francisco X. Andelmo, to be arraigned as soon as they could locate him. Wally and the rest of Ka Hui would need to distance themselves from this.

"Good luck with that, Wally," she said.

Distance; a good thing right about now. If today's cleaning job hadn't been related to Philo Trout, she wouldn't be here.

A beckoning hand from one of the scrubs guys ended her time online. She grabbed a small piece of luggage from among five other bulging luggage pieces and lifted it into the pressure cooker, then closed the cooker's lid.

Inside the facility she wheeled the cooker into a room barely large enough for a bed and a utility sink, where a body bag sat on a gurney.

"He's all yours," a scrub guy said.

She pulled some Tyvek over her loose, untucked blouse and her comfy jeans—her traveling clothes—and she zipped up. The small luggage piece also held her circular saw, cleaning agents, gloves and rags. Now to get to work. She unzipped the body bag as far south as the waist.

A surprise.

The indicted doctor, Andelmo.

Tanned face, capped teeth, his chest cavity splayed open. This was one way, she supposed, Ka Hui could distance itself from the organ trafficking allegations. It seemed her employers had no problem with eating their own contractors. Good to know. She turned on the circular saw.

Whirrr, whirrr, whirrrrr...

There would be a stop at Icky's restaurant to abandon the pressure cooker and its cooked contents, and another at a vacant lot to abandon her tools and her cleaning materials and her van, then a cab to take her and her luggage and her one-way ticket to the airport.

Her plan: say goodbye to Kaipo Mawpaw and hello to a new identity. Goodbye Mainland USA, hello unnamed Pacific island, for a layover long enough to catch her breath. And long enough to fashion a route to a destination she hoped would be too challenging for anyone, Ka Hui included, to find her.

* * *

Philo was awake inside the ambulance; he mustered a smile. Whatever drugs they'd pumped him with, his ribs hurt him less. The siren engaged, the wail low and tired, like Philo. The ambulance moved into street traffic. Its EMT attendant backed off to give Detective Ibáñez room next to him, both non-Philo occupants now hovering. Philo soon realized he'd apparently been answering questions, with the detective taking notes.

"Tell me again why you're here, Detective."

"Andelmo. His indictment. Your 'connection,'" the detective said with air-quotes, "per the ADA. You passed out at the wheel of your van, Mr. Trout, while you were on the phone with me. I was at the Sixth when I called you." She gave his battered body the once over, him strapped in tightly to the gurney. She shook her head. "Obviously my lucky day."

"Yes, it would appear so." He'd awakened only after the van's impact with the corner of a building, van against brick and glass, his face cut, but not badly. "Anyone else hurt?"

"Happy to say no, only you. You're a mess. I have more questions." She crouched down, assumed her close-talker persona. "Andelmo's missing. You have anything to do with that?"

The drugs made him a little giddy, made him want to confess everything that had happened in the past twenty-four hours that had done this to his body, was pretty sure he hadn't blabbed already, and now knew he wouldn't. The fight, the grain-elevator explosion. The organ trafficking. Kaipo, Wally. Grace's new lungs.

Detective Ibáñez best not know any of this.

And Hump. Dear, dear old Hump.

"Mr. Trout?"

"I threatened to rearrange some of Andelmo's body parts."

"Hence our interest, Mr. Trout."

"But I didn't. I hate the fucker. If he's missing, it wasn't me. How about this? Let's talk later," he said, his smile going lopsided on him, maybe even with some drool, "when I feel better. Lunch maybe?"

"Fine. Lunch it is, on me. At Pennsylvania Hospital."

"Works for me, Detective."

Her dark eyebrows tented. She again ran her gaze along his beaten body, head to toe and back, her hard cop eyes finding his face again, but this time they weren't quite so hard, were instead caring.

"Rhea, with an *R* and an *H*, Mr. Trout," she said.

"Excuse me?"

She straightened from her crouch, and whether she was aware of it or not she was no longer in his face, no longer talking close. "Call me Rhea."

"Nice to meet you, Rhea. Philo."

Philo let his consciousness desert him, the detective's softened, concerned expression and espresso eyes his last visage before drifting off. So exhausted. The rocking ambulance ride evaporated, was replaced with the sway of palm trees, a tropical blue sky, and gently lapping ocean waves caressing his legs and those of the dark-haired, sensuous woman lying next to him, her head on his shoulder, her arm across his chest.

Zero Island
Blessid Trauma Crime Scene Cleaners #2

Take a Hawaiian vacation, they told Philo.
Relax. Maybe keep a runaway mob cleaner alive while you're there, they said.
Try not to get killed while doing it, they said...

The Hawaiian mob isn't dead; they moved to Philly. And now one of their own has fled.

Hawaiian mob fixer Kaipo Mawpaw is incognito somewhere in the South Pacific, and she wants to stay that way.

A mobster wants her back and is willing to buy a small Hawaiian island that isn't for sale to make it happen. Miakamii, Kaipo's birthplace, where seashell jewelry made by the island's indigenous people are worth small fortunes, where there might be a cure for dementia, and where its inhabitants have been sheltered from outsiders since the 1860s.

But the island's quiet native citizenry is now under siege as bodies of current and former inhabitants start piling up.

Philo Trout, retired Navy SEAL, current crime scene cleaning business owner, and reluctant tourist, is about to get the vacation of a lifetime.

Get your copy today at
severnriverbooks.com/authors/chris-bauer

ACKNOWLEDGMENTS

In no particular order. Beverly Black and Jim Kempner for their assistance with some English-to-Spanish translations. Ryan Keawekane, for English to 'Olelo Hawaiian translations. Bobby Gunn, professional boxer who also holds the undisputed bareknuckle boxing record of 73-0. Respect to you, Bobby. The Bucks County (PA) Writers Workshop, especially Don Swaim, novelist and radio host, CBS Book Beat. The Rebel Writers of Bucks County (PA): Russ Allen, Dave Jarret, Martha Holland, Melissa (Mel) Sullivan, John Wirebach. Marita Vera for her July 22, 2010 *Popular Mechanics* article, "The Science of a Boxing Knockout." Dr. Anthony Alessi, neurologist and ringside physician for the Connecticut State Boxing Commission, quoted in Ms. Vera's article. YouTube, *National Geographic Fight Science*, "The Knockout Punch." Joe Frazier's Gym, now on the National Register for Historic Places; for the purposes of this novel the interior of the gym is fictionalized. Cleanertimes.com, regarding grain elevator cleaning. Sarah Krasnostein for her Nov. 24, 2014 article in narratively.com, "Secret Life of a Crime Scene Cleaner." A special shout out to Sandra Pankhurst, the subject of Ms. Krasnostein's article. Sandra, you are an inspiration. Mario Puzo, screenplay, Francis Ford Coppola, screenplay, *The Godfather*. William Goldman, author of *Marathon Man*, the novel, and screenwriter for *Marathon Man*, the movie. John Schlesinger, director of *Marathon Man*, the movie. KSHB, Scripps Media, for their October 31, 2011 Dr. Donna Hall interview regarding grain elevators. Dianne Small-Jordan for her March 23, 2016 article in decodedscience.org, "Organ Harvesting, Human Trafficking, and the Black Market." Reference to "the red market" comes from Scott Carney, investigative journalist, The Red Market, HarperCollins Publishers, 2011. Clint Eastwood for his portrayal of Philo Beddoe in *Every Which Way But Loose* (Warner Bros.

and The Malpaso Company), written by Jeremy Joe Kronsberg, and *Any Which Way You Can* (Warner Bros. and The Malpaso Company), written by Stanford Sherman and Jeremy Joe Kronsberg. Marinda Valenti (marindaproofreads.com) for her excellent copyedit. The author takes responsibility for all errors.

ABOUT THE AUTHOR

"The thing I write will be the thing I write."

Chris wouldn't trade his northeast Philly upbringing of street sports played on blacktop and concrete, fistfights, brick and stone row houses, and twelve years of well-intentioned Catholic school discipline for a Philadelphia minute (think New York minute but more fickle and less forgiving). Chris has had some lengthy stops as an adult in Michigan and Connecticut, and he thinks Pittsburgh is a great city even though some of his fictional characters do not. He still does most of his own stunts, and he once passed for Chip Douglas of *My Three Sons* TV fame on a Wildwood, NJ boardwalk. He's a member of International Thriller Writers, and his work has been recognized by the National Writers Association, the Writers Room of Bucks County (PA), and the Maryland Writers Association. He likes the pie more than the turkey.

severnriverbooks.com/authors/chris-bauer